THE FIRE TREE
BOOK 5
DESTINATION: INVERNESS
by Ken Kirk

Dedicated to the memory of Pamela Lang, Cydara Verrier, Margaret Beatrice Kirk & Cecilia Reynolds.

PROLOGUE

The story so far...

This is Book 5 of The Fire Tree series. While Books 1 and 2 are standalone stories in their own right, Books 3 and 4 directly precede this tale. Here is what you need to know if you haven't read them...

A hidden princess?

Janine believed herself to be nothing more than the daughter of poor crofters. When she found herself in the position of a personal maid to the Lady of Dunkeld Manor, she regarded herself as fortunate. When a senior officer, there, tried to force himself on her in the cellars, something astonishing happened. She heard tinkling bells, felt an overwhelming calmness, and lost consciousness. When she woke, her attacker lay dead in a pool of blood, brutally killed by an unknown assailant.

Fleeing the manor with a young butcher's boy named Callum, Janine was set upon and chased by robbers on the road. Again, the sound of the bells came, the strange calmness descended on her and she lost consciousness. When she woke, her main pursuer lay impaled and dead, killed by a mysterious protector. The other two fled in terror.

Exhausted and terrified, Janine was rescued by two kind-hearted brothers, Bruce and Brian, who picked her up in their coach and took her to Brech Woorlach, a grand mansion in the Lowlands of Scotland. There she met Francesca, who first pretended to be a maid servant but later revealed herself to be the daughter of the Duke and Duchess of Bo'Ness.

At Brech Woorlach, Janine began to feel strangely at home. She could describe places in the grounds she had never consciously seen. She possessed a beautifully crafted dragon ring that seemed far too fine for a crofter's daughter. Her mother had taught her to treat her dark hair with a special lotion, claiming that it prevented a family curse of baldness, but without its use Janine's hair turned a naturally golden blonde.

When mystical flames began appearing on her hand and around the dragon ring that she wore on a chain, Francesca and the others were in awe, explaining that such strange, mystical flames that had begun to appear to her were the same ones that had revealed themselves to the warrior queen 'Kiffan the Defiant' who had raised an army against the invasion of the Vikings, eight hundred years ago. Falling to their knees, they revealed to Janine that she had been brought to Brech Woorlach as an infant, hidden there for her protection during a period of upheaval in Scottish history. It was a time when traitors hunted anyone connected to the royal bloodline of the Scottish Highlands. It was revealed to Janine that she was not a crofter's daughter after all, but that she was the lost heir to the throne of the Queens of the Westlands in the Scottish Highlands. The woman, Annis, who currently wore that crown, they assured her, was an imposter.

It was further revealed to Janine that rather than having an elusive protector who rescued her from life threatening situations, she had – in fact – come to her own aid, using impressive martial art skills that had been hidden from her using ancient forms of mind control and that only surfaced when vitally needed.

Queen Annis and the Campbell Threat

Seven years ago, the powerful Clan Campbell murdered Queen Cydara in cold blood during what was meant to have been an historic reconciliation. They hunted for her daughter and apparent heir, the twelve-year-old Princess Annis, but a brave man named Leslie threw himself between the assassins and the young princess, giving his life to save hers.

Annis became the Queen of the West, inheriting a throne still warm from her mother's blood. The story finds Annis at nineteen years old, having spent seven years learning to be both a queen and warrior. The Campbells, however, remained unpunished and continued to threaten her rule.

When Queen Annis travelled to the River Spey to perform the ancient walking of her boundary to assert her sovereignty over her lands, she expected confrontation with her ancient enemies, the Clan Grant. Instead, in a moment of brutal honesty and courage, both sides confronted the true history of their eight-hundred-year-old hatred. The Laird Grant knelt before Annis and offered her his sword. He also pledged to raise her a cavalry force to guard her eastern flank.

At that precise moment, a great oak tree at the end of the meadow burst into flames. The Fire Tree had returned! It was the same mystical fire that had saved Kiffan the Defiant from a death sentence under the Vikings. The tree burned for all to see, without a single twig or leaf being scorched or burned. It was a divine sign that the ancient power approved of the reconciliation. The ancient feud was ended.

Reconciliation comes at a price and, as Annis stood triumphant, warning horns sounded. The Clan Campbell had launched a coordinated attack from two directions, striking at both the McRory camp and her new allies, the Grants. The Campbells saw the young Queen as vulnerable and the Grant alliance as a threat. The battle that followed was brutal and costly, leaving hundreds dead on all sides.

Though Annis survived, saved by a miraculous intervention when an eagle fell from the sky to knock aside a spear meant to kill her, she was gravely wounded. As she recovered, the truth became clear: the Campbells would attack again. This was only the beginning.

The McCarthy Stronghouse

Meanwhile, far from the Highland conflicts, an innkeeper named Hamish Pottle and a young soldier by the name of Alex Brennan, who had returned from 'The Long War' in Austria, found themselves in a dangerous situation.

Constable Ewan Burberry, on a secret mission for King James and carrying a royal warrant, had been captured by the lawless Clan McCarthy and held at their stronghouse in Coille Dorcha, the Dark Forest. He had managed to evade his thirty strong escort – drawn from the troops of the Lothian Pikes and Muskets and led by Captain McCleary – who had been sent by King James to protect him. He had, instead, gone 'exploring' on his own.

Hamish and Alex mounted a daring raid on the stronghouse to rescue the Constable. Just as success seemed to be impossible, the troops escorting the Constable had turned up. Victory was achieved and the Constable freed, but they found him to have been badly beaten by his captures and left with numerous painful injuries.

The constable's mission was revealed to be connected to the very fate of the Highland kingdom itself, involving plots and conspiracies that reached into the highest levels of power. His rescue would prove to be only the first step in unravelling a web of intrigue that connected the Lowlands to the Highland conflicts.

The Brydda

The Brydda are a secret society whose origins stretch back to the time of the ancients, dating back eight hundred years to the time of Kiffan herself. For the Brydda, service to the Queen is not merely a duty but a sacred calling, a faith passed down through generations. They believe the Queens of the West embody the spirit of Scotland itself. The Brydda would die to protect them without hesitation.

And Now...

Queen Annis has forged a new alliance with the Grants and has the prospect of a cavalry force on her eastern flank, but at the cost of making deadly enemies. The Campbells are preparing their next strike, determined to see her dead.

Janine has discovered her true heritage and possesses an ancient power she cannot control or understand. She knows she is connected to the Queens of the West, but is unsure of her destiny and the wisdom of challenging Annis for the crown.

The mystical flames have appeared to both women, marking them as chosen by the ancient power that has guided Scotland's destiny for eight hundred years.

In the shadows, conspirators plot. The Campbells sharpen their blades. King James watches from London, apparently uncertain whether to support or oppose one or other of the young women who claim the throne.

The story of Book 5 begins here, as these threads begin to weave together. Two women marked by destiny. Two bloodlines converging. One kingdom standing on the brink of a conflict that will determine not just who rules the Highlands, but the very fate of Scotland itself.

The three groups of people in this novel all having something in common: They all end up journeying to Inverness.

CHAPTER 1

Janine watched in fascination as an insect flew between the furry catkins of the nearby tree, pausing to scrabble around each one, before flying on to the next. After a while it flew off and she watched it grow smaller and smaller in the distance until it became the tiniest little dot and then disappeared.

She loved the grounds of Brech Woorlach. The very grand and imposing mansion was extremely impressive in its own right, but she favoured most the huge area of greenery within its boundary walls. The Duke and Duchess of Bo'Ness employed a small army of gardeners who tended to it and cared for it with an almost religious fervour. To Janine, it was a lush and splendid paradise.

Janine had sought out her favourite spot in the furthest corner. It was a place where she could be completely alone. She had sought it out as a place of sanctuary where nobody would be compelled to sit in silence while she was deep in thought. This kind of formal etiquette, observed by the people around her, had begun to make her feel oddly uncomfortable.

Stood in the shade of a weeping willow tree, its cascading branches falling around her like a giant umbrella, she closed her eyes and allowed her thoughts to drift.

She breathed in deeply and then let out a lengthy sigh. She felt cleansed. It was as if a giant weight had been lifted from her royal shoulders.

Closing her eyes and leaning back to rest her head against the trunk of the willow, she allowed her mind to wander. She recalled her arrival at Brech Woorlach and how, despite seeing it for the first time, she had felt confused and disorientated by how familiar it seemed. From the moment she had set eyes on the building, her mind had started presenting her with memories that seemed impossible.

Her mind was labouring under a heavy burden. She was striving to learn and reconcile her history in these surroundings. It was like watching an incoming tide making its slow but relentless progress in from the sea. Each new memory was like the waves rising up through a new outcrop of rocks and flowing into newly accessible pools. With each successive surge, the sea claimed more of the land. With each successive surge of her memory, her mind claimed more of her past.

The process of piecing together her earlier life had been disorderly, but it was a comfort to know that she genuinely had been here, at Brech Woorlach, as a young girl. She now knew, for certain, that she had arrived here as a baby, then returned as a small child and, again, at seven years old.

She stood, motionless, gazing towards an arched gateway in the wall of the grounds, but without actually seeing it. Her mind seemed to flit around like the insect she had been watching.

Despite her best endeavours, there was one great mystery that remained: She was unable to comprehend how she could have so completely disassociated herself from the role of Queen of the West. It was not like forgetting that she hated mushrooms or that she liked collecting pretty pebbles.

The job that Mister Chang had accomplished in so thoroughly wiping her memory had been extraordinary. She was the Queen of the West of Scotland. She was a monarch. She had inherited the right to wear a crown. Yet, all this had been completely and utterly forgotten. She was in awe of Mister Chang's skill and manipulation in rearranging her brain like that, for being a queen was not some tiny, inconsequential fragment of detail that could simply slip a person's mind.

Janine sighed and frowned as she recalled being a ladies maid at Dunkeld Manor, where the Chief of Arms to the Laird who had assaulted her and tried to force himself on her. He had dragged her down to the cellars. She had fainted and woken up to find him brutally slain. There had been blood everywhere. She and the butcher's boy had hidden in a departing wagon and jumped out and hurried away once they were out of sight of the manor.

Janine sighed and frowned, again, as she relived the moment of being accosted on the road by three robbers. She had run for her life to escape them, but had eventually been caught by one of them. She held her breath as she recalled fainting and waking up on the ground to find her attacker viciously killed.

Janine made an approving noise as she recollected her shock and horror at discovering that it was actually *she* who had hacked both men to death and *not* some mysterious protector! Mister Chang and his daughter, Genji, had – it transpired – taught her martial arts and hidden away that ability in a separate version of herself who only emerged when her life was in danger.

Janine smiled as she remembered how Bruce and Brian – the adopted sons of the Duke and Duchess – had gallantly rescued her from the side of the road, picking her up in their coach bringing her to safety at Brech Woorlach.

Janine set aside these thoughts and brought to the forefront of her brain the most profound implication of being a queen that she had not yet fully embraced: If she were a queen, then that meant that her mother had been a queen, too.

The title of queen, Janine knew, must have passed to her upon the death of her mother. This was the same woman who, in her childhood, had always studiously pretended that she was nobody of any kind of importance.

It suddenly hit her that she had only known part of her mother's life. Her mother had taken herself away, for around half of every year. Each Spring, she would wearily announce that she had to 'go and do the rounds'. This, her mother explained, involved visiting sick and elderly relatives and taking her turn to care for them.

Her mother's 'rounds' took her on a trek right across the Scottish Highlands and up into the furthest North.

Janine would beg to go with her, but her mother would always insist that her absence was a debt of honour that she fulfilled most reluctantly and that it was the most tedious, boring and tiresome thing that could ever possibly be imagined.

Each year, when the time came for her mother to depart, a group of men on horses would always come to call. They wore huge swords and had helmets and big, round battle shields of dark blue and gold with shiny metal domes in the middle. This was unusual, she knew, for her father had said that soldiers, here and about, had smaller oblong shields and only the more wealthy had claymores.

Janine recalled that, when these men came, they would act really strangely towards her mother. This used to confuse her, as a child, until it was explained to her that these men were "actors" and that they helped her mother to perform plays, to amuse and entertain the people she visited and tended. These men were just pretending, her mother said, because her own role was usually of a high born lady and these men liked to rehearse how they would behave in front of her when they were on a stage.

Once she understood the behaviour of these soldiers – who were also called 'travelling players' – it caused her great amusement. They were always bowing to her mother and would often drop to one knee in front of her. Even funnier was the time she had caught them kneeling on *both* knees, kissing their swords and offering them to her mother to touch! Now *that* had been hysterical!

Janine smiled at the recollection of those ludicrous antics. Then she stopped, suddenly puzzled. Perhaps her mother had grossly understated the importance of her role in those plays, back then. It seemed to Janine that her mother had been cast not merely as a high born lady, but as royalty! The smile froze on Janine's face. The actors had, in fact, always treated her mother as if she were a queen!

Janine put her hand to her mouth and, leaning against the trunk of the tree for support, she wondered how she could have failed to see this before. Her mother *was* a queen!

Janine cursed herself. She must have been an idiot! No, she hadn't been an idiot. That wasn't it at all. She had simply never been herself, before. Those memories were those of a child. She hadn't had a child's memory since forever. She had only possessed any conscious knowledge of that period of time since yesterday.

She smiled again, fondly. She had just conjured a particularly pleasant memory. It was the memory of the 'good man'. That is what she had always called the one who was the leader of the men who came to take her mother 'on her travels'. He always smiled at her with a genuine smile. The other men smiled at her with fake smiles. They used smiles that were sufficient for a mere child. They were the smiles they gave because she was her mother's daughter. The 'good man', though, smiled a true smile. His smile was one of fondness and kindness.

The other men did whatever 'good man' told them to do. The other men respected him. They didn't share the way he smiled at her, though. She strained to recall his actual name. It just wouldn't come to her. She knew it and she was certain she did, but she couldn't quite grasp it. For several minutes she stood with her eyes closed and tightly screwed up, trying to get the man's name to surface in her mind. In the end, she snarled at herself and clenched her teeth in annoyance.

Pushing herself away from the tree trunk, Janine leaned forward to resume a standing position, still cursing her memory for letting her down. As she did so, she became aware of another's presence.

She turned to see an old man watching her from a high arched gateway in the wall close by her. She was immediately intrigued by something about him that she could not quite place. He looked genuinely pleasant and amiable and had the glimmer of a smile on his lips. She could not help but smile back at him.

The old man touched two fingers to his brow in a salute. Janine smiled still more and made a little motion with her hands to grip an invisible skirt while bobbing slightly to insinuate a curtsey. The old man looked perturbed by her gesture. After a moment's pause he placed one hand on his stomach, the other behind his back and leaned forward into a deep, ceremonious bow.

Janine looked at him quizzically and could not prevent a frown from forming on her face. The man gave her a tight lipped smile and looked apologetic.

"Your grandmother was a fine lady," he said, "She had the most impeccable and refined manners. She was raised to the life of a lady and with a stern regard to her lofty station in life. She was a frequent guest of The Duchess Constance and would have been taught by her to never curtsy to a servant. I am sure that the current Duke and Duchess of Bo'Ness would find it fitting if I were to humbly prevail upon you to observe the same decorum. That is if you'll forgive me for such an impertinence."

Janine was instantly captivated by his quaint, almost archaic, turn of phrase. She found it, at one and the same time, both extremely endearing and almost pitiful. The man stood, serene and patient, waiting dutifully for a reply – if there were to be one – or for none at all.

"If you would show me respect," she replied, "I would have you speak to me without restraint."

The man appeared to gather himself, as if such an invitation as this were something momentous. He cleared his throat and coughed into his hand before speaking.

"Begging your pardon, Ma'am, I came to impart a warning."

Janine looked blank, utterly nonplussed.

"Beware the door left open," he said.

"Beware the door left open?" she asked, repeating his words in complete bafflement.

She heard the sound of approaching footsteps and turned to see who was coming. It was Bruce. He looked slightly confused.

"Who are you talking to?" he asked.

"I am talking to the old gentleman, of course," Janine replied, pointing a hand to the arched gateway.

"What old gentleman?" Bruce enquired, now intrigued.

Janine turned to the gateway and was shocked to see that there was nobody there. She looked back to Bruce, her eyes betraying her anxiety. She spun her head back to the gate, unable to believe her eyes.

"He was standing there!" she cried in disbelief.

Bruce looked from her to the gate and then back again, clearly perplexed.

"Very well," he said, his voice empty of feeling and his face tinged with concern.

"It's the truth!" she protested, "I saw him. He was standing there! We were talking!"

Bruce was plainly worried and knotted his brow. Janine was absolutely certain that there had been no time for the man to slip away. It would have been impossible. It would have taken a gymnast of extraordinary prowess to come anywhere close to that kind of agility.

She turned to Bruce with an imploring look.

"There was somebody there, Bruce, I swear it is the truth!"

"What did he look like, Your Ladyship?"

"He was an old man. He had a long, thin face and piercing eyes. He had a small moustache. He had ears that were slightly big and stuck out a little. He had a very square jaw. He had thin, greying hair with a high forehead."

Bruce shook his head and confessed that he did not recognise anybody from her description.

"He spoke strangely. He spoke very properly and formally. He put words together to form sentences that were oddly long. Does that sound silly?"

Bruce shook his head.

"No," he replied, "Not if that is what you heard."

"I can't describe how he spoke any better than that. Let us just say that he seemed to have a very old fashioned way of talking. Am I making sense?"

"Yes, My Lady," Bruce reassured her, "I am following what you mean."

"I saw him clear as day," Janine pleaded.

Bruce nodded sympathetically. Janine stood with a look of helplessness on her face and kept staring at the arched gateway, as if looking enough times might somehow bring the old man back. Bruce smiled, weakly, at her.

"Let us go and see Mister O'Keefe and Missus Keltie," Bruce offered, "They are the Butler and the Matron Housekeeper. They may recognise who it is that you saw."

With this, they made off to the rear of the house. Janine cast several anxious glances back to the gateway until they rounded a corner and it was out of sight. Bruce took her arm and squeezed it, reassuringly, but she could sense that he was worried.

CHAPTER 2

Bruce and Janine entered Brech Woorlach by descending a set of stone steps and using a narrow door at the bottom of them. Once inside, there was a regular flow of servants passing back and forth along the underground corridors, each hurrying about their chores. Bruce asked several of them where they might find Mister O'Keefe. The servants all apologised that they were unable to assist but, within a very short time, Mister O'Keefe suddenly turned up in person. He had evidently been advised of their quest by one of his staff and, on learning their identities, he had hurried to intercept them.

After politely bowing and greeting Bruce and Janine, Mister O'Keefe was eager to know how he could assist them. Janine began to explain her encounter and had only given him a couple of details of the mysterious old man's appearance, before Mister O'Keefe adopted a look of unease. It was obvious that he knew the person she described, but was quick to suggest that they draw on the assistance of Missus Keltie in trying to identify them.

A kitchen junior was despatched to find Missus Keltie and she arrived, soon afterwards, profusely apologetic for having kept them waiting, despite the fact that she hadn't.

Janine embarked on a fuller description of the old man and was only a little way into it before Missus Keltie, too, began to look distinctly unsettled. She listened carefully to the details and became progressively more apprehensive at each of them.

"He was old," Janine had said, "He had a long, thin face, a pair of piercing eyes and a small moustache. He was blessed with larger than usual ears that stuck out from his head. He had a distinctly square jaw and sparse hair that was going grey. He had a high forehead."

At the end of the description, Missus Keltie gave Mister O'Keefe a conspiratorial glance. He answered it with a grim, stony gaze and appeared to be distinctly troubled.

"I am certain that I know the man you describe," Missus Keltie announced, after some consideration, "But coming across him the way you describe is…"

Missus Keltie looked to Mister O'Keefe for support.

"More than a little surprising," Mister O'Keefe concluded.

"I can show you a painting of this man," Missus Keltie offered, "If you wish to view it. You can gauge his likeness yourself, Your Ladyship."

Janine accepted the offer and was instantly filled with a sense of foreboding. Mister O'Keefe excused himself and left the room for a moment. He came back carrying an unusual looking lamp. Behind the lamp's large, glass globe was positioned a round, highly polished reflector dish. The dish had a hinged arm that allowed it to be lifted up to concentrate the illumination of the flame in a given direction. The Matron Housekeeper looked at the lamp, took a long breath, swallowed, and led them out into the corridor with a second lamp of her own. Janine was fairly sure that she saw her give a little shiver.

The little group processed along the well-lit corridor to a door at its end and went through it in single file. They walked along a similar, but narrower, corridor and came to another door at the far end. This door had to be unlocked and Mister O'Keefe duly produced a bunch of keys for that purpose. Upon opening it, Mister O'Keefe and Missus Keltie raised the wicks of their lamps to provide more light for the next stage of their journey. Once through the door, Janine noticed that the temperature rapidly dropped until it was distinctly cold.

"None of the heating in the house reaches this far, any more," Missus Keltie explained, by way of an indirect apology.

"The paintings here," Mister O'Keefe advised them, "Are some of the less noteworthy ones from the hall's history."

"These are **old** paintings?" Janine asked, a little confused.

"Yes, they are."

"You don't have a recent painting of the man I met?"

Mister O'Keefe hesitated for a moment, "No. There is no such painting, I'm afraid."

They walked along the corridor with Mister O'Keefe leading the way, holding up his lamp to guide them. Missus Keltie, at the rear of their party, held up her own lamp, too, to offer extra illumination.

"So, you are going to show me a painting of a relative of this man?" Janine asked, "A painting that would show a similar appearance to him?"

There was a pause while the butler and matron housekeeper waited for each other to reply, allowing the silence to hang, before Missus Keltie gave in.

"If you take a look at the painting I have in mind, I am sure that you will be able to confirm if I am thinking of the right person from your description."

Janine detected the faintest exhalation of air through the butler's nose. His self-control had slipped for a second and he had narrowly avoided an unguarded snort at her reply.

They continued to walk until they reached a point approximately half way down the long corridor, a distance of around thirty paces. Here, they came to a halt. Ominously, the matron housekeeper and the butler exchanged glances, as if for mutual support.

Mister O'Keefe offered up his lamp to a particular painting and the flame flickered and wafted in the slight breeze.

Janine squinted through the semi gloom at the artwork. The face of the sitter was not very clear. After a few seconds, the lamp was withdrawn, its reflector was pulled up into place, and it was held aloft again.

Janine looked at the face on the canvas in front of her and gave a little, involuntary yelp.

"That's him!" she cried, "There is absolutely no doubt about it!"

The butler and the matron housekeeper looked at each other for a long moment. Their eyes loudly broadcasted to everyone present that they were not looking forward to whatever explanation they were about to provide.

"This is an uncanny family resemblance!" Janine insisted, still spellbound by the face that looked down at her.

"This is the butler to the original Duke of Bo'Ness," Missus Keltie advised, "His name was Angus Percival. He was held in such high esteem by his employer that, in recognition of the same, this portrait was commissioned."

Janine took Bruce by his wrist and drew him close to her, pointing up at the image hanging on the wall.

"His eyes, his nose, his chin!" she enthused, "All absolutely perfect!"

"The picture is by a very skilled and celebrated artist," Mister O'Keefe told them, "And would have been commissioned at some considerable cost."

Missus Keltie moved her lamp to the bottom of the painting where a brass plate, still quite shiny, gleamed its information for all who would see it.

"This is not a relative. This is the man, himself," Mister O'Keefe announced, "This is Angus Percival. He was an only child and never married, leaving no heirs. He was the last of his line."

Janine read the wording on the brass plate and shuddered when she came to the details of birth and death: *'Angus Percival: 1460 – 1522'.*

"It says he died a hundred years ago!" Janine exclaimed, her tone incredulous.

"Yes, My Lady, he did," replied Missus Keltie, visibly squirming with embarrassment.

Janine turned to Bruce, who was watching her the way a man might watch a dog he feared could, at any moment, turn on him and bite him.

"I saw him!" Janine exclaimed, "I spoke to him! He spoke to me!"

"And he looked and behaved like any normal, living person?" asked Bruce.

"Yes. Yes, he did. Except…." replied Janine, her forehead creasing in thought, "Except he spoke in a very odd, old-fashioned way. We only exchanged polite greetings," she lied, "His legs were strange, though…."

"He was renowned as a very tall man," Mister O'Keefe declared.

"No!" Janine objected, "He was of average height, if even that! I saw him clearly."

"He was a man of six feet and four inches tall, My Lady."

"He was? That is most strange…" Janine's voice trailed off as she tried to call to mind the image of him, there, by the gate.

The others waited patiently for her to continue. Bruce stared at the picture mistrustfully, while furtive glances passed between Mister O'Keefe and Missus Keltie, indicating worry and unease.

In a moment of sudden inspiration, the scene by the willow tree sprang into Janine's mind, presenting itself to her, vividly. She could see the man was standing on stumps rather than the whole of his legs.

"His legs were somehow not right," Janine announced, abruptly returning from her reverie, "He was stood next to the archway in the wall, at the far end of the lawns, the place where the path comes out next to the weeping willow."

Her audience all nodded.

"He wasn't on his feet, though," Janine explained, "The only way I can put it is that he was stood with his legs touching the ground a little distance below his knees. He had no feet."

The butler and the matron housekeeper looked blankly at each other. Janine had not expected this to make any sense and, very evidently, it did not.

"He was standing to the side of the doorway," Janine continued, "He was leaning against the wall, at first, then he stood tall when I spoke to him. He was, I would say, just two paces from the archway in the wall that surrounds the door."

Missus Keltie scratched her head. Mister O'Keefe rubbed his chin. They looked at each other for inspiration, but none came.

"He died in 1522," the butler murmured to himself, "The archway and the door would certainly have been there, back then..."

Missus Keltie nodded her agreement, then leaned forward and rubbed her head with the palm of her hand, as if trying to agitate her brains.

"The willows were there," Mister O'Keefe muttered, "Though not these we see, today. There would have been a lot more of them, back in his day..."

Missus Keltie suddenly gave a cry of excitement.

"The steps!" she said, triumphantly, "The steps!"

"The steps?" Mister O'Keefe asked with no sign of comprehension.

"Angus Percival died falling down the steps. There was an accident! The Duke had them covered over and the whole area was landscaped. The steps were replaced by a long, gentle slope. It rose up to the archway and the door beneath it!"

"That's right!" Mister O'Keefe agreed, "I've seen the old plans of the grounds. They show how the estate looked in 1510. The current path is higher than it was, but there have always been willows planted along that side of it, from back then right up to the present day."

Missus Keltie nodded vigorously and looked pleased with herself.

"The steps radiated out from the doorway," O'Keefe enthused, "They were a half circle that got wider and wider with each step, until they reached the level of the old path. There were, if my memory serves me rightly, either six or seven steps. So, if somebody were to be stood two paces to the left of the arch, they would have had to go down at least two of those steps."

Bruce gasped in surprise.

"He was stood where his feet *would* have rested, in his own time!" Bruce asserted, "So a man well over six foot tall would appear to be of only average height! The soil, as it is today, would be half way up to his knees!"

"My goodness!" Janine exclaimed in alarm, "I saw a ghost!"

"If you believe in such things!" Bruce cautioned.

"Do *you* believe in such things?" Janine asked.

Bruce looked coy and shrugged his shoulders.

"I do when it is dark!" he quipped.

"I have to believe my own eyes," Janine said, emphatically, "And I have to believe my own ears."

"My Lady, you only exchanged pleasantries with the man?" Missus Keltie asked.

"Yes."

The matron housekeeper nodded and gave this some consideration.

"I must confess that I do believe in such a thing as life beyond the grave, Your Ladyship," Missus Keltie admitted, "But, in my experience, those who appear to us, having departed this world, tend to want to convey something of importance to the living."

Janine feigned surprise and shrugged.

"I cannot recall him saying anything of any consequence," she lied, crossing her fingers behind her back.

Bruce observed the gesture and raised an eyebrow.

Janine pondered the actual words the old man had said to her: *'Beware the door left open.'*

Try as she might, she could not fathom any possible meaning from it.

CHAPTER 3

Ewan Burberry, High Constable of Edinburgh, was in very definite pain. As he sat outside the inn at Pitlochry in Scotland, propped up against a couple of hay bales, he eyed the army wagon before him with grim resignation.

He had travelled from Edinburgh in perfect health, sat astride a fine horse with a saddle so comfortable that it felt as if he were in an armchair. Both had been personal gifts to him from King James of Scotland and of England.

He was now in a thoroughly battered and bruised condition, however, and about to resume his journey northwards to Inverness in the back of a rickety military conveyance that had seen better days.

He closed his eyes and grimly reflected on the recent events that had delivered him to his current situation.

He had been instructed by King James to travel from Edinburgh to Inverness to oversee the trial of two people accused of treason. For his protection, the king had arranged for him to be accompanied by a detachment of thirty soldiers from the 'Lothian Pikes and Muskets', under the command of an officer by the name of Captain McCleary.

Unwisely, a little way into his journey, Burberry had slipped away from his escort and gone off on his own. It had not been long before he had encountered a band of thugs known as 'The McCarthys'. During a confrontation with them, he had shot their leader dead. The thugs scattered, incorrectly assuming that such boldness could only mean that he had his troops close at hand.

With the corpse slung across the back of his second horse, he made his way to a local inn, run by Hamish and Caitlan Pottle, and took rooms there.

The following day, he had gone exploring again. Just as before, it had been without the benefit of his armed guard. Crossing paths with the McCarthys that he had met the previous day, he was attacked and taken prisoner. Back at their hideout, they had severely beaten him but, to his surprise, they had *not* killed him.

Hamish Pottle, the owner of the inn where he was staying, was puzzled by his disappearance, as was Alex Brennan, a fellow guest, there. The two of them tracked him down and mounted a daring armed assault to free him. Captain McCleary and his troops – reaching them at the last moment – threw their forces into the conflict and the Constable was successfully rescued.

The constable knew that he was lucky to be alive. He had escaped death by a whisker. It was, however, depressingly obvious to him that the journey that beckoned was going to be an extremely uncomfortable one. He had a nagging suspicion that he might yet end up wishing he had *not* survived.

CHAPTER 4

Hamish Pottle and Alex Brennan – along with Captain McCleary from the Lothian Pikes and Muskets – carefully manoeuvred Constable Burberry into the rear of an army wagon. Despite their best efforts, he yelled frequent complaints and accompanied them with streams of profanities.

Positioning him at the front of the vehicle, propped up in the corner, they quickly withdrew, only too glad to leave him in the charge of the innkeeper's wife, Caitlan Pottle.

Burberry declared himself to be feeling like he had just been thrown down a well.

Showing saint-like tolerance and impressive patience, Caitlan padded out his sitting place with an abundance of straw, wood shavings and sacking, building them up until it looked like a throne.

Ahead of the vehicle, Hamish and the stable boy had hitched up four horses, rather than the normal two. This, it was hoped, would allow the inclines to be less of a struggle and avoid the need to rush at them to maintain speed.

Several soldiers busied themselves setting up huge metal hoops and a heavy sailcloth cover to shield the occupants of the wagon from the worst of the expected bad weather. This was, unfortunately, something that could never be escaped on any journey into the Highlands!

"There is no right answer to this situation," Constable Burberry told Captain McCleary, "Whatever we decide to do, everything could still go wrong."

Iain McCleary nodded and scratched his chin.

"The troops can either stay with you," the captain replied, "Or they can maintain a distance ahead or behind you. Thirty soldiers are going to be noticeable. There is no way of hiding them. They will either attract unwelcome attention and mark you out as a target or they will deter our enemies and keep you safe."

The constable looked up into the sky, studying the billowing clouds as they rolled slowly past. Every now and again, he grunted as he contemplated. Captain McCleary waited, as did Hamish, Alex and Caitlan.

At last, the constable dragged his attention back to activities at ground level and promptly made the *Scottish Noise*, a deep throaty grumble of annoyance.

"As I see it," offered Hamish Pottle, "We will be moving through some big hills and deep glens. They will present an ideal opportunity for our foes to ambush us."

Burberry grunted absentmindedly, seeming not to have heard him.

"Moses, in the Bible," said Burberry in a melancholy tone, "Had a pillar of cloud to guide him across the desert by day and a pillar of fire, by night."

Hamish and the captain looked at each other as if the constable had taken leave of his senses. The two of them then looked to Caitlan, who shrugged her shoulders and held up her hands to display her own confusion.

"I was reluctant to use these," said Burberry producing a small leather bag, the size of a man's fist, from his satchel.

"What is that?" asked Hamish, pointing to the bag.

"It contains seven small white stones and seven small black stones."

"Is that so?" mused Hamish, unsure if he had just received an answer or not.

The constable smiled and shook the bag, causing a vague rattling sound to emanate from inside it.

"As a young boy, I lived with my uncle, in England," the constable explained, "He was a man of the cloth. He was an enthusiastic believer in Saint Pierre Abélard of Notre Dame."

"Abélard was a Saint?" asked McCleary, cynically.

"He was, to all those who held that great man in high esteem," Burberry warned, with a hint of a growl edging his voice.

"Oh," said McCleary with mock innocence, "I thought that he'd done some things…"

McCleary's voice trailed off as Burberry turned to him and fixed him with a venomous glare.

"He was innocent of any seduction! He, in fact, was the victim of it!" Burberry declared, looking incensed, "In a moment of weakness he succumbed to the lure of the flesh!"

"I don't think the girl's father saw it quite that way," McCleary objected, mischievously.

"Sometimes we are tested. Sometimes we are weak. Sometimes we fail our test, but grow stronger from it," the constable asserted, almost pleading.

There was a brief, tense silence.

"There isn't a man who hasn't been haunted by temptation," Captain McCleary responded, his voice now conciliatory.

"My uncle revered Pierre Abélard. He studied him. He scrutinised everything he could find that mentioned him. Many times he travelled to London, most of a day's journey, to immerse himself in books about him in the great libraries, there."

McCleary nodded, looking a little bashful.

"There were times when Pierre Abélard was too ill to go to a holy place to pray for guidance. At those times, when he had a profound decision to make, he would search out his pouch of stones. One that looked something like this," Burberry revealed, holding up the little bag, "He would pray and then draw a stone. The colour of the stone would give him the answer he sought."

"I envy you for your faith," said McCleary, sounding miserable.

Burberry did not reply, but looked back to the clouds, moodily. McCleary looked at them, too. Hamish, Caitlan and Alex, seeing the two men's interest, found themselves staring skyward, as well.

"Sometimes," said the constable, almost to himself, "You just need to know for certain that you're not simply meddling and wasting your time, but that something real is driving you and calling you."

The five of them became still and silent, solemnly surveying the clouds. The clouds seemed oblivious to their sudden importance. They continued to slowly float along, drifting with unhurried nonchalance, like enormous fluffy sheep cropping at pale blue grass.

Without realising it, all their eyes fell upon the same cloud. It was a large white mountain of billowing cotton, sailing across a patch of blue, by itself. All of a sudden, completely contrary to the progress of its peers, it came to an abrupt halt. It paused for a moment, then – with spectacular disregard for the prevailing wind – shunted backwards a good distance, before resuming its original path.

McCleary gave a little gasp.

"Was that anything to do with *you*?" asked the captain, in awe.

"Aye!" Burberry responded, "I believe it was!"

"I don't think you need to draw a stone," McCleary enthused, "I believe you have your answer."

"I've never seen anything like that in my life!" Hamish exclaimed, "And I've spent many an hour gazing at clouds on long sea voyages. If you're on watch, there's little else to do. You either stare at the sky or you stare at the waves!"

"I feel confident, as Constable of Edinburgh, appointed by King James, that a far higher authority than anything on Earth has just confirmed that what we are about to do is right, just and honourable."

"Not only that," chuckled Hamish, "But, at least as important to me, personally, my wife gives her approval, too!"

Everybody laughed and the soldiers close by – unsure of the cause of the amusement – were happy to pick up on the good mood and laugh, too. Hamish caught Alex glancing across to the soldiers and slapped him on the back.

"Highland humour!" Hamish declared.

"A humour," his wife advised, with a twinkle in her eyes, "That results from the daily decision forced upon us in the Highlands, in response to the rain, the wind and the cold."

"The decision," Hamish crowed, "Is whether to laugh or to cry!"

They all laughed, again, and the skies began to bless them with a light drizzle, as if in confirmation. Everyone turned up their collars or raised their hood.

"Our Holy Mission," McCleary announced with a deliberately shaky voice, jovially mimicking an elderly priest addressing his congregation, "Must now commence!"

With this, the captain gave a shout and twirled his finger in the air like a lasso. The soldiers moved to form into a column and the lead vehicle pulled away ahead of them. It then drew to a halt thirty paces distant.

"A priest once told me that if we avoid suffering in this life, then we must endure it all the more in the next," said McCleary.

"I have heard it said," replied Burberry, groaning and rubbing his back.

"Well, no matter how noble our cause," Hamish warned, "I'm afraid you're going to be thrown around in the back of this wagon like an ant in a tin trunk."

"My past sins must be catching up with me!" the constable guffawed.

"Aye," agreed Captain McCleary, smiling broadly, "The road is flat out of Pitlochry but climbs steeply beyond Calvine and Dalwhinnie and that is just the start of it. Our route takes us either over or around at least twenty sizeable hills. As if that were not bad enough, it then takes us down and through at least a dozen glens, some with steep sides."

"Our own wagon," Alex said, casting a hand, accusingly, at Burberry's conveyance, "Will force us to stay on the roads and prevent us from striking out over the hills, themselves."

"And this awful track that we'll be travelling on gets worse and worse the further we go," Hamish added.

"So," said Burberry, sarcastically, "Apart from this seemingly endless list of good news…?"

The two soldiers hauling the canvas up onto the hoops looked at each other, sceptically. It wasn't difficult to read their minds. This was not going to be an easy trek.

"If we are lucky," McCleary grumbled, "Getting a wagon over this kind of territory will take us three days. If it rains badly, on the other hand, and we get bogged down, we'd need to add at least one extra day to that."

Burberry grimaced and sucked air noisily through his teeth. Captain McCleary stood idly kicking one of the wheels of the wagon while clenching and unclenching his jaw. His oversized, black, slickly oiled mariner's coat – which he favoured over any official army attire – looked slightly strange on his slim frame. With his hands stuffed into its pockets – which was his favourite pose – he looked like some kind of baggy insect. His piercing blue-grey eyes kept a systematic watch on everybody around him, as if he suspected they might leap at him if left unobserved for too long.

"With the best will in the world," the constable said, at last, "If I were to climb onto a horse, I'd be in mortal agony and falling to the ground in a heap within the first minute."

"We will keep all of the wagons to the road," McCleary said, "We may be slower for it, but that will not be at any risk to our mission."

Everyone nodded their agreement.

"We would be better travelling without displaying any lanterns as we pass through the denser of the forests," McCleary suggested, "It would attract a lot less attention. In just under an hour, it will be light enough to set off without them. The sun is rising fast. If the clouds break, we could be away sooner, still."

The captain's eyes darted from man to man around their group. Once he was certain that nobody was about to spring at him, out of disappointment, he turned and began to walk away. After a few paces he stopped and spun on his heels. The two soldiers, who had just finished rigging the wagon cover, looked at him apprehensively.

"Go and set expectations amongst the troops," he instructed them, "And make sure we have no stragglers when we move off. If anybody falls behind, they are to shout up. There are no exceptions."

The two men jumped down and hurried away to follow their orders. Iain McCleary, his coat billowing, strode after them. Burberry, Hamish and Alex exchanged glances but, though sorely tempted, nobody commented on the captain's coat.

"From his twang when he speaks," Hamish told them, "He's a man from the Isles. A MacDonald, to be sure."

"I'll take your guidance on that," Burberry replied, "If he is, it will certainly and most surely prove no disadvantage to us in the northern parts."

Hamish and Alex traded a long, purposeful look and each raised an eyebrow for a second. Burberry caught their expressions and grunted with the merest hint of annoyance.

"I don't question the troops on their allegiances," the constable growled, "If that's what you're suggesting."

"They are the King's men!" Alex declared with a wry grin, "Good and true!"

"As are we all!" Burberry responded, "To a man. Every last one of us."

"And to a woman!" quipped Caitlan from her vantage point, sitting by the pump.

"And to a woman!" Burberry acknowledged, tipping an invisible hat to her.

Caitlan Pottle stood up, with leisurely elegance, and walked over to where Alex and Hamish stood by the wagon. She trod with the grace of a cat. Burberry looked at her, with a flicker of curiosity in his eyes, and pursed his lips appreciatively.

"Gentleman," she said, her voice almost purring, "If I could trouble the constable with a couple of questions before he leads my husband off into certain peril?"

Constable Burberry nodded and smiled a sardonic smile. Caitlan smiled back, the movement of her lips coming deliciously close to a pout. Burberry was genuinely startled by the difference he saw in her from the woman he had previously met. He smiled, again, but this time it was the smile of a man openly and honestly communicating his approval and admiration for a woman who – he now realised – had so effortlessly duped him into underestimating her.

"Constable Burberry," she said, enticingly, "Can I presume upon your time to ask you something?"

"Of course," he replied, amiably.

"The three men currently residing under the soil in the woods at the back of the inn," she cooed, "They were here to find you and, without a doubt, to kill you?"

It was clear from the stress on particular words that this was not actually a question at all. Burberry nodded and narrowed his eyes slightly.

"I am a mere woman, but can I just observe that the McCarthys, up at their Coille Dorcha stronghouse, resisted what must have been an overpowering urge to shoot you dead on sight."

Burberry nodded, again, this time more slowly and with considerable deliberation.

"Would I be right in saying that you have not one enemy, but two?" she asked with a disarming smile, "One enemy who wants you dead, whatever it takes, and one enemy who wants you kept good and alive at all costs?"

Burberry held her gaze and, staying silent, gave her a wide smile that would not have looked out of place on the face of a crocodile.

Hamish, mimicking an initial introduction to a stranger, gesticulated towards Caitlan with a flourishing sweep of his arm.

"I'd like you to meet my wife!" he said.

Constable Burberry reached for her hand, and she gave it to him. Lifting it to his lips, he kissed it.

"I am honoured to make your acquaintance, Ma'am," Burberry said, with mock formality, "I fear I had mistaken you for someone else."

"Most men do," she said and smiled like an innocent.

Burberry gave a genuine laugh, "I am sure that they end up regretting it!"

"Sir," she said, dropping a polite little curtsy, "You put me in a challenging position."

Reaching into her apron, she pulled out a pistol. It was a duelling style weapon with a long barrel and an arm that could be pulled up and drawn back to rest onto the bearer's wrist to steady the device for aiming.

Caitlan Pottle cocked the sparking drum, flipped open the charge pan and brought the steadying mechanism into play against her forearm.

The eyes of all three men went to the watering can, sat on a bench a full twenty strides away, and then back to Caitlan. Levelling the weapon in the direction of her target, she paused for scarcely a second before squeezing the trigger. There was a flash and a loud report, and the barrel lifted for a moment as it shot. They all watched in amazement as the watering can lifted into the air and tumbled backward, landing upside down in the dust.

"Just in case you thought that it was a lucky shot...." she said, leaving the sentence unfinished.

With a swift, elegant movement, she produced a second pistol – a perfect match for the first – and, with the same unhurried rapidity, prepared it, aimed it and fired it. The weapon loudly discharged a round towards the watering can. The target kicked over on its side, skittered along the ground, and then lay spinning wildly like a humming top.

With a look of satisfaction, Caitlan turned back to Constable Burberry.

"While I can defend myself – more than adequately – from an assailant, I fear that the people who came for you will return with a substantially larger force. They may come at me in too great a number for me to subdue them so easily as this!"

With deft, sure and practised movements, Caitlan quickly packed up the pistols and stowed them back into her apron.

"While you are away on your mission," Caitlan declared, with her hands on her hips, "I have two maids, two cooks, a labouring man who limps from age and a young stable boy with me here, at the inn."

Constable Burberry flapped a hand to indicate his surrender.

"I will send urgent word to Perth," Burberry promised, "I will advise the County Sheriff that he needs to have the laird appoint a new band of Rangers to stand guard at your inn, on account of the previous ones all being dead."

Caitlan shook her head, waved a hand, dismissively, and spoke calmly and assertively.

"To ensure the safety of the inn and its staff I will require six of your soldiers to remain here, five at the very minimum."

The constable looked at her in amazement and had to remind himself to close his mouth, which had dropped open in surprise.

"I can have someone ride to the County Sheriff, this very minute," he assured her, "And I can have him use my authority to have temporary Rangers appointed immediately and for them to take up their posts without delay, but I regret that I cannot spare the soldiers."

"Very well," Caitlan said, lifting her head, haughtily, "I am obliged to yield to your authority."

Constable Burberry narrowed his eyes, suspiciously. This sudden compliance did not ring true to him. Caitlan turned and began walking towards the door of the inn. After five paces, she called back over her shoulder to him.

"I will need you to wait for me while I get my travelling bag and my heavy cloak. My horse is already saddled."

The mouths of all three men now dropped open.

"Caitlan!" Hamish protested.

His wife stopped dead in her tracks and feigned surprise.

"Why, thank you!" she said, "You're very kind."

Hamish looked at her in confusion.

"You're very kind to offer to get my things for me," she said, "I will wait here for you."

After a moment of exasperation, Hamish trudged off into the inn and returned, a minute or so later, with the said bag and cloak. He placed these into the back of the wagon, underneath the covered section at the front, and performed a formal bow to his wife. She smiled graciously, in return.

Caitlan stood, patient and unflustered, by the rear of the wagon as the stable boy emerged from the side of the inn with her horse.

"You can ride with the driver, up front, and tie your horse to the back of the wagon," Hamish offered.

"If it's all the same to you, Ma'am," Burberry said, grimacing from his discomfort, "I would welcome a fellow traveller in the rear of this vehicle. Mostly for the benefit of your very pleasant company – of course – but, if you would oblige me, also for your help in preventing me from knocking myself unconscious over the ruts and potholes."

Caitlan smiled and, raising one foot a little way off the ground, froze in that pose. Alex promptly took the foot and helped to boost her up onto the flat back of the wagon. Jumping up after her, Alex took several sacks of feed and arranged them to make her a little three-sided refuge. Stuffing some hay into an empty sack, he fluffed it up to function as a cushion for her.

Once arrangements in the rear of the vehicle were concluded, the driver checked all the harnesses and straps. Once satisfied, he told the horses to set off and, very slowly, they moved away.

Constable Burberry winced at the first jolt and closed his eyes as the wagon rocked and swayed. Caitlan shuffled across and grabbed another bag of grain, which she pushed up alongside him to prevent him from slewing and sliding. Burberry grunted his thanks.

The remaining wagons, carrying army supplies and troops, moved out behind them. The soldiers on horseback rode mostly ahead, a few dropping back to follow the last of the wagons. All of the soldiers – mounted or on foot – had their muskets at the ready and prepared for any trouble. There was an unmistakable tension in the air.

CHAPTER 5

Queen Annis was pleased when, the following morning, she received some reassuring news. Her nearly fatal battle injury was healing well. While she was not yet recovered enough to ride her horse, she was well enough to travel in her personal wagon.

Her wagon, as Annis called it, was far more of a large, rustic coach. This and her domed circular tent were a home away from home for her. When she was growing up, they were where she spent her best times with her mother. She associated the tent and the wagon with all of her fondest memories of childhood.

Her mother – who had been murdered by the Clan Campbell – had been a deeply religious person. She had often said that, if she were not born to be Queen of the West, she would have gleefully become a nun. Regardless of her title and position, she did not completely turn her back on this calling. From October to February, each year, her mother would announce that she was leaving Annis in the charge of her personal maid and would head off to France to live with a religious order at an abbey. Annis would continue their nomadic lifestyle, in her absence, and would only head for their family stronghouse at Fort Augustus when full Winter had arrived.

Annis and her followers would remain at the stronghouse until the first signs of Spring. She always looked forward to leaving the shelter of stone and mortar to return to the open air. She felt closer to her mother when she was in the outdoors.

Annis ventured into the nearby meadow, where the sound of a curlew greeted her. She closed her eyes and lifted her face to the sky. The bird's mournful cry pierced her heart, for it held tragic memories. The bird sang and sang, and as she listened, she began to sob. With a lump in her throat, she recalled what her mother used to say:

'One day, when I am freed from this mortal body, when I have cast off these chains of flesh and blood that bind me to life, I will be a curlew and I will soar in the sky, I will swoop across the glens and I will make people weep for the pity of my plaintive song.'

She could never hear a curlew without fondly imagining that it might be her mother come to see her to make sure that she was well. She breathed a few heartfelt sighs, wiped her eyes and tried to push her sadness away from her.

Close by, there was a rustle in the bushes. Annis stiffened and her hand moved instinctively to her dagger. She looked across to her nearest guard. He looked back, unconcerned. If anything, he was slightly amused by something. She was not pleased. Annis cast her eyes back to the bushes. Her brow creased in puzzlement as the noise came again.

"Who is there?" Annis called.

After a few moments, a small figure emerged, timidly, from the undergrowth. She could immediately make out the face of the little girl, Wild Flower. Annis beckoned her to approach.

"Your men swept me up onto one of their horses, after the battle, Your Majesty," said Wild Flower, looking contrite.

"Oh, I see."

"They said that they needed to take care of me."

"Just so."

"They insisted that they rush me to safety."

"Were these my men with the bronze helmets or with the steel helmets?"

"The steel helmets, Your Majesty. They were your ordinary riders."

"They make me proud," Annis declared, "For when they act to defend the poor, the meek and the humble, they serve me best."

"I thank you, Your Majesty."

"They must have thought you were cut off from your clan, the Grants."

"Yes, Your Majesty... but...." Wild Flower's voice trailed off.

"But what?"

"It is of no importance, Your Majesty."

"Tell me. You need not fear speaking plainly to me."

Wild Flower drew in a breath and held it for a few moments before letting it out. Then she spoke in a timid voice.

"I was, indeed, a distance away from the Grants, my clan, Your Majesty," she faltered, looking at the ground, "But it caused me neither worry nor distress. The truth is, these past few days, I have felt best and most at peace when I am close to you and to your people."

"Do the Grants ill treat you?"

"No, Your Majesty."

"Do they beat you?"

"No, Your Majesty."

"Do they make you go hungry?"

"No, Your Majesty."

"Do they make you sleep in the cold?"

"No. I have no complaints about their care of me."

"Come here," Annis said, pointing to the grass in front of her, "Sit down with me."

"Thank you, Your Majesty."

"You don't have to call me *'Your Majesty'*. I give you leave not to do so."

"I am honoured, Your... My Lady."

Wild Flower walked across to her and sat down, a greater distance away than Annis had intended.

"I can arrange for a rider to take you home, if you wish. It would be no trouble."

"No, My Lady. No thank you."

Wild Flower looked thoughtful and made a thin line of her lips as if concentrating hard.

"My Lady, Clan Grant does not feel as much like my home as it always has," said Wild Flower looking embarrassed.

"Does anywhere feel like your home?" Annis enquired.

"Home feels like wherever **you** are, My Lady."

Annis smiled a broad, warm smile and held out her arms to embrace the little girl. Wild Flower shrank back and looked first to the guard on her left and then to the guard on her right. Both men looked back nonchalantly, clearly unconcerned.

"I am unworthy," Wild Flower whispered.

"Nonsense!" Annis scolded.

Wild Flower dropped to her knees and walked forward on them, but only a little way, intending to sit back down, but – once she was within reach – Annis leaned forward and pulled her into an embrace.

"For all that I am and all that I represent," whispered Annis, "I am nothing more than the same flesh and blood as anybody else and – if the truth were known – I am, at times, lonelier than you can imagine."

"My Lady, I am honoured, that you should trust me with your confidence."

"You may stay here, with my camp and my followers, for as long as you choose. You are most welcome to join us, Wild Flower."

"You know my name!" Wild Flower gasped in genuine amazement.

"Why, yes. I heard somebody address you by it."

"And you remembered it!"

"Yes, I remembered."

"You know my name!" Wild Flower said, again, with no less astonishment.

Annis smiled.

"I am a queen, but I am not some lofty and distant person in a tower who has no idea and no care for what happens on the ground."

"My Lady, your mother is so very proud of you."

"Do you not mean that my mother **would** be very proud of me?"

"No, My Lady, your mother **is** very proud of you. I know this."

Wild Flower cocked her head and touched her ear, as if listening. At that exact moment, the curlew sang its woeful song, again.

"Your mother is never far from you," Wild Flower declared, "She is always close by."

Annis stared at Wild Flower in surprise. The look of shock and amazement that had been on Wild Flower's face was now transferred to her own.

"Your mother's love will endure to the end of time," Wild Flower assured her, "Her love will last until the end of all things that have been, all things that are, and all things that will be."

Annis took a deep breath and steeled herself not to cry.

"She needs you to be strong, My Lady."

Tears brimmed in the queen's eyes.

"She knows how strong you can be, My Lady. It was she who made you so strong. She prepared you."

Annis' lip trembled. The two sat in silence for a while.

"Wild Flower, tell me about yourself."

The little girl, so very much older and more grown up than her apparent years, began to tell the story of her life and Annis listened, enthralled.

"I was born on an island, to the Southwest of Scotland, called Ellan Vannin. It sits in the sea, midway between Scotland and Ireland. It is a place with a long Viking heritage. That heritage is much celebrated. It is a source of pride for them."

Annis gave her a quizzical look, as if something she had said, a phrase or emphasis, had not rung wholly true. Wild Flower realised that her face might have betrayed her real feelings and gave the queen a very grown up look and a grim smile.

"When the Vikings first arrived, My Lady, in the year 798, they were a brutal scourge on Ellan Vannin. They plundered, they burned, they stole and they brought much death and destruction to our island."

Annis nodded, accepting this version as more sincere.

"I was the youngest of six children, My Lady…"

"Why do you say, 'I *was* the youngest'? Why do you not say, 'I *am* the youngest'?"

Wild Flower looked surprised, "That is exactly what I should have said," she acknowledged, "I wonder why I did not?"

The queen waited for the answer, but an answer did not come. Instead, the little girl seemed to be fascinated by her slip of the tongue, and appeared to marvel at her own words, rather than seeking to explain them.

"You know what it is, My Lady, to feel like you have been here before?"

"Yes," replied Annis, astonished.

"And to feel like you may have lived this life already?"

"Yes," Annis confirmed, still in awe of her insight, "But how could you know that?"

"I wish I knew," Wild Flower shrugged.

"Yes," said Annis, nodding thoughtfully, "It is a strange thing. I have felt it, too. I know what it is to know things that I surely cannot know."

"I caused my mother and father much worry and concern with my gifts. I told them things that I could not possibly know. I saw things in the future before they happened."

Queen Annis nodded.

"My family was very poor. It was a struggle to survive. One year was even harder than usual. There was a harsh Winter and most of our crops failed due to frost. To make matters worse, there were many weeks of very poor fishing. We went hungry a lot."

Annis made a sympathetic noise.

"It was around that time that I started seeing and hearing fairies. This amused them, but did not worry them, until…"

"Until?"

"Until I started hearing the bad fairies. From then on, My Lady, people started to worry what powers I might have secretly learned. My family was close to starving and they had a daughter who made some of the local people frightened. In the end, my father sold me to some visiting traders."

Annis looked saddened.

"They did what they had to do, My Lady. By selling me, my father may well have saved me from being accused of witchcraft and being burned for it."

"Life has not been kind to you," Annis said, "And yet you show everybody around you love and kindness. Love is the most powerful thing in the world. To be loved is a precious thing."

Wild Flower appeared to consider this, for a little while, before speaking.

"The two girls who attend you, My Lady. They love and adore you. They worship the ground you walk upon."

"How do you know of them? You have not seen them. Have you?"

"No, but I know of them, still. I know of many things that I cannot explain."

"Jet and Jade are young," said Annis, "They are but nine or ten years old. This cruel world has not yet taught them to hate."

"Their love for you is way beyond their years."

Annis smiled and sighed.

"You found them by the road, My Lady. You rescued them."

"You know that, too?"

"Yes, My Lady. It has come into my head," replied Wild Flower, looking contrite for such an intrusion, "They were cared for by their grandparents when their mother and father died of the fever."

The queen nodded, sadly, vividly recalling the day in question.

"They were left by the side of the Great North Road. When your caravan drew level with them – your wagons and riders ahead and behind you – they came to a halt."

Queen Annis nodded.

"You did not give your driver a command to stop?"

"No."

"But he stopped, even so."

"Yes."

"Why did your driver stop?"

"Because he knew that it was what I would have wanted."

"You did not see the children?"

"No."

"You were completely unaware of them?"

"Yes. I had no idea that they were there. I had not looked out of my window for some time. I was reading a book."

"Your driver, making the decision himself, brought your caravan to a stop because of two abandoned children, with dirty faces and with filthy matted hair, shivering and clinging to each other for warmth, sat by the side of the road?"

"Yes."

"He did not fear a reprimand?"

"Absolutely not."

"The miserable, desperate life that those girls had known was swept away and replaced by love and kindness."

"I am proud to say so, for there can never be too much love or kindness in the world."

"My Lady," said Wild Flower, with a note of melancholy, "The girl of the two who is shorter by a thumb's length, she has a sadness that she hides deep inside and does not share."

"I have sensed it," replied Annis, knowing that she was referring to Jet.

"More sorry than you would say aloud, My Lady."

Queen Annis turned to Wild Flower and put on a pretence of haughtiness.

"They are just servants," she said.

"Aye. They are," Wild Flower responded, with a crooked smile, "Or they would be, if **you** were **just** a queen."

"Am I so transparent to you?"

Wild Flower smiled, again, kindly and reassuring.

"Your goodness, My Lady, is more beautiful than a butterfly, than a flower and even more than the loveliest of sunsets."

"Your kind words are beyond my deserving of them."

"The hearts of those two girls are pure. Pure as the whitest snow on the highest peak. They love you for who you are and not because you wear a crown."

"I hope I deserve it."

"My Lady, they are just servants," mimicked Wild Flower.

Annis laughed to be taunted with her own words.

"The soldier," Wild Flower said, pointing to Balgair, who stood at the foot of the meadow with his back to them, organising some troops, "He is most fond of you, too. Most fond indeed."

Wild Flower spoke with the merest hint of roguishness in her voice.

"His heart leaps high enough to vault those trees when he looks at you," she said, motioning to a line of tall firs.

Annis sat tall in order to look stately and regal.

"Is that so?" she asked, trying to appear unconcerned.

"Why, yes, My Lady. You are the reason that he is glad to wake up in a morning."

The queen could not suppress a glimmer of a smile at this and her cheeks began to flush.

"He is a fine man, My Lady. A fine man, for sure."

The curlew sang again.

"And your mother approves, too!"

The two of them laughed and laughed. The guards looked baffled. Twice, the two girls managed to regain their poise and restraint, but only to lose it again, in another fit of laughter.

At last, Wild Flower and Annis were able to maintain straight faces. Within a few moments, Wild Flower held up a finger, as if listening to something. It soon became evident that it was not a sound that absorbed her. It was something she was feeling.

"There is a messenger coming," she said, "He is a soldier, but he is not a soldier. This messenger is not any ordinary kind of messenger. He conveys only things of greatest importance. Things of importance to the King."

"Is he far away?"

"No, he will be here shortly. He brings with him a piece of paper. It is a document. An important document."

Wild Flower looked up into the sky and her eyes flickered as if trying to wake from a dream.

"The document he brings bears the seal and signature of King James."

Queen Annis looked alarmed.

"This document is for me?"

"Yes," Wild Flower said, reluctantly, "It is not a good thing. There is a dark shadow in its wake."

Annis whistled and, when the guards turned, she raised both hands and made a sweeping gesture in the air. The soldiers immediately shouted to their fellows, stationed at intervals, and the alarm was then passed on until it reached the perimeter guards.

It took only moments for Balgair to learn of matters and he quickly sent word that whoever was approaching was to be brought to him, without delay, when they arrived.

Within ten minutes, a well-dressed man in what appeared to be something like a uniform, arrived and he was immediately presented to Balgair. The man was riding a superior quality horse with an expensive saddle. The saddle had paniers attached and both of them bore the Royal Crest of the King of Scotland.

CHAPTER 6

Balgair waited while Annis went to her wagon to be dressed by Morag, her maid, and her two helpers, Jet and Jade. She had decided that it would be appropriate for her to receive the King's courier in formal attire.

There was a buzz and a palpable sense of excitement around the camp by the time the courier was brought before the queen.

Annis was well acquainted with the kinds of politics that prevailed when people came to see her. Some men – and it was usually men – were slightly reluctant to bow to her, failing to appreciate that it was an obligation. At times, they needed the encouragement of hearing her guards drawing their swords, to bring them to their senses.

Annis found those men who were her lairds to be especially interesting in their behaviour. Some were eager to bow, some even insisting on kneeling, although this was in no way something she required. This kind of laird regarded their loyalty and deference to her as a badge of honour to be flaunted as an enhancement to their own status. She was aware that this was often done so that others might interpret them as having a special relationship with their sovereign and, thus, implying favour.

Some lairds, however, tried to be slightly aloof. It was as if they were declaring that a girl of her age could not possibly be due full credit for their royal station. She had learned not to acknowledge this kind of person straight away when they were presented to her. She would delay any form of interaction with them until they had demonstrated some measure of reverence. Such men keenly valued their status and leaving them standing had a sobering effect on them. The implication that they were not important enough for their presence to register would always hasten their compliance. Losing face was a disaster to their way of thinking.

Destination: Inverness

The Royal Courier appeared to be a master of diplomacy. He approached her at a slow and careful rate, allowing time to see if she would look up before he committed himself to coming within ten paces. At her glance, he continued, but delayed any gesture or motion until he had assessed her deportment and attitude.

Queen Annis sat stiffly erect, her head held high, looking cool, calm and very slightly detached. She held her features completely neutral with neither a smile nor a frown.

The courier reached three paces from her and bowed with extravagant graciousness while doffing his cap to her with a swooping flourish of his arm across his belly.

Annis made no move and remained expressionless. The courier waited for a mere heartbeat and then fell to one knee, lowering his head and looking no further forward than his own toes.

Annis continued to wait.

The courier waited, too.

Annis made no noise and did not move a muscle.

The courier lowered his head, still further, and – after an exquisitely timed pause – greeted her loudly and clearly.

"Your Royal Highness," he said, "I bring you greetings and salutations from His Majesty King James of Scotland and of England. He extends to you his warmest regards and his most profound good wishes."

Annis allowed his words to hang in the air, waiting for just long enough for her silence to make him uneasy before she replied.

"Please return to His Majesty my own greetings and salutations and convey to him my sincerest wishes for his health, his happiness and his good fortune."

She could sense the courier's surprise at her perfect accent, with no trace of Gaelic inflection, and her impeccably precise pronunciation.

The man whispered his shock to himself, softly, under his breath.

"Pisse sur mon âme!"

This, Annis knew, meant *'Piss on my soul'* in French. The courier, she assumed, had felt certain that – said so quietly – his vulgar French curse would have been inaudible to her. Irrespective of that, he had clearly been under the impression that his words would be completely incomprehensible to someone from Scotland. He had reckoned, however, without her astonishingly acute hearing and without her commendable grasp of the French language.

Queen Annis leaned forward in her seat and spoke in a low, throaty tone to the courier.

"Allez dire au roi que j'ai ôté mon gant et que je vous ai frappé le visage de ma main nue." she told him, menacingly.

The man froze. All colour drained from his face. He was certain that her instruction to *'tell the king that I took off my glove and smacked you across your face with my bare hand'* was a bad omen.

"Seize him!" she shouted.

Several of her soldiers grabbed the courier and hoisted him to his feet.

"Cut off two fingers from each of his hands," Annis told them, "And send him back to the king with them in a bag around his neck."

"No!" the man shrieked, "Please! Your majesty!"

"Then, once it is done," she continued, "Ride him down to the border and send him blindfolded across into Northumbria."

"Please! Please! Your Majesty! I beg you for your mercy!"

Annis held up a hand and stabbed her index finger towards the ground. The soldiers dropped the courier, unceremoniously, face down into the dirt. The man got up onto his knees, keeping his head down. It was obvious that he was shaken.

"It's a long way back to London," Annis told him, "I wouldn't want you dying of an infection, from wounds such as those, on the way."

"Thank you! Thank you! Thank you!" the man gushed.

"I have a question for you and I warn you to answer it truly. If you don't, then you won't simply be heading South without some of your fingers, it will be without your hands and without your feet. Do you understand?"

"Yes! Yes, I do, Your Majesty!"

"Comment parlent-ils de moi à Londres? Qu'est-ce-qu'ils disent?" she asked.

The courier weighed up her words: *'How do they speak of me in London? What do they say?'* And looked up at her warily.

"Take care," she cautioned him, "For you are far more likely to lose your life by making your words too kind than by making them too harsh."

The man looked at her distrustfully. On the one hand, he was frightened to dilute and soften the truth, on the other, he was just as frightened to incur her wrath with the level of frankness she demanded. His face crumpled into dejected misery.

Annis laughed and taking a dagger from out of her sleeve, she pointed to a tree where a metal weather charm was swinging back and forth in the breeze at the end of a string. She threw the knife with a flick of her hand, pinning the string to the trunk of the tree, midway through its swing. The man glanced at the dagger in the tree and appeared to quake.

"Sir, if you wish to test me, I have another dagger beneath this skirt, tucked into the laces of my sandal."

The man looked down, wide eyed, to the approximate location she described.

"The first moment I think you are deceiving me, I will ask you to count aloud to three, as quickly as you can. I wager you that I can have my blade out and your nose split down the middle before you finish."

The man gulped and nodded his head, nervously.

"Now," she urged, flashing him an innocent smile, "Answer my question."

The courier looked positively ill and took a deep breath before speaking.

"They say that you are..." he began, and gave her a pained expression and swallowed hard.

"Yes?" Annis asked, inclining her head to one side, quizzically.

"They say that you have an impression of your own importance that is grossly inflated."

Annis raised her eyebrows and lifted her chin in encouragement. The man closed his eyes for a moment, manifestly wishing to be somewhere else, before reluctantly continuing.

"They say that you would benefit from..."

The man's face dropped and he looked imploringly at her.

"From?" she prompted.

"From being put over somebody's knee and spanked."

He looked as if he were beseeching the ground to open up and drag him under it. Annis lifted her hands to her chin, interlaced her fingers, and rested her chin atop them.

"Good," she said, "I am glad that we are able to have this kind of frank and open conversation."

The courier looked mightily relieved.

"You, Sir, can be assured that your chances of getting away from here alive, have just hugely improved."

The courier gave her a pained expression and looked pitiful.

"But, I must insist, that you continue," she demanded.

The man closed his eyes, breathed deeply and gulped, with difficulty, before proceeding.

"They say that you are an impudent and ill-mannered child."

"I lied," said Annis, "I'm going to kill you, after all!"

The man visibly shook and gave a little whimper.

"Stop!" she cried, "Do not worry! That was just me being an impudent and ill-mannered child!"

There were some muffled laughs from the gathered soldiers around them, but the man wisely chose to ignore them.

"They don't like me. That is clear," Annis told him, "But I want you to convince me just *how much*. Ensure that you do not hold back."

The man looked sick to the very pit of his stomach. Her soldiers and senior officers looked on in eager anticipation.

"Talk for your life," she ordered.

With grim resignation and grave misgivings, the man embarked on an account of how people at Royal Court regarded her and her seniors. His disclosures appeared to be full and ruthlessly honest. The queen, herself, even winced in a couple of places at some of the details he provided.

The courier never attributed anything said to the king, in person, but presented everything as a general patchwork of remarks, insights and comments. At some points, however, he lowered his eyes, which suggested that some of the remarks might well be those of the king. Surprisingly, these words were not filled with the vitriol she had expected and – at times – some of them hinted at a grudging respect.

At the end of his ordeal, the man seemed to have physically deflated, as if he were a pig's bladder that had been inflated and then punctured. He stood, head bowed, and awaited her response.

"Show me a mother in childbirth who, at the end of her agonies, delivers a stillborn offspring, and I will weep," Annis told him, "Show me a soldier who buries his comrade, lost in battle, and I will weep. Show me an old man, taken low by the fever, who struggles but fails to make it through the night and I will weep. Show me the heartbroken child who has watched their mother weaken, fail and die from the pox and I will weep."

The queen recited a lengthy list of the things that broke her heart. The courier lifted his head and looked at her. His gaze was, initially, one of confusion, but it slowly turned to intrigue. As she spoke, the intrigue became respect. As she continued, still further, the respect transformed into admiration.

"Tell me, Sir, how it feels to cradle a dying friend and tell them not to fear what is to come. Tell me how it feels to be unable to find the words that would give them comfort and stem their terror. Tell me how it feels to watch the force of life inside them drain relentlessly away, leaving you utterly broken and alone. Tell me how it feels to be haunted by their memory and despise yourself because you could not console them at their last. Tell me and my heart will ache for you."

The man was quiet.

"I am a queen. I am a queen as verily and as fully as any king is a king. I have killed and I have ordered people to be killed. I have slit a man's throat as he wept to be spared and cried for his mother. When my people go hungry, so do I. When my people go thirsty, so do I."

The man was quiet.

"I do not look down on the poor from the windows of some fine banquet hall, drinking wine and eating game as those people starve. Nor do I sing and dance as their children die for the lack of milk. I pity the sovereign who feels so remote from human suffering that, instead of a heart, they have a lump of stone in their chest."

The man was quiet.

"You can tell the king that I wear a crown but that I wear it as a duty and that I am humbled by the love of my people and would take not one copper coin from them that would stop them from eating."

The man nodded.

"Your Majesty, I will tell the king that I have met a queen who could not be truer to God."

"My servants will feed you," Annis told him, "They will give you hot water to wash and they will tend to your horse."

"I am grateful, Your Majesty, but I have not yet given you the document I carry from the king."

"It will wait," she said.

The courier looked surprised.

"Yes, Your Majesty, of course," he replied, looking distracted and ill at ease.

"The document is urgent?" she asked, playfully.

"Yes, Your Majesty."

"All the more reason for it to wait, then," she retorted, "For the business of the king, whilst important, is not so pressing as my own."

The man allowed himself a hint of a smile.

"Of course, Your Majesty."

The man saluted her. Annis nodded in acknowledgement.

Annis knew that the courier was of a military rank, though not an official part of the army. She knew that there were a range of courtesies he could have extended to her short of a full salute. The salute, being neither required nor wholly appropriate, was an act of genuine respect.

CHAPTER 7

That night, remembering what Wild Flower had said, Annis ordered that rather than just Morag being in her tent, both Jet and Jade should sleep there, too. The girls were completely delirious with joy for the honour.

The night was still and quiet. The forest was calm and peaceful. Annis opened her eyes in sudden wakefulness and heard the muffled sound of Jet whimpering in her sleep. Annis made her way across the floor of the tent, guided by the dull red glow of her fire, and cradled the girl's head in her arms, gently rocking her until she stopped.

A little later in the night, Jet began to sob in her sleep. Annis crawled across to her pallet and gathered the little girl up against her chest. Propping herself against one of the outside poles of the tent, she drew Jet into her lap and held her in her arms like a mother might hold an infant. Jet snuggled against her and gave a little sigh. It was the sound of contentment. Annis bent and kissed her hair and stroked it until she was fully settled and then fell asleep herself.

In the morning, Jet's sister, Jade, woke first. The light was still dim and vague, but she was able to make out the scene before her. She stared at the queen, who sat cross-legged, with her sister in her arms. Tears ran down Jade's face. She made no noise. She cried in complete silence.

After a minute, Jade crawled across to the queen and, reaching beneath the jiggy blanket that Annis had wrapped around her legs, as a barrier against the chill, she uncovered a royal foot. Annis woke but said nothing. Jade gently cradled the foot in her hand and then dropped her face to it, kissing each of its toes, one by one. Annis could feel her tears falling on her skin as she did so.

Annis reached out and tousled Jade's hair. Like accomplices in a crime, Jade helped Annis to put Jet back beneath her blanket again, and – once Annis had crawled back to her own pallet – Jade tucked her in.

There was a minute of complete silence. Until she spoke, Annis was sure that Jade must have fallen asleep.

"My sister fears the darkness," Jade confided.

"I can have a candle or a lantern lit if it would help her," Annis offered.

"No," said Jade, solemnly, "Not that darkness. The other darkness. The darkness beyond the grave."

Jade and Annis cried.

CHAPTER 8

Janine found that breakfast at Brech Woorlach was almost too sumptuous an affair for her to cope with it. The endless supply of bacon, ham, eggs, fried potatoes and batter cakes overwhelmed her. At Dunkeld Manor, where she had been a maid, they had enjoyed living life to the full, but had never managed this kind of spread!

Gluttony, as they all knew, was a sin, and these were – in all respects – good, God-fearing people. This made such an immense bounty all the more confusing and not a little shocking. It had not been long, however, before she had learned that there was a very particular reason for the grand scale of breakfast. Once she was aware of the reason, she made a point of always asking for more of everything she was served, even if she had no intention of eating it.

It had been on her third day at Brech Woorlach that she had discovered the benign nature of this sumptuous excess. Following breakfast, on the morning in question, she had imposed on Francesca to walk with her in the gardens. They had exited via the servants' entrance, which was not an unusual route for Francesca. This was on account of her being both the daughter of The Duke and Duchess and of her regularly adopting the role of a household servant.

It was on their way out that she had happened to see the staff loading up the panniers of a pair of mules with the abundant leftovers. She asked Francesca what was happening and it was revealed that whatever food was left from breakfast was distributed to the poor and needy up and down the banks of the River Forth.

The morning breakfast, it turned out, was a celebration and a thanksgiving for their family's good fortune. It was also one that culminated in this act of typical Brech Woorlach generosity.

It was a regrettable truth that, amongst the gentry and aristocracy of Scotland, benevolence was not always looked upon favourably. In fact, it was often regarded as a sign of weakness. The extravagant flaunting of wealth and privilege, on the other hand, was almost universally well received!

The ludicrously excessive breakfast at Brech Woorlach was used by The Duke and Duchess as a method of boasting their affluence and of showing their complete disregard for cost. The servants, there, were encouraged to ensure that this "decadence" was well broadcasted when they accompanied their employers on stays at other stately homes. The disposal of the remnants, conversely, was kept a closely guarded secret.

Janine was conscious that her call on Francesca's time diverted her from other things that she might otherwise be doing. Francesca was always gracious about this and was careful to assure her that there were always people who could fill in for her. This didn't make Janine much happier about it, until Francesca disclosed that the senior house staff were always delighted to take on her role and that they looked forward to it, eagerly.

Francesca would often gently chide Janine, using an expression to which she had become very much accustomed: *'There is nothing for which you cannot ask and nothing that you would ever be refused.'*

Janine did not find it easy to be a queen but had finally stopped begrudging them the pleasure of treating her with unlimited kindness and generosity. The love she was constantly shown went far beyond the loyalty of subjects to their sovereign. They were not simply driven by some sense of obligation. They all truly and genuinely loved her.

She had once mentioned, completely offhand and as nothing more than a whim, that she wished Francesca could sleep in her bedchambers with her. It had been a mere dreamy and fanciful idea of no consequence, but Francesca had promptly adopted the maid's couch in her chambers as her bed. Janine had quickly had this swapped for a proper bed.

The two brothers, Bruce and Brian, were equally obliging and would miss no opportunity to please her. They were both eager to go the second mile when asked to do even the simplest thing.

Genji was the same and would never leave any avenue unexplored when it came to executing her wishes.

The Duke and Duchess were every bit as keen. They were delighted to do whatever they could to make Janine's life easier, happier or more comfortable. Much to Janine's relief, they had now become accustomed to not constantly bowing to her. She had made it clear that this displeased her.

Janine would lay awake at night and think about her situation. She was a queen. She was of royal blood. She was an important person. She had lived here, at Brech Woorlach, twice before in her young life. Now she was home, again. She was truly home. She was at the place where she had found the most profound peace and joy. Despite all this, she also felt a nagging restlessness that she could not describe. It was as if she had unfinished business.

Janine had not seen the flames, again. They had been completely absent. She quizzed Francesca, The Duke and The Duchess, Bruce, Brian, Mister Chang and Genji and none of them had seen the mysterious tongues of fire, recently.

Janine had taken to wearing her mother's ring on her finger, rather than having it around her neck. The dragon on the ring was a precious symbol of her childhood. She would often look at it and recollect those happy times.

Janine had not stopped being happy when her family had fallen on even harder times, forcing them to move to a different, much smaller, cottage. She had even been happy when the new home had meant going from poor to extremely poor. She wondered if her life could have continued like that – being so very poor but so very happy – and if she could have grown up with her mother and father, like any normal child. She knew that, in the end, this had not been possible. She knew that things had turned out very differently because life had required it. She knew that she had been in danger from a powerful band of bad people and that she had been forced to come back to Brech Woorlach as a place of sanctuary.

Janine stopped herself. She held her thoughts still in her mind. It was like pausing while half way over a stile, one foot on one side and one on the other. There was something wrong. There was something missing. She had a gnawing intuition that her memories were incomplete.

She opened her eyes in the dark. She pinched herself to make sure that she was awake. It hurt. There were just vague shapes around her in the gloom. There was the dull glow from the windows where a light, from outside, was filtering through the curtains. The source of the glow was a brazier, alight in the yard, that kept the night watchmen warm. As she listened, she could hear Francesca's breathing, slow and rhythmic.

Janine closed her eyes and concentrated. Her mother had been away the fateful night that her father had died. A sudden pang of pain shot through her at the recollection. It was like a shard of ice piercing her heart. Her father had come to her bedside and woken her. He had gathered her into his cloak. It had felt warm. She remembered that, distinctly. It meant that he had to have been recently wearing it. Their home was cold, unless they sat by the small, smoky peat fire. Her father always slept away from the fire so that she could be close to it. He had taken her outside and it had been raining. The rain had fallen on her face and she had cried out. Her father had kissed her and tugged his cloak down over her, to shield her against the wind and rain.

The man had been there. The good man. The kind man. The man whose smile made her feel safe. He was the man who always had time for her. He wasn't related to her father. He was not, she knew, any kind of near or distant relative. Her father trusted him, though. Her father handed her to him. She felt safe in her father's arms. She felt safe in the good man's arms. Her father trusted this man with his life. Her father trusted this man with **her** life. That was something **far** more valuable to him. There was nothing in his world that was of more value.

The good man was on a horse. It was a tall horse. It was a strong horse. It was a fit and healthy horse with long strides. They had never owned a beast anything so fine, themselves. They had once, before they came to this cold and damp house, had a tired old donkey. It had grown too weary to get up onto its feet, one morning. Her father had told her that the donkey had grown tired of living. The donkey had gone away, her father said, to the place where donkeys could be with the angels. She recalled they had had meat that week. A lot of meat, in fact. They seldom had meat and they salted a lot of it to preserve it for later. It was tough meat, but it tasted wonderful.

The good man on the horse had pulled her close to him. He had moved something across, behind her. It was a strap. It was a strap to hold her safe and close to him. He had kissed her head. He had told her that she was safe. She would have known what he was saying, even if the words meant nothing to her, for she had a rapport with the good man.

Janine searched her memory and strained to bring the moment back. She was seven. Janine frowned. Why was she seven years old but feeling so frail? Why was she so weak at that age? She fought the darkness in her mind. She scrabbled to grip the memory that eluded her, trying to take a hold of it and drag it through into the present. She was young. She was a young girl in a feeble state for a seven-year-old. Why? She was sick. That was it! She was sick! She had developed a fever. She had been suffering with the fever for a while.

Her mother was away, trekking around elderly and infirmed relatives in her extended family. Her mother knew about healing. Her mother knew about making medicines. Her mother could have saved her, but her mother wasn't there. Her mother was gone, and her father had been left alone to care for her.

Her father was out of his mind with worry. Her father had sat holding her and rocking her all night and, sometimes, he had cried. He had sent his brother to fetch the good man. He didn't know what to do, himself. He had sent for the good man to save her life.

Janine held her breath. She screwed up her eyes and knotted her brows. What had happened? She had overheard her father speaking to her uncle a few days before. They had suddenly become friends, again, united by a hatred of the evil people who wished to harm both Janine and her mother. Janine was at risk of dying from her illness. She now knew that she had, also, been at risk from assassination by the bad men. Her father had feared for both her health and for her safety. Her father was in danger, too. She remembered that. She remembered her father getting up, repeatedly, during the night to look out of the shutters into the darkness. He had stood and listened, keeping watch in case the bad men came. One night, he had stood and watched through the shutters for so long that he had fallen asleep on his feet and toppled over.

Janine let her breath out. She had heard Francesca stir. She breathed as quietly as she could. She breathed shallow and with her mouth wide open to minimise the noise. She heard a rustling. She felt rather than saw Francesca approach her.

"Is anything wrong?" Francesca asked in a soft whisper.

Janine tried to answer, but she could muster no words. Her eyes were filled with tears and there was a lump in her throat. It felt as if there were a boulder inside her chest. She sniffed and gave a little gasp, then shook her head.

She felt a movement of air and Francesca landed on the bed beside her. She had jumped nimbly over Janine, from the far side, by the chair. She felt herself drawn into Francesca's embrace.

"It's okay," Francesca cooed, "I can love away the hurt."

Francesca drew back the covers, briefly, and Janine felt her slide in beside her. She felt the warmth of Francesca's body against her own. She was always warm, no matter how cold the weather. *'My little furnace'*, Janine had taken to calling her. Janine felt Francesca kiss her hair, draw her close, and put one arm behind her neck.

"Your little furnace is here," Francesca whispered.

Janine gave a little laugh that came out as a sob through her tears.

CHAPTER 9

"When I was a little girl," Janine said, "When I was seven. When I came back here. There was something important. Something I can't remember. I have been trying to remember it, but it makes me so very sad to think of it."

"I'll be quiet and just hold you, then," Francesca whispered, "I'll let you think."

Janine could feel Francesca tenderly stroking her hair and then felt her kiss the side of her head. Janine reached out and found Francesca's cheek in the dark. She squeezed it, then she turned Francesca's head to face her and leaned up and kissed her. She felt Francesca's smile flood across her lips.

Janine looked up at the ceiling. The ceiling was invisible except for the occasional flicker of light from the brazier outside. She felt Francesca stroking her hair, again, and it felt wonderful. She tried to marshal her thoughts. She grappled with her reminiscence. As she did so, she felt Francesca's motion of stroking slow down, then gradually stop. She heard Francesca's breathing suddenly become deeper and more measured and she knew that she had fallen asleep.

It was wet and windy back on that dreadful night, when she was seven, Janine told herself. The good man had started forward on his horse and then stopped. There was another man with him. The other man had given a low whistle. It was a warning. She knew it was a warning. The good man and the other man both stopped. Their horses' breath was billowing clouds of steam. She remembered watching the steam. She remembered that she had pretended that they were dragons. She smiled to herself at that tiny splinter of memory.

Janine tried to bring back the moment. The rain. The wind. The horses. The plumes of steam from their breath. What had happened? The bad men. The bad men had arrived! That was it! The bad men had found their house. The good man had told her not to make a noise. She had trembled with fear.

He had pulled her close to him. There was a smell. He had a smell. What was the smell? Janine inhaled deeply in the dark and suddenly she could smell it. She could smell the smell from twelve years ago. It was camphor!

Janine was genuinely frightened from the recollection of the emotions from that night. There had been noises and shouting and her father's voice cursing. There was the sound of a struggle. The good man squeezed her hard. She could hear the clang of metal. There was a cry of pain, and somebody called out. It was her father's voice! The good man put his hands over Janine's ears and held them there, tight. He lifted his cloak, further, to shield her view, but the wind blew it back down. The good man didn't realise and went back to covering her ears. Then she saw it. Then she saw what happened. She cried out, involuntarily, in the dark. She sobbed. She gasped. She saw one of the bad men kill her father. He held her father's head and drew his knife across his neck, slitting his throat. She saw him writhe and squirm. She saw him arch his back. She saw him die. Janine suddenly saw the bad man's face, in her memory, as clear as day, as clear as if he were right there in the room. She screamed.

Francesca was awake in a split second.

"What is it?" she asked, panic stricken.

Janine couldn't find her voice. She screamed again.

Francesca vaulted off the bed and, in a single stride, had reached the window. She dragged open the curtains and shouted through the gap in the open window.

"Alarm!"

Francesca ran to the door and drew the bolt back with a bang. Within a moment the door flew open and two men, dressed in black from head to foot and their faces covered in pitch, sailed into the room through the air, landing like cats on the carpet. They spun around, scanning the corners of the room, their eyes piercing the darkness.

There was a flash of light as Francesca struck a flint to light a lamp and, in that split second of light, Janine saw one of the men aim a pistol at Francesca's head. In that moment, she realised that the man in black had feared the spark to be an attempt to fire a weapon.

"Stop!" shrieked Janine.

Francesca cried out in alarm and dropped to the carpet. Unseen, the man picked up her flint and striking rod and, mustering a spark himself, he lit the wick of the oil lamp.

In the blossoming light, they saw the first of the two men spring across the room to the door of Janine's personal water closet and land with absolute silence. The second man in black checked under the bed and in the wardrobe. Both men then padded across to the window. They exchanged nods and visibly relaxed at their mutual confirmation that there were no intruders.

"It was a nightmare!" Francesca shouted, "I could not be sure what was wrong, at first, and did not tarry to think it over."

"Thinking time is dying time!" the first man replied.

"Always act. Don't think. You did exactly the right thing," said the second.

The two men in black made their farewells and walked soundlessly back out into the corridor. The moment the door was closed, Queen Janine unburdened herself to Francesca.

"When I was seven, the men who wanted to kill me, murdered my father!" she exclaimed, "That's why, as a child, I always called them the *bad men*. There was a friend of my mother whom I called the "good man". I remember him from when I was very little. I remember him even from before I first came here. He came to rescue me. My father sent my uncle to ask him to come. I was gravely ill. I had a fever."

"I'm so sorry!" Francesca said, hugging Janine as she put her back to bed, "Those are terrible memories to recall in the complete darkness!"

Janine returned Francesca's hug and snuggled her head against her shoulder.

"You had a very bad fever, My Lady, when you arrived here."

"You remember?"

"Yes. I remember. I remember for a particular reason!"

"What reason is that?"

"I sneaked down to the dormitory and I climbed into bed with you!"

"While I had a fever?"

"Yes. I am unlikely to forget it. My father was furious! He was shaking with rage! He set about Riley, the Nursery Matron, with a vengeance for allowing me into the dormitory. It was the first and only time that I ever saw my father use violence against a servant!"

Janine cringed.

"My father was devastated, afterwards, at his own behaviour."

"The poor servant!"

"Riley would disagree..."

Janine tilted her head in question.

"He gave Riley a guinea," Francesca revealed.

"A guinea!"

"Yes, a guinea in silver pieces. Riley said she would happily take another such beating for even a quarter of a guinea!"

"I don't feel quite so bad, in that case, despite it being me to blame," said Janine.

"No, I was to blame," Francesca protested, "It was my fault."

"I was the person behind it, though."

"Please be consoled by the knowledge that Riley has received a silver crown, each and every Christmas, from then on."

"Ah…" Janine replied, uncertainly, now unsure if she were being offered the credit for the outcome rather than the blame for the mishap!

Francesca smiled and squeezed her hand.

"You could have died, Francesca!"

"Yes, I know," Francesca admitted, lowering her head, as if in repentance, "But I was so distraught at your condition."

Janine reached and squeezed Francesca's hand. Then, pulling back the cover of the bed, she patted the space beside her, invitingly.

"I don't think I would have wanted to have lived, Your Majesty, if you had died!"

Janine looked at her friend disapprovingly for using such a formal address. Francesca hopped into bed beside her and kissed her full on the lips. Janine was shocked but didn't pull away. Francesca lingered over a second kiss for several long seconds, which seemed to take an age to pass, and then drew back, looking ashamed of herself. Janine cupped Francesca's chin in her hand and leaned forward and kissed her back. The kiss lasted a long time and, when it was finished, both girls looked a little flustered. After a strained and awkward exchange of goodnights, they sank back into their pillows and quickly drifted off to sleep.

CHAPTER 10

The next day, after a mighty breakfast, Janine set off to walk around the grounds of Brech Woorlach, following the perimeter wall. It was a distance she was sure she could complete in little over an hour. She was made to take Sykes, the shoe cleaning boy, with her. This was at the insistence of Mister O'Keefe, the butler.

The young lad had taken only a single pace, when O'Keefe grabbed him. Holding him painfully hard by the ear, the butler warned the boy of all kinds of dire consequences if Janine were to come to any misfortune.

Janine set off at a slow pace, perceiving this to be more 'ladylike', but was soon striding purposefully. Sykes was more than a little surprised by her gait but did not venture to comment. After they had been walking like this for three or four minutes, Janine stopped and turned to him, questioningly. The boy, who was not yet ten, looked at her apprehensively.

"You are happy to go this quickly?" she enquired.

"Oh, yes! Yes, My Lady!" Sykes responded, taken aback, "Of course! Anything you say. Anything at all!"

She smiled a kind smile at him and he relaxed considerably.

"That's good," she said and started off again.

The boy grinned at her and stomped off behind her. He was perfectly delighted to be escorting a young woman who liked to walk at a gallop, rather than creeping along behind some elderly, tottering guest.

As they walked, the boy fumbled with his ear, apparently still painful from its violent interaction with Mister O'Keefe. Janine turned to the boy and he looked up at her expectantly.

"Am bu mhath leatsa mo chuideachadh? *(Would you like me to help you?)*" she asked, mischievously teasing him in perfect Gaelic, "Is urrainn dhomh do chluas eile a tharraing dhut, ma thogras tu? *(I can pull your other ear for you if you wish?)*"

The boy looked stunned and gaped at her, open mouthed. He had most certainly not expected such a lady to speak the first language! Janine smiled, amused at his consternation.

"Chan eil. Chan eil buidheachas dhut. Tha thu glè chaoimhneil. *(No. No thank you. You are very kind.)*" he replied, still gathering his senses.

Janine laughed and the boy laughed, too, evidently relieved that his manners had been sufficient.

For the rest of their journey, the boy walked tall with his head high and shoulders back.

As they came around the furthest corner of the grounds, on the last straight, there was the sound of a trotting horse coming up the decoratively cobbled drive from the gates. They both turned to see a rider in a military style uniform on his way up to the entrance of the hall.

The boy made no attempt to disguise his astonishment. The rider carried a red sack, which Janine knew to be called a 'royal mail', across his lap. The boy may not have been able to recognise this kind of bag, but the deportment of the rider gave a very good indication that his mission was one of great status and importance.

"Gabh. Rach air adhart. Faigh a-mach dè a tha a 'dol air adhart. *(Go. Run ahead. Find out what is going on.)*" Janine ordered, gesturing that he should cross the lawn.

The boy set off at a good speed, running directly across the immaculately trimmed and lovingly tended grass. He seemed to take a good deal of enjoyment in doing this. His route quickly brought a loud reprimand from one of the gardening staff who hollered abuse at him through cupped hands. The boy shouted something back, without slowing, and pointed towards Janine. The shouting man clapped his hand to his mouth in alarm and threw himself into a series of vigorous bows in her direction.

"Loisg mi teine na bhriogais! *(I have lit a fire in his britches!)*" Janine called, amiably.

On a sudden whim, she amended her course from the gravel path to take her across the same area of intensely cosseted grass.

The arriving rider had reached the bottom of the steps at the formal frontage of Brech Woorlach, with its grand marble facade. A footman hurried across to receive him and the man dismounted. From the way the two stood, the horseman manifestly judged himself to hold a loftier rank than the footman. From the footman's begrudging deference, she guessed him to be correct.

Another footman appeared at the top of the marble steps and shouted something to somebody in the doorway at the bottom of them. A few moments later, Mister O'Keefe came out. The boy, Sykes, had now reached the little group and could be seen making enquiries and pointing to Janine. Mister O'Keefe, being a party to Janine's true identity, as Queen of the West, patiently spoke to the shoe boy. The boy nodded energetically and trotted back to her, gasping for breath when he finally reached her.

"It is a courier from King James!" he exclaimed, excitedly, "He carries a message to be delivered in person!"

Janine thanked the boy. It was something that was evidently unusual, for he was profusely grateful. It seemed that he was far more used to dismissal by a wave of the hand, a curse or a blow from a crop or cane.

Janine reached the gleaming white steps and began to climb them. As she did so, she reminisced back to the few short days ago when she had arrived. Everybody had been so very kind to her and had gone out of their way to make her feel welcome. The warmth and kindness that permeated this entire place was a credit to The Duke and Duchess.

As she neared the top of the steps, her good mood wavered, and her mind went back to the courier's arrival.

A message from the king to be delivered, by the courier's own hand, to The Duke of Bo'Ness? This had to be either very good news or very bad news. She was far from certain which option she favoured as the most likely.

As Janine came in through the main entrance into the marble hallway, she saw Michael, the footman who had met and welcomed her the day she arrived. His face lit up when he saw her, and she gave him a little wave and a big smile. Michael looked a little rattled by her greeting but came across to her and bowed magnificently.

"Your Ladyship," he said, "I am most honoured to see you, again."

"Thank you," she replied, "I am on my way to see The Duke and Duchess, fresh back from my walk. I believe they have important news that has arrived, just now?"

"Yes, Your Ladyship, I am told that a royal courier has arrived," he declared, proudly.

"I will take myself away, then," she told him, "I am eager to learn what he brings."

"If you wish to reach the apartments of The Duke and Duchess quickly, Your Ladyship, you can go down the side corridor and through the door half way along it."

"I can?"

"Yes, there is the servants' passage, there. It is behind the door with the two brass knockers. To open the door, turn the two brass knockers outwards, in opposite directions."

Michael demonstrated an approximation of the required movement, using his gloved hands in the air.

"Very well. Thank you, Michael. I am grateful."

Michael beamed at her, evidently thrilled that she had remembered his name, and he delivered her another bow with a flourish. Janine intimated the merest hint of a nod, careful not to offend Michael's refined sense of decorum.

Hurrying out of the hall into the side corridor, Janine was grateful not to have to navigate the main hallways and encounter the inevitable groups of curtseying and bowing servants along her route. She had been a maid, herself, and was not particularly fond to be on the receiving end of such copious volumes of polite greeting.

Janine admired the numerous paintings on her way and looked into a couple of cabinets containing stuffed birds and animals. She shivered. She had never been fond of dead animals that stared back from beyond the grave with unblinking, beady eyes.

A little less than half way along the corridor, she spotted the door that Michael had described. Exactly as he had said, it had two brass knockers in the middle. She reached up and turned the two knockers, in the prescribed manner, and the door opened. She gingerly stepped through it.

The door led into another corridor. This one was narrower and dimmer. It appeared to be lit by sunlight from the outside, directed down long horizontal shafts. The shafts ended in a line of windows just below ceiling height. She made a mental note to look for the entry point of the light the next time she was outside.

She stood and waited for her eyes to become accustomed to the relative darkness. After about twenty seconds, she felt comfortable enough to start walking.

Janine had the overwhelming feeling that she was an imposter. Absurdly enough, even though she was the queen, she felt that being 'caught' was something to be avoided. She deftly reached down and, taking off both her sandals, hung them over her shoulder by their laces. She walked quickly, treading as quietly as she could in her stocking feet, running the tips of her fingers along either wall.

The light appeared to be getting no brighter. Closing her eyes, Janine found it strangely pleasing to rely only on the pressure of her fingers for guidance as they slid over the polished wooden panelling. She could feel that the walls were punctuated, at intervals, by doors. These, she surmised, led into guest rooms as an entry point for servants to discretely service the accommodation.

Janine decided to keep her eyes closed as she moved. Half a minute passed before she considered opening them, again. By this time, she was most of the way to the other end of this strange passageway. On finally opening her eyes, she discovered that they had become far more sensitive to the dim light and was able to see quite clearly.

She closed her eyes, again, and continued along the passage. As she went, she started to build up speed and it wasn't long before she was on the verge of running.

Suddenly, she stopped dead in her tracks and froze, like a statue. The voice of the apparition she had seen by the willows came into her head.

'*Beware the door left open,*' the old man had warned.

Just ahead of her, a mere two or three steps away, she could see a bright slit of light. It was one of the access doors into the apartments and it had been left slightly ajar. She could hear voices on the other side of it. Her heart leapt in her chest as she realised that she would have banged this door shut with her trailing hand had she not shown the caution that she had been advised.

Hardly daring to breathe, Janine crept to the door and put an ear close up to the gap.

"We must be cautious," said a man's voice, "We must not raise any kind of suspicion."

"Yes, you are right," agreed a woman, "We have invested too much time and effort to be discovered, now."

"We must invent a good reason for not accompanying The Duke to Inverness," the man asserted.

"Then we can go on ahead and keep a watch on him there."

"Exactly so," the man replied.

"The colonel will be most pleased with us!"

"Yes, indeed, he will!"

"This will finally mean the downfall of this place."

With that the two left the room.

Janine closed her eyes and forced herself to memorise the voices. She repeated their words in her head, over and over. Neither had what she regarded as a particularly strong accent, but there was, nonetheless, something strange about the way they talked. There was something in the background of their speech, a vague pattern that she could not identify. Again, she repeated their words to herself, until they were firmly committed to memory.

Abruptly, a thought came into her head. The door with the two brass knockers and this 'secret corridor' were not things that would be common knowledge. Michael, the footman, had told her about them because he had known her to be a highly trusted person. He did not know that she was a queen. He thought of her as a prominent lady favoured by The Duke and Duchess. Still, he knew that she was *one of us* and not an outsider.

She debated with herself if she should go back and find Michael, bring him to this door, and ask who would have been in this room. She dismissed the notion. She sensed that these had not been guests speaking in their own room. They had, she felt, simply stepped inside a vacant room to talk privately. They could be any one of the guests currently residing at Brech Woorlach.

She needed to find The Duke and Duchess and speak to them about the conversation she had just overheard.

She broke into a trot, hurrying down the passage as quickly as she could. All of a sudden she stopped, halting as if she had run into a rope. She retraced her steps, back to the door, and gently closed it. Then, taking a pin from her hair, she scratched a cross into the wooden frame of the doorway. Content with her work, she raced back along the corridor until she reached the end of it.

Janine turned the doorknob of the end door cautiously. Nothing happened. The doorknob rotated freely with no purchase on any mechanism. Janine stood and listened, trying to determine if anybody were in the hallway at the other side of the door. She reached up, stroking her hands up the middle panels of the door, until her fingers found two knurled knobs. She twisted them, turning the left one clockwise and the right one anticlockwise. To her great satisfaction, the door now opened effortlessly. She stepped out into the corridor of the North Wing, directly across from the entrance to the private suite of The Duke and Duchess.

Janine knocked on the splendidly decorated door and The Duke's voice called for her to enter. The Duke bowed to her, forgetting her instructions not to do so. He seemed to be agitated. The Duchess appeared from a side room and she, too, looked to be out of sorts.

"Your Ladyship," the Duke said, carefully resuming the protocol Janine had requested, "I have sent servants out to look for you urgently."

"For what reason?"

"A courier, sent from King James, has arrived," the Duke explained, "He advises me that he is to deliver to you, personally, a most important document."

Janine blinked in astonishment.

"A document from the king!" she exclaimed, "For me?"

"Yes, Your Ladyship," the Duke confirmed, apologetically.

"The man is in the next room," the Duchess announced, gesturing to the door from which she had just emerged.

Janine gulped and drew a deep breath.

"I suppose I should see him without delay?"

"You can make him wait as long as you wish!" objected The Duchess.

Janine thought for a moment and then shook her head.

"It is best for my peace of mind that I find out what he brings as soon as possible."

"As you wish," replied The Duchess.

"It is your decision," the Duke agreed.

The Duke and The Duchess escorted Janine into the room with a dignified formality and with bows to Janine so gracious that they made the courier feel awkward. Smartly saluting her, the man then followed their lead and bowed low. Advancing the three paces it took to reach Janine, he kept his eyes downcast. Then, opening his bag with calculated care, he offered her the sharply creased and folded, pale fawn parchment it contained.

Janine took the document and looked at it, uneasily, as though worried it might become an angry wasp. The courier stood tall, his hands stiffly at his sides, and gazed purposefully at a vacant patch of wall by the door behind her. The Duke knew, from experience, that the man's anxiety did not bode well.

"You are dismissed," the Duke told him, curtly.

The man saluted, stamped his foot to bring himself to attention, and then marched from the room with a little too much haste for The Duke's liking.

They heard the man's heels clattering down the marble stairs and then across the marble hall to the doors. As

Janine stared at the royal communication in her hand, The Duke and Duchess quickly crossed to the window. There, they were in time to see the courier leap onto his horse.

They watched as he galloped away towards the gates as if the Hounds of Hell were behind him. The hooves of his mount hammered on the stone tiles as he rode close to full tilt. He was evidently intent on putting as much distance between himself and the recipient of the message as quickly as he could.

The Duke and Duchess exchanged a worried look and wordlessly agreed that a departure such as this was a bad omen.

Janine, managing to recover herself, began to open the document, breaking the red, royal seal at its rear. She unfolded the heavily creased paper and read the sparse message it contained. Her eyes grew wide at what she read and she staggered slightly, feeling suddenly unsteady. The Duke and Duchess were at her side in an instant and each took hold of an arm.

"It is a summons," said Janine, distantly.

The Duke and Duchess quaked inside.

"I am to go to Inverness," Janine disclosed, "To stand trial."

The Duke and Duchess were furious.

"Summoned you!" the Duchess said, scathingly, "Like a common criminal?"

"A warrant of summons from the king?" the Duke asked in astonishment, "Sent to someone whose public rank is that of a mere servant girl?"

"No," replied Janine, "It is addressed to me as Queen of the West."

The Duke's mouth dropped open as he stared in disbelief, his mind in turmoil as a dozen questions cartwheeled through it, competing for priority.

"How on Earth and by all things holy," he demanded, "Did the king have even the first glimmer of an idea as to your true identity?"

No sooner had he spoken than the answer occurred to him. He quickly covered his mouth with his hand and his eyes bulged with shock.

"We have a spy!" he groaned.

CHAPTER 11

As Captain McCleary's convoy set off, the sun was trying its best to peek through the clouds but was losing the struggle. Way off in the distance, the first mountain rose up, its peak invisible behind a shroud of dense mist. The first stirrings of a fitful breeze were making little impact on clearing it.

The captain sent out the first pair of scouts and they clattered off up the road, their horses striking sparks on the pebbles and small stones with their shoes. They had only made it a little way up the hill, before the sound petered out as the quality of the track rapidly deteriorated.

McCleary gestured to one of the leading riders in the main group and, in a moment, there was a toot on a horn. In response, their party began to move forward.

Lumbering along with them, Constable Burberry's wagon soon began to lurch violently, causing him to curse loudly from the rear.

The convoy made slow progress up the incline, as it steepened, but managed to make it most of the way before it came to a stop. At that point, the front wheels of the lead wagon dropped into a narrow rut, and it came to an abrupt halt. The iron rims of the wheels were gripped, as if in a vice, and no amount of urging the horses could free them.

A couple of soldiers jumped down from one of the following wagons and rummaged about in the heavy stowage chest built into its rear. After a brief search they hauled out poles, pickaxes and spades. With these tools, they quickly set about digging and levering the wagon out of the offending rut.

As they waited for the wagon to be freed, Caitlan settled herself more comfortably beside the constable. She had noticed his increasing discomfort and the way he seemed burdened by more than just physical pain.

She thought back to when he had first appeared at the inn she ran with Hamish, her husband. She remembered what he had said. The Constable carried a royal warrant and was, he had declared: *'On the king's business'*.

Later, he had been beaten half to death by the McCarthys, but they had not killed him. They had not, it seemed, *dared* to kill him. There was more to this man's story. She was certain of it. There was much that he had not yet revealed.

"If I might make a suggestion?" she offered.

"What might that be?" asked Burberry, grimacing in pain.

"It might serve you better to endure your discomfort if you were to distract yourself from it."

"Distract myself?" gasped the Constable, "How might I achieve that, when I am in mortal agony?"

Caitlan shook her head, "God help men if they had to endure childbirth," she muttered, a little too loudly to be discrete.

The man roared with laughter, then contorted himself as waves of vicious hurting immediately punished him for his loss of control.

"My grandfather," Caitlan persisted, "Had a game he would have my brothers and I play. It absorbed us and held our attention and would subdue our skittering minds to give him some peace."

Burberry found himself holding his breath to spare his ribs, but nodded rapidly for her to continue.

"My grandfather would have us tell him all about ourselves, as if we were another person with full knowledge of our lives, and as if he knew nothing what-so-ever about us. We spoke as if he had never met us before and addressed him as if we were a stranger."

Burberry frowned as he appeared to consider the proposal. Caitlan began to have her doubts at to whether it appealed to him, but his face suddenly brightened and he seemed to be won over.

"Let me think how to start," he said, his face knotted in concentration.

After a minute without him saying anything, Caitlan decided to help him out.

"My grandfather would sometimes start us off, then we would take over..." she suggested.

"Yes, thank you. That would be good," he responded.

Caitlan took a deep breath and embarked on a preamble for him that she hoped would lift his spirits.

"Constable Ewan Burberry was a jovial, bear-like, mountain of a man, with a commanding presence and a charm that won him friends easily," she announced, "His deep voice had a certain quality about it that made people feel calm, safe and happy."

Burberry grinned and pretended to fan his face to cool a non-existent blush.

"Ewan Tiberius Burberry had lived a life that passed through different phases," he began, "It had been – at different times – boring, repetitious, adventurous, challenging, dangerous and death defying."

Caitlan smiled encouragingly.

"Ewan Burberry was born in Scotland in the small town of Paisley. It sat on the bank of the River Clyde, to the east of its vastly greater neighbour, Glasgow. His mother had been a teacher and his father a vicar. This upbringing blessed him with an education denied to all of the children around him. Their focus of their parents was the struggle to put bread on the table and clothes on their children's backs. For them, anything but the most superficial learning was a thing wholly out of reach."

Caitland nodded appreciatively and, after a few moments of thought, he continued his tale.

"Burberry's father and mother were in a habit of making regular trips up to a place called Crianlarich, a few hours journey to the north. There, they told him, they tended to the medical needs of the poor, his mother being an accomplished healer. Ewan was somehow aware, even from a very early age, that these trips were somehow wicked and disreputable. Still more so, the hushed conversations and mysterious meetings between his parents and certain folk who came to visit them from Crianlarich. A strange thing for a pious vicar and a reputable teacher!"

Caitlan raised her eyebrows.

"Ewan Burberry was strictly forbidden to witness or overhear any of his parents' meetings and his father assured him that he would go straight to Hell if he did. The young Ewan, however, out of natural curiosity, several time crept to the door of the study and listened. He was disappointed to find himself unable to comprehend anything that was being said. They spoke in what, to him, was a foreign language. A language he later discovered to be Scottish Gaelic."

The cart went over a particularly deep rut and there was a pause in proceedings as Burberry growled and cursed in pain and Caitlan soothed him and adjusted his back support.

"One day," he resumed, "Midway through one of those meetings – with young Ewan banished to the outhouse – a gang of angry men arrived, shouting, cursing and screaming. They kicked down the doors and smashed the windows of the cottage to gain entry, then dragged the people they found there, outside."

Caitlan looked shocked and leaned forward in anticipation.

"Ewan Burberry peeped through a gap in the wooden door of the outhouse and could see that his mother and father had been dragged out of the house, too."

There was silence and Caitlan patiently waited while the story teller gathered his resolve.

"To Burberry's horror, the men promptly killed everyone. One of the men came marching across to his hiding place and Ewan quickly forced himself out the back, between a couple of loose boards. The man flung open the door, grunted at finding it empty and stomped back outside to circle the little structure. Hearing his footsteps, Ewan hurriedly squeezed back inside and drew the boards together again. The man loudly declared to his companions that there was nobody to be found."

Caitlan looked relieved.

"Those men spoke the same 'low tongue' as Ewan himself and, from their rantings, he became aware that his parents had belonged to some kind of secret sect. The men loudly declared that such people were 'traitors' and 'betrayers'. His parents were members of the Brydda. He didn't know who the Brydda were or what they did, but it seemed to him that those men seemed to hate them more than Satan."

Burberry gave a cry of pain, followed by a groan, as the wagon lurched. Absorbed in his storytelling, he resumed the tale without delay.

"Over the next week the young lad, Ewan, survived on wild berries, the odd rabbit he was able to snare, and stealing food from his neighbours' pantries."

Caitland nodded, sympathetically.

"It was soon after that when a man turned up, looking for him. Ewan didn't recognise him, but the man shouted for him by name. He man seemed to be kindly and gentle and, eventually, Ewan dared to come out from hiding."

Caitlan looked expectant.

"The man," Burberry revealed, "Turned out to be the lad's uncle and, together, the two of them made the long journey to Hampshire, which was in southern counties of England, below London. Ewan was relieved to find that everyone talked the low tongue, even if it was with a strange and bizarre accent. His uncle, a priest like his father, had lost his wife the previous year and was happy for Ewan to live at his tiny house next to the church."

"Is this going to be a happy ending?" Caitlan enquired.

Burberry swayed his head, weighing up the possibility, "Well, as far as endings go, I can say that it's not an *unhappy* one."

"That will suffice, then," his travelling companion replied, with a smile.

"Ewan Burberry's working life started the day after they arrived, at the age of eight years old. He worked as message carrier for the army. His job, which he loved, was to convey messages for the clerical orderlies in the Writing Room at the barracks. He would run, usually at full tilt, back and forth to the administration hall, the officers' quarters, various briefing tents, the training field and the regimental headquarters."

Burberry smiled, seeming to relish the memory.

"The lad knew his way around the military base at Aldershot, so well that he felt certain that he could likely carry his messages around the base with his eyes closed. In fact, on a couple of occasions, he had attempted to do just that."

Caitlan laughed. Burberry joined in.

"The lad's attempts were rewarded with a sound thrashing from indignant officers – with whom he collided – having failed to find his behaviour either amusing or entertaining."

Caitlan mimed applause.

"In truth, the lad got up to all kinds of antics – most of them harmless – but I must confess that there is one in particular that stands out. The lad, at the grand old age of fourteen, managed to accidentally interrupt a lieutenant who was enjoying an intimate moment with the wife of his major."

Caitlan feigned shock.

"When the lad was ordered to bend over a table for a sound whipping, his compliance was a little *too* prompt and without protest for the lieutenant's liking. It was obvious that beatings were *not* going to be an effective threat to gain his silence. Instead, in exchange for swearing to take what he had seen to his grave, the young Burberry was promptly elevated to the dizzying ranks of the Army Courier Corps. That was most definitely the dream job of any message runner!"

Caitlan applauded for real. Burberry responded with a grin.

"Not only did the young lad's lips remain firmly sealed, but he began to broadcast invented tales that promoted the virtue of the major's unfaithful wife. In those slanted versions of reality, she slapped the faces of men who suggested improper acts and scolded them loudly. In one particular made up story – one of which was most proud – she emptied a bucket of ice over the head of a man who attempted to touch her leg under the table at a dinner dance. Her mythical virtue became the stuff of regular camp gossip, causing any accounts of the actual truth to be dismissed as mischief, jealousy and envy."

"I can report that the young Ewan spent the next eight years as a courier and was shot at – while galloping on a horse with a red mail sack across his lap – more times than he would ever care to count. His courage and daring began to earn him notoriety and his exploits soon became the subject of wandering story tellers. Before long, he came to the notice of some very highly placed people working for the king. Soon, they arranged for him to be drafted as a *royal* courier. His continuing heroism was such that he was regularly chosen by the king, himself, to carry his personal letters."

Burberry leaned forward conspiratorially.

"It was around this time that he found himself selected by his superiors for a job that was the very essence of danger."

Burberry looked dramatically to left and right, as if to check for spies, before continuing.

"He was given a job where, to serve amongst the ranks of the people who did that job, was a huge and significant honour in itself. They were the members of what rapidly became known as *'The King's Secret Service'*."

Caitlan raised her eyebrows in acknowledgement.

"That" Burberry confided, "Was the confidential name for a team of people who did things that were, officially, never done. The majority of their acts – the lad would soon discover – were strictly against the law. This, by coincidence, was another role where he found himself being regularly shot at."

Burberry took a swig of whiskey from a flask that Caitlan offered him.

"That young man's audacious and daring adventures in his new position would deliver him the most danger, the most excitement and the most gut-wrenching fear of his entire army career."

Burberry, again, pretended to check for spies.

"It would also earn him an astonishingly grand reward from King James. As a sign of His Majesty's royal gratitude, Ewan Burberry was appointed to the extremely prestigious office of Constable of the City of Edinburgh."

Caitlan smiled broadly, looking genuinely impressed, and the Constable saluted and bowed to her to accept her mouthed congratulations.

"The little boy who had once cowered in an outhouse while his parents were slaughtered, was now a man of power, influence and authority," Burberry beamed, "He had become *'High Constable Ewan Burberry'* and he made it his mission to find out about the Brydda. His early attempts were met by an impenetrable rock face. Nobody would talk. Nobody would admit to knowing anything. Nobody would trust him."

"It was only a little while before Constable Burberry discovered that his new job put him in ultimate charge of a group of citizens known as the *Lantern Men*. These were people – all comfortably above the lowest rungs of Edinburgh society – who took an active interest in maintaining the King's Peace. They patrolled the streets of the city in an evening and at night, dealing out a primitive and rudimentary form of justice. To light their way – as their name suggested – they each carried a lantern."

"The Lantern Men were the 'go-betweens' for lesser groups of law enforcers who had a reputation for liking blood and violence. These unsavoury characters, known as 'Bruisers' – for obvious reasons – were every bit as happy to split an offender's nose or break their fingers, as to merely crack them around the head with a cudgel or give them a couple of licks of a cane. Without the right to approach a magistrate, these roughnecks had to deliver people accused of more serious crimes to the Lantern Men."

"The Bruisers' activities were confined to the poorer parts of Edinburgh and, unlike the Lantern Men, they demanded a fee from the local taverns, eating houses and bawdy hostels for their services. The Bruisers' idea of justice was a little vague, by all accounts, and they were reputed to seize and batter just about anybody on even the flimsiest of grounds."

"They sound like evil people!" said Caitlan, scowling.

"They were indeed," Burberry confirmed, "But, regrettably, they were a necessary evil."

Caitlan motioned for him to brace himself and he did so as the wagon suddenly thudded and bounced over a rain trench dug across the road.

Burberry recovered himself from the jolt, took a deep breath, and continued his tale.

"The newly appointed Constable Burberry heard repeated rumours of the Bruisers' dishonesty. It was widely held that they were open to bribes and prone to abuse the power they wielded. He heard many accounts of them extorting money and of them selling targeted beatings as a means by which people could exact revenge or punishment on others."

"Constable Burberry was none too happy with the frequency with which the Bruisers arrested people who had been accused of being members of the Brydda. Burberry made it known to the Lantern Men that anybody coming to their attention as possible Brydda members should be brought to him, personally. His own parents had, as far as he could tell, been members themselves. In England, it had been extremely risky to enquire about the Brydda and he had learned to bridle his curiosity. Since moving back to Scotland, however, he had been very cautiously delving into them and had become captivated by their history and their dogged allegiance to a woman with flowing golden hair known as *The Queen of the West*."

"Slowly, Burberry began to exact retribution for his parents' death by ensuring that those who accused people of being members of the Brydda eventually came to grief. This was achieved by both fair means and foul. The foul means sometimes involved anonymously hiring the Bruisers to indulge in some of their favourite activities."

"I am sure that nobody blamed you," said Caitlan, "And I am sure that other people would have done far worse."

"I like to think so," Burberry agreed, grateful for her confidence in him.

"Week by week and month by month," Burberry continued, "The Constable established a network of spies and watchers who reported to him. Using these sources of information, he carefully drew up a map of the accusers of Brydda members and with calm, cool precision delivered his answer to their harassment and persecution. He arranged to spare the lives of certain criminals – amongst them arsonists and burglars – on condition that they leave Edinburgh and never return. Before their departure, however, they would be obliged to undertake a couple of *special assignments* for him, to show their gratitude."

"Constable Ewan Burberry concluded that danger, excitement and gut-wrenching fear were grimly determined to follow him wherever he went in life. For this reason, he was relieved and pleasantly surprised when, after five years in Edinburgh, he was ordered by King James of England and of Scotland to go on a mission, himself. He was to go to Inverness and convene a *Special Court of Justice* at the Fortress, there, and oversee the trial of several people accused of treason."

"When he had set out from Edinburgh, he had hoped that this task would turn out to be boring and uneventful. He had hoped that being accompanied by Captain Iain McCleary and thirty soldiers of the Lothian Pikes and Muskets – known widely as the Blue and Greys – was a needless precaution that would turn out to be a waste of manpower. The constable's journey, however, proved to be far from uneventful!"

Caitland grinned and clapped her hands with glee, for she was well aware, already, of this part of the tale.

"Adamantly refusing to allow the Blue and Greys to do their job, by letting them stay close to him, he had gone on ahead and, near Pitlochry, had encountered a group of thugs called the McArthys. He and they had taken an instant dislike to each other. He knew by their demeanour and way of speaking that they were arrogant bullies. He had later found out that they were, in fact, the local Rangers. The Rangers, or 'The Watch' as they were often known, were appointed across the Scottish Highlands by local lairds to maintain some crude semblance of law and order. The McArthys' greed, drunkenness and love of violence, however, had meant that law and order had been in very short supply in their territory."

"Having exchanged some ugly words with them, our hero, Constable Burberry, made to ride away, only to hear the rumble of hooves behind him. Turning around he had found the leader of the McArthys bearing down on him with his sword drawn. Deciding it best to be firm with them, Burberry pulled out his huge, double barrelled pistol and blew a hole in the man from front to back. The remaining members of the McArthy gang had promptly scattered. They were well aware that he had arrived with an armed escort and presumed that he would not have dared risk such a bold and brazen act without those troops being close at hand. They were wrong. He had been alone."

"Burberry calmly gathered up the dead man and slung him over the back of his second horse. This animal had been brought in case he'd had the good fortune to hunt down a deer while on his travels. Loaded up and ready, he made his way further along the main track to an inn, a little way ahead. Much to the consternation and annoyance of Captain McCleary, he took lodgings there. During his stay he became firm friends with the inn keeper, Hamish Pottle, his wife Caitlan and a fellow guest, a young soldier by the name of Alex Brennan, who had just returned from the 'Long War' in Austria."

"I have heard good things about the innkeeper's wife," quipped Caitlan.

"Yes, so I have," laughed Burberry, "Many speak highly of her."

Caitlan pretended to fan her face with her hand to cool her blushes. Burberry laughed, again.

"The next day," Burberry resumed, "As if wanting to demonstrate beyond doubt that his earlier encounter had taught him nothing what-so-ever, Ewan Burberry slipped away without his escort again, strolling and exploring on his own."

"Foolish man!" jibed Caitlan.

"Pig-headed I would say," Burberry agreed, grinning broadly before continuing.

"Whilst the foolish man was away from the inn," Burberry adapted, "Three hired killers arrived, seeking him out. Little did these men realise that the owners of the establishment were not timid, helpless victims. Within the hour, the would-be assassins were laying face up beneath damp forest soil to the rear of the inn."

"Constable Burberry, creeping around in the forest, was suddenly pounced upon by the self-same Ranger thugs he had encountered the day before. Using the advantage of surprise to full effect, they took him to the ground, bound him, gagged him, and bundled him off to their lair."

"Finding Burberry missing, the inn keeper and Alex, the young soldier, set out to track him down. On a hunch, they had gone to the forest stronghouse of the McArthys. Just as the two of them were launching a foolhardy rescue attempt, Captain McCleary and his Blue and Greys turned up, and promptly mounted a full scale assault."

"Despite having been badly beaten by the McArthys, Constable Burberry had insisted that he resume his journey to Inverness. Since he was unable to ride, Captain

McCleary had put a cart at his disposal and had padded it out with hay and sacking. Battered and bruised, he had been lifted up into the vehicle and made as comfortable as his injuries would allow."

"Resigned to this undignified method of travel, the constable had thought himself about to make farewells to the inn keeper, his wife and the young soldier. Instead, they had boldly announced that they would accompany him to Inverness. Despite all efforts, he had been unable to persuade them to reconsider."

Caitlan raised a hand and interjected to take over the role of narrator in the unfolding story.

"There was no doubt in any of their minds," she began, "That their paths had crossed due to the influence of a divine purpose and not by mere chance. This divine purpose had manifested itself, several times, in the form of golden flames. This mysterious spectacle was one that echoed the time of the legendary 'Kiffan the Defiant'."

Burberry nodded his approval of her version of events and she took this as permission to continue.

"Kiffan," she announced, "Had lived around eight hundred years ago and was a hero whose name was still spoken with awe. She attacked and harassed the Vikings as they began to expand downwards through the north of Scotland. The Norse invaders had grown accustomed to most Scots and Picts fleeing before them when they attacked. Kiffan, however, had succeeded in uniting the people into a devastatingly effective strike-and-flee army and personally led them into battle. After a long series of bloody confrontations and a lengthy campaign of daring raids, Kiffan began to earn the grudging respect of the Vikings. Before long, they began to refer to her band of fighters as the *'Brydda'*, which – in Old Norse – meant 'annoy'."

Quickly, before Caitlan had time to object, Burberry jumped back to the role of narrator.

"Constable Burberry's fascination with the Queen of the West and the Brydda had rapidly become an obsession," Burberry announced, "His studious cultivation of Brydda contacts and his campaign to rid them of their enemies had not escaped their notice. Before leaving Edinburgh, his final triumph had been to be accepted by them as a brother in their cause. Their parting gift had been to swear him into their order. He was adamant that, from that day on, his life had taken on a new and deeper meaning."

"To Burberry's utter astonishment, when he had been rescued from the McArthys, he had seen the legendary golden flames of the Brydda."

"Really?" asked Caitlan, surprised and fascinated by this revelation.

Burberry nodded enthusiastically to confirm it.

"They flames had sprung to life before him!" said Burberry, triumphantly, "They had curled and gyrated in the air, illuminating the face of his captor, thus enabling a shot to be aimed at him from outside. The musket ball that delivered the death to the man who held Burberry was fired from a distance that defied both logic and mechanics in its uncanny accuracy."

Caitlan nodded, appreciative for his disclosure.

"Suddenly, Ewan Burberry felt part of something greater than his own life and more momentous than anything of this world."

Caitlan stared at him in stunned silence. She thought back to what she and Hamish had discussed. The Constable's mission was, they were certain, connected to plots and conspiracies at the highest levels.

Now she understood.

It wasn't just that Burberry was *investigating* conspiracies. He was *part* of one of them. *He was* a conspirator! He was treading a dangerous path. He was sworn to the Brydda. He was working for King James. He had worked in the King's Secret Service. He had connections to the French that could get him hanged as a traitor if they were discovered. Whose word did anybody have but *his own* that he had been spying on the French for the king?

"You must be very careful," she whispered, "If anyone were to learn about the... the French..."

Burberry nodded grimly.

"I deliberately never speak French but, unfortunately, when I relive those times, when I contemplate the things I did back then, my mind begins to *think* in French."

Caitlan gave him a worried look.

"One slip of the tongue," he acknowledged, "A single stray sentence with the wrong choice of words and I could be a dead man."

CHAPTER 12

Captain Iain McCleary studied the contour of the trees in the distance. It was clear from their sweeping curve that the road turned west to avoid the line of towering summits ahead of them. The top of the first mountain was still obscured in billowing low cloud and the next three had caps of dense grey mist on them.

When they eventually reached the top of the incline, it came as no surprise to anybody that the view beyond it turned out to be more of the same terrain, stretching way off into the far yonder.

Soon, another wagon dropped into a particularly deep rut and it, too, refused to dislodge under horsepower alone. Eventually, it was roughly handled out of its trap and rolled a little way forward to be wedged stationary with a set of wooden chocks. A little way ahead was a far worse rut. The soldiers gathered rocks and stones and dropped them into the cavernous trench until it was full. Once their work was complete, they let the wagon roll back, again, to give it a run up over a series of humps. After a lot of shoving and pushing from the soldiers and straining by the horses, the wagon resumed its journey. There was a little cheer from those around it.

The first scouts returned, signalling that all was clear ahead and another cheer erupted. McCleary motioned for his Second-in-Command to come alongside him and the two entered into a discussion about their route. The Captain periodically leaned across and set his finger to points on the map his junior was holding open and aloft. From time to time, the man with the map would lean forward and use a long twig that he was holding, clenched between his teeth, to touch the map to indicate this or that spot of interest.

Burberry was vaguely amused at how the horses of the two men were fully trusted, by them, to take them forward without any need for human interaction. The two beasts, devoid of guidance from the reins or heels of their riders, picked their way expertly along the muddy highway, negotiating dips, ruts and holes with obvious care. Now and again, one or other rider, would reach down and pat or stroke their steed in encouragement or congratulation. In response, the two animals would look and nod to each other, exaggeratedly, as if confirming between themselves that they were doing well.

Burberry felt a pang of envy. He had been a courier, both as a boy and, later, as a young man. He had started out on foot, running messages around a large, expansive army camp, but later graduated to a pony for covering wider distances. Years later, he had got to ride a proper horse, and he recalled that he loved that creature with all his heart. He and the horse were almost joined together as one.

Burberry happily reflected on his courier days and, as they rumbled and lurched on, he was completely absorbed in his recollections, losing all track of time.

Many were the occasions, Burberry recalled, that he had gone hungry in order to feed his horse. As a fully appointed and commissioned army courier, he could call upon citizens on his route to provide assistance to him. This included food, water and, on occasion, lodgings. He would never over extend his requests and would always avoid burdening poor people by making demands on them that would cause them to suffer. This was not something that could be said for all of his colleagues in the courier service.

Burberry's belly would often rumble from lack of nourishment, but – when the need to levy food was upon those of limited means – he would not hesitate to ask for nothing more than oats for his horse, declining any offer of food for himself. He hated, with a passion, the idea of ever eating food that would leave the giver hungry. This was especially so where they had children.

There was a sudden jolt and Burberry returned to his senses to find that they had dropped into yet another deep rut. The soldiers lurched and rocked the vehicle, backwards and forwards and from side to side, but the horses pulling them could not overcome the grip of the rocks on the wheels. There was a ringing of hooves against stone and laboured grunts from the soldiers with their shoulders against the rim of the rear wheels. The vehicle did not budge.

Burberry knew the routine. Everyone, including the driver, got down from their seats. The driver went to take charge of the horses, on foot, and everybody else took up their stations leaning their weight against various parts of the wagon. Burberry was taken to sit up against a tree by the side of the road. The troops ahead and behind came along with poles and levers and set them to the wheel rims of the vehicle.

Burberry sighed, annoyed that he was forced to be a spectator rather than a participant. As he watched, he was more than a little impressed by how the drivers didn't whip or flog their horses. Instead, they took hold of their harnesses about their shoulders and hauled on them, to help the horses, and shouted encouragement to them, delivering only the occasional slap to urge them on. The wagon still did not dislodge.

The driver fetched a bucket, filled it with water, and took it to each of the horses in turn. Burberry was amazed at how the animals reacted. They look genuinely disappointed in themselves and it was unmistakable that they felt they had let the driver down.

The driver spoke to each of the sorrowful horses in turn, patting and stroking them for solace.

Next, the driver went to one of the other wagons and came back with a sack. The sack appeared to be half full of something. The driver took it to each horse and let them put their nose into its neck. The horses sniffed and, whatever was in the sack, the horses were delighted by it!

The driver went six paces ahead of the horses and reaching into the sack, he withdrew a dozen round objects, three for each of the four horses, and laid them on the road at the four corners of a square. To each of these clusters, he added a handful of another treat. The horses trod the ground and snorted, breathing heavily and becoming very alert.

Burberry looked from the horses to the bounty in the road and then back again. The driver visited the horses with the water bucket, once more, but each of them declined to drink, one even dismissively pushing the bucket away with its nose and huffing. All four of the horses had eyes only for the juicy, red apples and tasty carrots sat in the road.

This time – almost as if in support of the horses – even more people clamoured around to help move the cart. For this attempt, long poles were passed underneath the cart and grabbed by a pair of soldiers at each end. These, the constable recognised, were 'dragon poles'. They were used, he knew, as long as a thousand years ago. They were supposedly for the purpose of carrying home dead dragons, slung beneath them, that had been fought and slain. These poles were extremely sturdy and the fact that dragons had never actually existed, except in fanciful legends, did not prevent them from retaining their name!

The moment came and, much to the relief of the eager and impatient horses, the pushing and pulling recommenced. The soldiers swayed as they exerted themselves, chanting "One, two, three…" with the emphasis and exertion on the 'three', each time. To the delight of Burberry – from his vantage point beneath his tree – he could see that the horses quickly took up the rhythm, matching the tempo, as they strained in time with their human collaborators.

After a little while, the constable's positivity began to wane. He, too, found himself moving in time to the beat, swaying and grimacing with the pain that it caused. This spectacle, he decided, must have been what it was like to watch the slaves of ancient civilizations moving great stones for their masters. Burberry mentally calculated thirty seconds and slumped back against the tree, now almost certain that he was witnessing another failure.

Suddenly, there was a loud creaking and groaning of tortured timber, and the wagon unexpectedly jerked up and out of the rut, bouncing in the air to knee height as it went. It landed with a sickening cracking sound. The horses immediately dragged the wagon forward to reach the apples and carrots. The vehicle dropped to the ground, collapsing with a thud, as both front wheels came away. The wheels fell to the road, left and right, as if a giant had just flipped a pair of huge coins. The front axle had completely broken.

Without even hesitating, the soldier who was the carpenter and wheelwright, ordered one of the dragon poles to be hauled to the side of the road. A pile of rocks was constructed to raise one end of it from the ground and, without delay, axes were produced to begin the job of cutting it down to size to form a new axle.

Hamish, Caitlan and Alex, panting and breathless from their exertions of wagon shifting, came to sit beside Burberry. After issuing orders to several of his troops, Captain McCleary came to join them.

"There are soldiers going ahead of us and to our rear to set up a watch for anybody approaching," the captain told them.

The six of them sat and watched as the horses were changed around. The offending ruts, further along, were filled in with small rocks and pebbles and then stamped down into place by a dozen pairs of boots. It took only half an hour before, through some impressive teamwork and masterful woodworking skills, the defective wagon was repaired.

The driver of the wagon examined the refurbishment and, from his gestures and the fact that he shook the carpenter's hands – both of them – he seemed to be very well pleased. McCleary's junior officer came across to them and confirmed that all was ready for them to restart.

Everyone stood up and dusted themselves off. The Captain placed himself before Caitlan Pottle and, bowing low and graciously, swept an arm in the direction of the wagon.

"Madam," he trilled to her, "Your carriage awaits."

The innkeeper's wife curtsied deeply and formally, then offered her hand. Sweeping his massive coat to one side and ignoring the tails of it levitating in a gust of wind, Captain Iain McCleary took Caitlan's hand and escorted her to the wagon. There he knelt, for maximum gallantry, for her to place a foot on the knee he offered as an aid to her ascent.

Hamish, her husband, turned to Alex and lifted his nose in the air in the manner of an aristocrat and addressed him in an affected, whiny, nasal tone:

"Good servants are so terribly hard to find, these days!"

Alex and Burberry bellowed with laughter, the latter telling him off for the hurt this caused him in his ribs. McCleary, meanwhile, strutted back to them in a parody of a nobleman of haughty disposition, much to the amusement of all.

"Sir," said McCleary, bowing to the constable and swirling his hand in the air in an elaborate motion, "If you would care to join us in this splendid, stately carriage?"

Burberry gurgled with a mixture of amusement and pain as he grasped his sides. Hamish and Alex assisted McCleary in conveying their friend back to the wagon and helped him into the rear of it. All the while, they chatted to each other like simpering aristocrats, much to the entertainment of all those around. Once the constable was deposited onto the tail board of the 'splendid, stately carriage', Caitlan took hold of him underneath his armpits. With as much care as could be employed, she dragged him to his straw bed at the opposite end.

"You've over filled this bag of turnips!" she shouted in rebuke, putting on a fierce face, "I can hardly move the damned thing!"

There was more laughter and more groaning with pain from the constable. Caitlan helped him to get as comfortable as he could in his corner and built up a wall of straw around him. Meanwhile, the Captain sent a rider to recall their rear guard.

Everybody else mounted up or clambered into wagons and waited for Captain McCleary to give the order to move off. McCleary shifted himself to sit high in his saddle and flopped a hand in the air, towards the rise ahead of them.

"Gentlemen!" he yelled, attempting to mimic the voice of the English gentry, "Let's go leap some fences and ditches!"

Everybody roared with laughter and the troops hurled good natured abuse at their leader, which he fended off – maintaining his adopted character – with outrageously flamboyant retorts.

It took a while before everyone tired of this ribaldry and, when their main column reached the men of their fore guard, beyond the hill, those individuals were thoroughly confused at the repeated outbursts of chuckling and sniggering from their colleagues.

As they descended into the valley floor, any remaining gaiety was rapidly quelled by the danger of ambush as they passed through the narrow gap between the mountains.

In the distance, the road continued along, by the river, until it could be seen climbing up to crest a wide range of tall hills. This, they knew, would be an extremely risky section on their way and nobody spoke until they reached its base.

As the road began to rise, Captain McCleary stopped them and ordered them to widen the gaps between each cart and each escorting pair of riders as they ascended.

No sooner had they begun to labour their way up the hill, proper, than their Captain raised his hand and brought the leading riders to a dead halt. He held up his hand and wagged a finger side to side in an exaggerated motion. This was for the benefit of those further back, who repeated the gesture for 'stop', signalling it to those at the tail end of the convoy.

The captain looked around, suspiciously, but could not pinpoint anything out of sorts. Nobody spoke and nobody moved. They waited for a minute and a half, which felt more akin to ten.

McCleary looked to his second-in-command who rocked his head, side to side, to indicate a lack of inspiration. McCleary lifted his hands in the air, where he mimicked the action of grasping invisible reins while riding a make-believe horse. Pointing up to the brow of the hill, he extended two fingers and threw them forward in the air to indicate the two scouts who, earlier, had gone ahead of them. He then shrugged his shoulders and raised both palms, questioningly. His junior performed a similar pantomime to indicate that he, too, had no idea what might have happened to them.

They waited a little longer, but the scouts did not return, causing the feeling of expectation in the air to grow still heavier.

Captain McCleary lifted his index finger and touched his right ear with it before flapping both hands in the air like a pair of wings. His second-in-command lifted his chin and nodded. He understood the observation. They had entered a forest, with tall trees on either side of the track, but all the birds in it were completely hushed.

McCleary held up two fingers, representing two men, and wiggled them in the air to represent them walking forward. Then, he pointed up and beyond the rise ahead, directing where the men should go. Finally, he placed a finger vertically against his lips, to emphasise the need for them to move quietly.

His second-in-command, using similar gesticulations, communicated the order to two of their foot soldiers, sending them on up ahead as lookouts and fiercely commanding them to make the minimum possible noise. The two men, with their muskets at the ready, set off, cautiously.

They only got halfway to the top of the rise when, from beyond it, came an urgent alarm. It took the form of a pair of hollow wooden tubes clacking, over and over, as they were forcefully knocked together. The noise violently shattered the silence, bringing a shocking end to the quiet.

They watched as the two men who had been sent ahead dived into the trees, one either side of the road. Captain McCleary held up both arms over his head and urgently gestured for the rest of his troops to scatter, off the track, in similar fashion.

Captain McCleary signalled for everyone to find cover. Riders quickly jumped to the ground and led their mounts off the road. Soldiers leapt out of wagons and ran for cover. A group of four of them – seeming to have been charged with the constable's wellbeing – hauled him out of the wagon, as kindly as circumstances would allow, and hurriedly carried him into the cover of the foliage.

A full two minutes passed, dragging by – moment by moment – with nerve jangling slowness. Suddenly, they heard the screeching of whistles from the second pair of scouts as they sounded another warning.

All at once, ahead of them, and far too close for comfort, came the very clear sound of galloping horses. Their riders were making no attempt to disguise their approach. The galloping suddenly slowed, the horsemen apparently now very close to the horizon of the road. They could be heard to assume a steady walking pace.

Appearing in the middle of the road, a pair of unidentified mounted soldiers brinked the hill. They were both holding long poles aloft. From the ends of the poles, long pennants fluttered and flapped in the breeze. The light behind them was too bright for any details to be visible. Everything was bleached out to a murky black and white.

"How many of them are there, do you reckon?" McCleary's second-in-command asked him, in a loud whisper.

"A lot."

"I agree."

"Too many."

"I agree."

"If we fight, and I think we may have to, we may be facing defeat."

"The men will fight to their last breath, captain. They won't let you down."

CHAPTER 13

"Dear God," said Annis, dropping a small square of material from her old cloak into the stream, "I cast into the water this fragment of material that I have worn and which may have absorbed my spirit or the essence of my being and I ask that you allow it to convey my prayer to the ocean, into the darkness of its oblivion, and, from there, into the light of your glorious eternity. Please bless my mother, Cydara, taken from us before her time, and let her dwell with You in paradise."

She stood and looked around her at the forest and took a deep breath. The birds were singing in the trees and bees were contentedly buzzing around amongst the flowers. She always found the forest to be a very peaceful place, just like a church.

She walked up the short rise into a little clearing in the forest. The two Honour Guards who shadowed her remained at a good distance and she was grateful for their efforts not to intrude on her quiet moments.

When she had finished, Queen Annis turned and was puzzled to see Wild Flower standing a few paces from her. She felt certain that nobody had been there a few seconds earlier. The clearing was surrounded by ferns and bushes and was strewn with leaves and twigs. Annis was sure that she should have heard anybody approaching.

Wild Flower's presence, however, was wholly reassuring and caused Annis no alarm. Wild Flower exuded a calmness and a gentle warmth that was profoundly comforting. She seemed to always bring with her an extraordinary sense of peace and love.

'Love?' Annis thought to herself, 'My life is one of duty and has no space in it for love!'

Without wishing it, Annis suddenly thought of the strong, tall, handsome Balgair and smiled.

"He is one of three, but he does not know it," Wild Flower said, gently.

"Who?" Annis asked, certain that she had said nothing aloud.

"Balgair. Balgair McRory. He is one of three, but he is unaware."

"How did you know I was thinking of him?"

Wild Flower ignored the question, for she knew most things.

"Balgair is an only child," Annis insisted, "He has no brothers or sisters. He told me so."

Wild Flower smiled her soft, indulgent smile.

"He is one of three because he is bound to two others," Wild Flower replied, "He is bound to them by fate. I have seen his two others. They are not his family, but they all look a little alike."

Annis looked slightly puzzled.

"You, on the other hand, My Lady, are one of two. You are one of two and you do not know it."

"I, too, am an only child!" Annis objected.

"I see a face with your same eyes. I see lips with your same smile."

"It is a mere coincidence."

"No."

"You'll be telling me next, my Sweet Wild Flower, that she has this very same hair!" retorted Annis, twirling some of her golden locks around a finger.

Wild Flower raised her eyebrows at this reply but made no comment.

"The courier, from the king is one of two," Wild Flower said, "I have seen his other in a dream. He is as big and as strong as a bear. When he talks, people listen. When he smiles, the whole room is alight with his charm."

"He sounds impressive."

"He is impressive. The royal courier has not seen this man for years and years, but the two of them will know each other, instantly, on sight. You must take the king's courier with you to Inverness, for that is where he will meet his other."

"We are not going to Inverness," Annis protested.

"We will be," Wild Flower smiled.

"I have decided to go home to Fort Augustus. That is where we are going. This year, we return ahead of the approach of Winter."

Wild Flower closed her eyes and lifted her face to the verdant canopy above her. She paused, appearing to commune with some spiritual force, then opened her eyes and looked back to Annis.

"King James would have you go to Inverness. That is the message carried by the courier. The king's purpose, there, is contrary to God's purpose. God's purpose, however, is that you should meet your other and this will serve to achieve it."

Queen Annis shook her head, slightly perplexed by the conversation.

"I have no *other*," Annis insisted.

"People can be bound together in different ways," Wild Flower replied, "By their beliefs, by a common purpose or by blood. You will find your other at The Fortress of Inverness. She is unknown to you, but she will be revealed."

Annis looked at Wild Flower with a mixture of wonder, annoyance and dread.

"The courier and his other are seekers of the truth. His other has found that truth and it burns within him like a fire. His faith is a true faith but one that is not yet accepted. It is his destiny to save your life. It is your destiny to save his."

Annis looked puzzled.

"My Lady, God never asks anything of us that we cannot deliver. His ways are as wonderful as they are baffling. We do not need to understand in order to obey."

"I am wounded and unfit," Annis said, in a small voice, "I am completely and utterly useless to Him."

Annis hung her head in shame.

"A power has been sent into this world," Wild Flower said, her voice trembling, "It is a power that is beyond the imagination of mortal people. It is a power that has no limitations and no constraints!"

Annis felt a warmth beneath her arm where her wound was located. It still pained her, from time to time. Sometimes it would ache for hours on end. Her greatest fear was that she might never be able to properly wield a sword again. It was a fear that she forced down and buried in a dark, deep space inside her.

Annis felt the wound on her arm suddenly begin to tingle, then tremble and quiver. The sensation progressed until it seemed to be vibrating. It was as if a deep note were being plucked on a harp. Finally, there was a brief, stabbing pain and then it was all over and she felt nothing more from it.

The queen looked at Wild Flower, shocked by what had just happened. Wild Flower smiled back, sweetly. Annis knew, with absolute certainty, that the girl was aware of what had just happened.

"No limitations," said Wild Flower, firmly, "No constraints."

Annis felt, urgently, for her wound through the fabric of her tunic and, for the first time, touching it caused her no pain. She pressed her fingers, hard. It no longer hurt. Almost in a panic, she grabbed at her flesh, savagely digging her nails into it, but it still did not pain her.

"Impossible!" Annis cried.

"No limitations," Wild Flower repeated, "No constraints."

The queen's hand trembled as she loosened the cord around her cuff. With fumbling fingers she managed to pull up her sleeve. There, where the wound had been – fierce, red, and angry – was just pale, unblemished skin. She let out a sound that was halfway between a yelp and a moan.

"When we say the Lord's Prayer," Wild Flower told her, "We say: *'Your will be done, on Earth as it is in Heaven'.*"

Annis nodded, only half listening.

"You must understand, My Lady, that God's will is a potent force in itself. It is an authority. It is His will brought to life. It is His active envoy. It causes things to happen and people to act."

Annis nodded, her mind now in turmoil. Wild Flower sat down on the ground, cross-legged, and stared into the near distance, her eyes taking on a faraway look as she spoke.

"The English will come – in ten or twenty years – with a mighty army. They will not be the same English that we know, now. It will be in a period of history during which Scotland and England will cease to be heads and tails of the same coin. It will be in a time of hostility. When it happens, the Queen of the West **must** be ready."

Annis nodded, again, feeling a desperate need to be strong.

"I must go and see this courier from King James," Annis said.

Wild Flower stood up and stepped closer to the queen, whispering beneath her hand for secrecy.

"The king *knew* the courier for his true identity. It is an identity that the courier keeps completely and utterly secret. The king's advisors, at court, believe the courier to be nobody other than the person he portrays himself to be. The courier is an ally of your allies and an enemy of your enemies."

Annis opened her mouth to speak, but Wild Flower held up her hand, motioning for her to hear more.

"When I close my eyes, I see faces in semi darkness. I see men with hoods drawn up to hide their faces in shadows. They are the friends of your enemy. It is an enemy that has not yet revealed himself to you."

Wild Flower paused, again, as if she were listening to something out of range of normal ears.

"There are two men who travel with the king's courier, but they are not amongst his fellows. He is in danger from them. These men who accompany him do not wish him well. Their loyalty is not to truth and justice, but only to money and power."

Wild Flower closed her eyes and breathed in deeply, inclining her head, again, as if drawing the truth out of the air. Suddenly, her eyes flew open and she bared her teeth.

"These men despise you! They scorn and detest you because you are a woman. They respect nobody in authority unless they are a man!"

Wild Flower's voice changed and she spoke like she was one of the men.

'Women should cook food, scrub floors, fetch and carry, and bear children. Women should be beaten if they answer back!'

Wild Flower screwed up her face and pushed spittle from her lips with her tongue. Then she spat. It was as if having the men's words in her mouth created a bad taste.

"My mother was a mighty queen," declared Annis, proudly.

"She was," agreed Wild Flower, "And so are you."

"I am merely a shadow of her greatness," said Annis, miserably.

Wild Flower smirked.

"Not when the moment calls you. Not when your blood courses through your body. Then you are glorious!" she said, gleefully.

Annis looked at her, uncertainly.

"I am tormented by doubt," the queen confessed, "I lay awake thinking about my mother and how wonderful a queen she was and how I can never compare."

"Your mother was a truly great queen," agreed Wild Flower, "But you will be the greatest queen ever. You will become the Greatest of the Great."

"No!" cried Annis, "Do not say that!"

Her face was contorted with fury and she jabbed a finger at the little girl as if it were a spear.

"Those words are reserved to describe Queen Kiffan!" Annis reprimanded, "For *she* and she alone is and was the Greatest of the Great!"

"Yes. I know it," said Wild Flower, calmly, "I have chosen my words carefully."

Annis made a grumbling noise in her throat and turned away, to calm herself.

"My Lady, when the moment calls, you are glorious."

Annis turned back, tears brimming in her eyes.

"Am I?" she asked in a tiny voice.

"Glorious!" Wild Flower assured her, "Magnificent!"

"People speak, in tales told around the campfires, of my mother's glory," Annis whimpered.

"People tell such tales about **you**."

"They do?"

"Yes, My Lady, but they will sing songs around their campfires, for centuries, about what you do today."

"What I do, today?" asked Annis, flexing her sword arm and looking at it, dubiously, "It will be a while before I have much chance of glory."

"Are you sure?"

Annis adopted a fighting stance and lunged a few times with an invisible sword. Her eyes widened and she regarded her sword arm with wonder. She swung again, more energetically, and leapt forward and sideways, cutting and slashing. She looked at Wild Flower, aghast.

"My Lady, whatever needs to be, will be."

Annis twirled around, put her right hand to the grass and sprang from it in a tumble, landing nimbly and then, as if inviting disaster, performed a one-handed handstand on it.

"The courier is important to your destiny," said Wild Flower, "But the men who escort him will take his life if they suspect he has good will towards you. He is in mortal danger."

Annis screwed up her face and made a tortured smile before she replied.

"Sweet Wild Flower, I have abused the courier and treated him harshly. I do not think he feels any affection towards me."

"My Lady, he sees through your anger. He sees the person you truly are. He is no ordinary man."

"Very well," said Queen Annis, standing tall, "I will talk to this courier, but – before I do – I will see if there is any word of these men who accompanied him. I will deal with them, first."

Wild Flower blinked hard, several times, and shook her head violently for a second, as if she had seen something spectacular.

"Oh! My goodness!" she enthused, "Yes, My Lady! Yes, you will indeed!"

CHAPTER 14

Annis sat on her throne. It was an imposing wooden chair with brass and copper finery. It was adorned with a bearskin, but nothing akin to the grand scale that might be found in a palace or a castle.

The queen had set up her "chamber" in a large clearing at the edge of the forest. Clay had been strewn and hammered hard to form a floor. Canvas sheets – once the sails of an ocean-going schooner – were stretched and roped overhead to form a canopy.

Annis looked around and heard the soft call of songbirds and the gentle tumbling of water in a nearby brook. She felt that no monarch had ever sat at a more wonderful or inspiring court.

Balgair and Gavin appeared, escorting two elegantly attired men. The men had a mean and cunning look that Annis found both distasteful and disturbing. Immediately her eyes fell on them, Annis could sense the aura of evil that surrounded them.

Both of the men wore riding breeches, tall, shiny leather boots and impressively embroidered capes. They had two swords apiece, a long horseman's sword and a close quarters sword. They were both clad in light armour. Each carried a pistol, a powder horn and a leather satchel.

The two men were ushered to stand in the centre of the cleared ground, facing Queen Annis on her throne. They adopted a relaxed, informal pose that affected no kind of respect or reverence.

Annis waited while the silence became a little uncomfortable. The men continued to stand, now adopting almost a slouch, and looked unconcerned. Annis looked the men up and down, allowing her displeasure to show on her face.

This seemed to annoy them. After a while, Annis spoke, keeping her voice low so that the men had to pay attention to hear her.

"I am Annis, Queen of the West," she said, softly.

The men looked uninterested in her words.

"You will kneel," Gavin told them.

The two exchanged looks of scorn and the taller of the two addressed Annis, directly, placing his hands on his hips to emphasise his disrespect.

"If **you** are a queen, then **we** are both kings!"

Balgair and Gavin drew their swords in unison. The sound of metal sliding from leather appeared not to concern the two visitors. One of them gestured contemptuously towards Balgair and Gavin and curled his lip in a sneer.

"Don't think," he told Annis, "That I could not run these buffoons through and easily make it to you in three strides."

"Your Majesty," Balgair pleaded, "One word and I will leave them both a bloody mess on the ground."

"We," said the second man, "Are the finest swordsmen in the land. We could each take three of your best, slice them to pieces and not be out of breath."

Annis ignored their boasting, which appeared to further infuriate them.

"Who are these men?" she asked of Balgair, "What is their business? Were they begging?"

"Begging!" the first man shouted, incandescent with rage.

Everyone followed the queen's example and ignored them both. This only raised their hackles, still more.

"They were brought in by our scouts, *Your Majesty*," Balgair announced, placing emphasis on her title, "They were looking for a courier who carries a message from King James. They are his escort."

"The courier is my guest," Annis said, offhandedly.

"He is their concern," Gavin announced, "They and he – so they tell us – are guaranteed safe passage and may demand food and shelter of whomsoever they wish, throughout Scotland, by the authority of King James."

"I'm sorry," Annis said, feigning misunderstanding, "So you're saying they **are** beggars?"

This provoked a chorus of laughter from all those around. The two men clenched their teeth and snarled, now utterly enraged.

"We represent King James and you will show us deference!"

Balgair, looked to Annis, his eyes pleading, his fist clenched so hard on his sword that his knuckles were white. Annis gave him an apologetic look and shook her head.

"In a round about way, I am a subject of King James, myself." Annis declared, "I am also a monarch within my own realm. King James of England and of Scotland has never, previously, had any problem understanding or respecting this circumstance."

"You are privy to the king's orders," the taller of the two men said, arrogantly, "They have been delivered to you. You should go about doing as the king has commanded."

"As the king's **commands**?"

"Yes! Commands!"

"The matter of any…" Annis pouted sardonically, casting her eyes heavenwards, "Of any **requests** is something still to be dealt with **at my leisure**, and I have not yet allotted time to read anything so tedious as such a correspondence, irrespective of its source."

The two men bristled with indignation.

"My two officers will make you welcome," she told them, cheerfully imitating cordiality, "While I decide if I have sufficient time to tend to my correspondence."

Balgair and Gavin guided the two of them away.

CHAPTER 15

Annis summoned the courier. When he appeared, he stood before her looking neither defiant nor compliant.

'Here', Annis thought to herself, 'Is a man who is resigned to his fate.'

"Good Sir, I would have you deliver to me the document from King James," Annis said, plainly and without emotion.

"Yes, Your Majesty," replied the man.

He reached into his tunic and revealed a knife. Immediately, the hands of both Balgair and Gavin shot to their swords. Annis waved her fingers, giving the courier permission to proceed.

The man opened his bag by breaking a lead seal with the knife and then pulled a metal wire through a brass eye to free the clasp. He then withdrew a small leather pouch from inside the bag. The pouch was also sealed. This time the seal was a concave metal disc with wax set solid in its pan. He handed the pouch to Gavin, who strode over to the queen and presented it to her.

Annis held the pouch, with its seal upward, while Gavin dug out the wax and unhooked a wire clasp from beneath it. Inside the pouch was a waxed envelope. The envelope had its own, individual seal, placed where its flaps intersected on its reverse. The seal took the form of a large circle of melted wax with an image embossed into it.

Annis beckoned the courier to come forward and held up the envelope so that he could see the wax seal.

"Is this how it should look?" she asked him, with charming frankness.

"Yes," he replied, plainly charmed to be asked, "Yes, it is, Your Majesty."

"I presume that you have seen a lot of these?"

"Yes, indeed," replied the courier, "A great number of them."

"You note," Annis said, leaning forward confidentially, "That I trust you to authenticate it?"

"Yes, Your Majesty."

"And you note that you are still alive?"

The courier looked a little uneasy at this question but replied after gulping to restore his voice.

"Yes, Your Majesty."

"If it were permissible for a queen to apologise for her behaviour to somebody below her, then I believe that – in your case – it would be warranted. Life, however, is how it is and not how we would wish it to be. I am restricted in my actions for the sake of appearance. As a queen I am not as free as you might think."

"No, Your Majesty."

"The two men who rode here with you, have been found searching for you."

The courier stiffened, visibly, and looked nervous.

"Tell me, my man, would you wish them to find you?"

The courier looked at her, hesitantly, and – after some thought – shook his head.

"Then, I guarantee you, that they shall not," she replied.

The courier glanced to meet her eye, but looked away, immediately.

"I don't think that they are friends of yours, are they?"

Again, the hesitation, the thinking, then a shake of his head.

"Have you ever fought with two men at once, with a sword, and won?"

The courier stood a little taller and a little straighter before he responded to the question.

"Yes."

"Have you fought three men with a sword and won?"

"Yes."

"Four men?"

The courier paused, before touching two fingers to his lips and then to his forehead.

"Only just, Your Majesty, and I escaped with my life only with God's good grace."

"These two men, the ones who seek you, could you defeat either one?"

The courier looked a little shaken and gulped, again.

"No."

"They are good swordsmen?"

"They are amongst the finest you could ever imagine."

"They are amongst the finest swordsmen, but not the finest of people?"

"They take pleasure in inflicting pain and suffering."

Annis looked the courier directly in his eyes and moved her face closer to his.

"Then I will kill them," Annis assured him, "And you may watch."

The courier tried his best to stifle his disquiet but failed. Annis saw his face contort with the effort of it and she laughed aloud.

"Do not worry, they will not see you," she promised.

The man looked at her imploringly.

"Oh!" the queen cooed, softly, "You fear not for *your* safety but for *mine*?"

The man's expression changed to one of deep concern.

"Your Majesty, they will kill you," he implored.

"You think so?"

"I know so. It is what will happen."

"Fear not," Annis assured him, "For I am a 'David' and they, for sure, are no Goliaths."

Gavin and Balgair, laughed. The man looked relieved and managed a hesitant little chuckle. Annis raised her head and gestured to her two officers.

"Leave us," she said, abruptly.

Balgair and Gavin withdrew. Annis looked at the man, coolly and levelly, and he looked away.

"You may look me in the face, Sir," she told him, gently.

The man looked back to her with a flicker of fear behind his eyes.

"You fear that I confide in you too much," she said, "You fear that I do this because you will soon be dead and unable to speak of my babblings."

The man did not reply. He just continued to look at her with the same expression in his eyes.

"You are safe," she said, "I do not take pleasure in killing."

The man looked at her intently as if he might see her soul if he looked hard enough. Annis smiled.

"I take it," she said, "That history has seen few Kings of England who could say the same."

The man contorted his lips into a haggard smile but said nothing.

"The men who have come looking for you," she asked, "What are their names?"

"They are Robert Taylor and Victor Haviland, Your Majesty."

"I feel that their presence in Scotland makes Scotland a less pleasant place to be."

"It is their first time in Scotland, Your Majesty, and they do not welcome being here. They speak of it with disdain."

"They are your enemies," Annis declared, "They will die for that reason. For, if they are *your* enemies, then they are *my* enemies, too."

The man looked at her with incredulity.

"Go," she said, flinging a hand in the air, "Go to my officers and tell them that it is my wish that you watch while I kill your enemies. I will do it with my own hand."

The man gave her a desolate look, bowed deeply, then turned to go, but she called him back.

"Stop. You have come north to Scotland with an escort. Now, will return without them. That will make things somewhat difficult for you. Will it not?"

The courier thought for a brief second and then smiled a dismal smile.

"Yes, Your Majesty. It's not like losing my handkerchief or reporting that my dog has gone wild."

Annis laughed and the man did his best to laugh with her.

"I will make you a wager," she told him, "If I do, indeed, kill these two 'outstanding swordsmen', with my own hand, then will you accompany me to Inverness?"

The courier looked astonished, his eyes fixing on the envelope he had brought, which was still unopened in her hand. The final seal, he was certain, remained unbroken. She could not know its contents! His face was a picture of consternation. Annis smiled at his confusion and the man distractedly nodded his agreement to their bargain.

"Good!" she said, "When I am done with them, if either has a horse better than your own, you may accept it as my gift."

The man bowed elaborately and left. When he had gone, Annis broke the seal on the envelope and extracted its contents.

It was a warrant, signed by the king, directing her to go to The Fortress of Inverness to stand trial.

CHAPTER 16

The two men who sought the courier were hustled back before Queen Annis. They were still every bit as pompous and stood with the same swaggering arrogance as before.

"You are ignorant men," she told them, without preamble, "But you are not fools."

The two men looked at her with smouldering fury.

"As men, you are ignorant of the value of life, for you cannot give birth to it. You are ignorant, too, of the merit of mercy, for you disdain it."

The two men glowered at her.

"So, with my own hand, I shall take from you the one thing and withhold from you the other."

The two men laughed a scornful, contemptuous, derisory laugh.

"You'll need more men to help you than just these!" the taller scoffed, scanning the five soldiers around them.

Annis gave him a withering look as if he were the village idiot.

"Not *them!*" Annis snapped, "*Me!*"

The men laughed viciously, then sneered, then spat.

"I will cut you to pieces!" the shorter man growled.

"I will run you through and mount you like the whore your mother was!" the other snarled.

Annis leapt to her feet and her face contorted with simmering venom.

"You shouldn't have mentioned my mother!" she warned.

With a swirl of her hand, Annis tore back her brilliant white tunic, revealing her white armour glinting beneath it. Gavin and Balgair ran to her side.

"Your Majesty," Gavin implored, in a harsh whisper, "Do not do this! They deceive you with their slouching! I see them truly as they are! They are exemplary swordsmen, both!"

"Thank you for your concern and for your loyal service, but word of this will reach London while I am at The Fortress of Inverness and the king will know my worth!"

"No! No! No!" Gavin begged, "This is folly!"

Balgair looked at her with desperation, with sorrow and with a heart about to break.

"Your Majesty," he said, "Don't!"

"I must!"

Balgair leaned close and whispered in her ear.

"My Queen, if you die, I shall never marry!"

She smiled and then winked at him and whispered back.

"Then nor shall I!"

Balgair looked on in disbelief as Annis walked forward, calmly and serenely, in the direction of her opponents. The two men regarded her with a sneer.

"Mister Taylor and Mister Haviland," Annis said, with mocking civility, "I hereby accuse you of the crimes of robbery, rape and murder. Will you choose Trial by Combat and fight me to settle judgement?"

"With the greatest of pleasure!" said Robert Taylor.

"Nothing would please me more!" said Victor Haviland.

"May God be your judge, then," said Annis.

"I'm going to enjoy this!" declared one.

"Not as much as me!" the other challenged.

Annis laughed.

"**I** am a queen. **You** will soon both be corpses."

"You are as good as dead already, stupid wench!" said the first.

"You? Kill us?" the other scoffed, "You're just a woman!"

The queen's eyes blazed. She bared her teeth. With an elegant motion, she reached behind her and drew her twin swords, one in each hand, and held them aloft. She bit back her fear. She could not allow herself the luxury of doubt and these men must not see even a glimmer of it.

'Feeling fear will harm your chances,' her mother used to say, 'But showing fear will damn them.'

Annis took a deep breath. Then, invisible to the men, curling fronds of fire began to dance and spin in little eddies from the tips of her swords, gleeful and exultant.

"I'm not **just** a woman!" Annis bellowed, startling both men with the power of her voice.

Throwing her head back and crying out each word as if it were a whole sentence, she hollered her rebuke.

"No…

"Woman…

"Is…

"Just…

"A…

"Woman!"

Birds launched in waves from the trees, all around as her words echoed across the valley, striking the walls, and booming back.

With the sublime flow of an athletic dancer, Annis took two steps and launched herself into the air. The first man, quick as a bolt of lightning, pulled his sword from its sheath and lifted it to meet her impending blow.

Annis watched, dispassionately, as if she were a bystander, feeling as if the whole world had switched speeds and become incredibly slow.

The sword in the queen's right hand came down in a blur, a streak of golden flame trailing from its edge. The man's expert move soared up, the edge of his sword aimed for the underside of her own. His action was a textbook example of total precision.

With the merest hint of effort, Annis, flicked her sword from cutting edge down to its flat face down. She watched and counted in her head, awaiting the exact moment to react. The two weapons struck each other, mid swing, and Annis braced her arm for the shock. Her blade began to ring like a bell as her opponent's sword collided with it, but, at the precise moment they touched, she flicked her blade back to lead with its cutting edge. The action was so deftly performed and its timing so precise, as to defy explanation. Her sword began to run down the length of the tall man's steel.

She looked into his sullen, black eyes and – with all action now progressing at a languid crawl – could tell that he knew he had mistaken her level of skill. Her blade sang with shrill glee as it slid like a flat pebble skimming across a pond. The man's eyes widened. As her blade touched the handguard of his sword, she tipped her weapon to assume the perfect angle. It glanced off the handguard, sailing towards his face. His eyes, already wide, now expanded yet further.

The tip of her weapon smashed through his teeth, shattering them as a hammer might destroy the ice of a frozen waterfall. She watched the shards spin this way and that, twisting and tumbling with sublime slowness. Annis leaned onto her sword as its blade slid still further, piercing his tongue, and pushing through his gullet. As its razor sharpness met his spine, it was severed like nothing more than a twig.

The light of life extinguished from his eyes and his inanimate corpse began to tumble to the ground where it would land with a thud.

Annis had made a very careful calculation as to how much time she had available to engage each man. In this bizarrely lethargic dimension, the maximum allotted time had almost elapsed for her first strike.

As she had assumed, the second man's blade was already desperately close to her as she switched her attention to him. She was amazed by the speed of his reactions. He was as swift as a snake. Annis thrust her left sword downwards and, instantly became a spectator, she observed its sluggish progress, cutting through the air to the point of interception.

Her blade deflected the other's weapon, narrowly avoiding her kneecap being cut off. He had come as close to her as the thickness of her little finger.

Despite abhorring the man, she could not be anything but impressed that he had been able to judge her motion so well and launch at her with such incredible rapidity.

Annis whirled her legs, as if treading water, desperately seeking the ground that was coming up to meet her. She landed, cat like, behind the man and dropped gracefully into a crouch. He was already turning, and she was shocked at his nimbleness and wondered if he, too, were seeing things slowed to a fraction of their normal speed. She judged it to be extremely likely.

His sword was sweeping across the space between them and she realised that he had seamlessly transformed his lunging cut at her leg into a gliding swoop to her head.

Annis leaned back, placing a hand to the ground, and dropped herself below the level of the blade. She heard it whistle passed her face, alarmingly close, and felt a waft of air from it. She was now certain that this man saw things at the same dawdling pace as she was seeing them.

Invigorated with a new urgency, she kicked her foot across to strike the leg that bore his weight as he carried through the arc of his blade. She felt resistance and lifted her hand from the soil to transfer more momentum, finally pulling her other foot a little way aloft, too. The man's leg gave and he started to fall forwards. She felt him spontaneously correct his stance to compensate, but she was already driving her sword towards his knee.

Her unexpected replication of his original move had taken him completely by surprise.

She had been shocked at his agility. Now he was shocked at hers. His eyes registered the ferocity of her attack and the speed of its delivery. She felt a crunch as metal met bone and her blade bit into his knee. There was the most infinitesimal pause as sufficient momentum built up to break his knee cap and the edge of her sword buried itself into the joint. She heard his cry of pain as it gathered in his throat and lungs. She felt the air vibrate to its sound.

His eyes popped open like a pair of saucers and she could see his gaze had transferred to above her head. She became aware that her right sword was cruising down towards him. The move had been a mere consideration at the back of her mind. A flash of inspiration. An exploration, in a glimmer of time, of her next possible move. She was astounded to see it translated into action.

The dawning realisation that he was doomed registered on her victim's face. His eyes began to narrow as he focussed on her lips. She found this odd, as her mind had not yet enrolled the use of her mouth. The word she was forming had been spurred purely by her subconscious.

Just as her sword penetrated the front of the man's skull and its tip began to plunge into his brain, Annis managed to decipher the syllables she was uttering.

Some primitive and vindictive part of her mind had decided to taunt this man while life exited his body and as his last moments expired. He was a hater of women. He was a degrader of women. He was an attacker of women. He had promised to do all sorts of unspeakable things to her, because she was a woman.

The final recognition of what she was saying occurred to both her and him at the exact same moment.

A look of disgust hit the man's face. The word that came from her mouth, and which was the last one he would ever hear, was *'woman'*.

CHAPTER 17

Janine waited, patiently, for the Duke of Bo'Ness to fully vent his anger.

Her role as the rightful Queen of the West – a title still honoured and celebrated in the Scottish Highlands – was a very closely guarded secret and one that the Duke had gone to great lengths to conceal. It was a secret known to only a very select few people. It had, therefore, shocked and angered him to learn that her identity had been discovered by King James, the monarch of Scotland and England.

The greater part of his fury, however, had stemmed from the fact that, as Queen of the West, Janine had received a summons from the King to stand trial in Inverness for treason.

The Duke sat in an ornate, finely crafted armchair by the fire. With his head tilted back, his face glowered at the ceiling. His breathing had more or less returned to normal.

The Duchess for her part, had controlled her temper a little better and had recovered her composure a little quicker. She now sat opposite her husband, at the other side of the hearth, with her face unusually stern. Periodically, she pursed her lips and grimaced.

Janine, who was sat on a beautiful red and gold sofa with exquisitely carved spiral legs, mentally relived the momentous events of her recent life.

Only day or so ago, she had been the personal maid of Lady Dunkeld, at Dunkeld Manor. It had been a job that she had much enjoyed, until she started to attract the unwelcome attention of the Laird's Chief at Arms. One day, she recalled, he had dragged her down to the cellars, where he had assaulted her and then almost raped her.

Janine shivered, involuntarily, at the memory of it. She glanced to the Duke and Duchess of Bo'Ness and was relieved that, engrossed in their own thoughts, they did not appear to have noticed.

Janine recalled how she had fled from Dunkeld Manor in panic when her attacker had been found dead in the cellars. At that time, being no wiser, she had presumed that she had blacked out while fighting him off and that somebody had intervened to defend her, killing her assailant in the process.

Janine trembled as she remembered her encounter with the three thugs who had accosted her as she made her way along the road to Perth. They, too, had most certainly been intent on rape. She had run from them, only for one of them to catch her just as she thought she had escaped. Again, she had lost consciousness and woken to find the perpetrator dead.

Making her way back to the road, she had stopped a fine coach, carrying Brian and Bruce, the adopted sons – formerly nephews – of the Duke and Duchess of Bo'Ness. These two witty, charming and intelligent men had brought her here, to the fine mansion of Brech Woorlach, where they had fussed over her and doted on her like their little sister.

On arrival at Brech Woorlach Hall and on meeting the duke and duchess, Janine had been overcome by the opulence and splendour of her surroundings, but – at the same time – had been worryingly comfortable with being a part of it. It was almost as if Janine, a lowly maid, had previous experience of the elevated status of being a lady.

Janine reminisced, with a fond smile, how she had met the beautiful and elegant Francesca, daughter of the Duke and Duchess. Francesca had pretended to be a mere maid, tending to Janine dutifully and diligently up to and – at Francesca's own insistence – beyond the revelation of her true identity.

Janine smiled, again. This time the smile was fractured and bitter. The subject of her true identity was a harrowing one for her. It had not been long after discovering the real Francesca that she had discovered the startling truth of her own self.

She had been introduced to a Chinese man by the name of 'Mister Chang' who confessed to having, seven years earlier, taken control of Janine's mind and created a new character and existence for her. This had been her persona as the maid at Dunkeld Manor.

Still more shocking was the fact that Mister Chang and his daughter, Genji, had trained her in the oriental fighting arts to a level of impeccable proficiency. She was, it turned out, able to fight expertly with her hands and feet, with knives, swords, spears, poles, ropes and chains. In fact, with anything that might come into her grasp!

It had turned out that her secret protector, who had saved her life multiple times, had – all the time – been nobody other than she, herself, in her other mental guise.

To Janine's horror, the reason for having had a secret other self was revealed. She had been living as a maid to keep her hidden and safe from people who were her enemies. Her false persona had been created so that she could not accidentally betray herself and give away her real role in life.

Janine reminded herself that it transpired that she was the direct descendant of the legendary hero, Kiffan, a Pictish Queen who, almost eight hundred years earlier, had fought and resisted the onslaught of the Viking invasion of Scotland.

Janine could not suppress a little chortle of amusement at her abrupt transformation from a lady's maid to a queen. The noise she made, however, was louder and a little merrier than she had intended. In response, the Duke and

Duchess of Bo'Ness simultaneously emerged from their individual reveries.

Seeing the queen in their presence, they both began to get to their feet, wearing looks of intense embarrassment for having somehow ignored her. Janine motioned her hand for them to remain seated and this appeared to only add to their awkwardness.

"I have something important to tell you," she announced, "And it is of grave consequence."

The Duke and Duchess looked at each other with a mixture of surprise and foreboding.

"The other day, I was walking in the gardens, at the far end where the willows stand by the gate in the wall. There, I had a conversation with an old man. The man, it turned out, was not of mortal flesh but an apparition."

"You know this for sure?" asked the Duchess.

"Yes, I do. Your butler and the matron housekeeper recognised him by my description and took me to view a portrait of him that hangs on a wall beneath Brech Woorlach, in one of its basements. That picture celebrates the life of your grandfather's butler, Angus Percival. A life that ended over a hundred years ago."

The Duke and Duchess looked intrigued.

"The old man gave me a warning, but it was one that made no sense to me until only ten minutes ago."

"What did he say?" enquired the Duke.

"He said: 'Beware the door left open'."

The Duke and Duchess looked duly baffled.

"Today, I heard a rider arrive on horseback, moving at a fast pace, and, on seeing that he was a royal courier, I hastened to learn what news he might bring. Seeing my hurry, a helpful servant confided in me a quick route to reach your chambers. It was down the hidden passage that runs the length of the guest rooms with secret doors into them either side of it."

The Duke and Duchess eagerly leaned forward in their chairs.

"The passage was very dim and I could hardly see," Janine recounted.

"The servants use lanterns," said the Duke, helpfully.

"As I went," Janine resumed, "I was pressing my hands against the walls, to my left and right, for guidance. One of the doors had been left slightly open."

"The warning!" exclaimed the Duke and Duchess, together.

"I heard a man's voice in that room," said Janine, "He was talking to a woman. He said that they needed to be cautious and not raise any kind of suspicion. The woman replied that they had invested too much for them to be discovered, now."

The Duke and Duchess were wide-eyed with amazement.

"The man said that they must make up a reason for not accompanying you to Inverness," Janine revealed, pointing to the Duke, "So that they could go on ahead of you. They agreed that someone they called 'The Colonel' would be pleased with them."

The Duke and Duchess both leapt to their feet in horror.

"This is outrageous!" the Duke declared.

"It is diabolical!" the Duchess gasped.

The two had spent a quarter of a century studiously giving the impression to the world that the college they happened to run at Brech Woorlach, was doing nothing more than turn out impeccably trained and exemplary servants.

Whilst it could not be denied that the servants they produced were exceptionally good, there were those who suspected – quite rightly – that one of their functions was to gather information by carefully memorising and reporting on conversations they might overhear. Nobody, however, had any inkling that they were all actually highly skilled spies and exemplary assassins.

It hurt the pride of the Duke and Duchess more than they would admit that, catastrophically, they had managed to unknowingly play host to a pair of other people's spies.

Janine deeply regretted that – having never seen them – she was unable to help identify the culprits or offer any real clues about them at all. It was, however, agreed that anyone who would be expected to accompany the Duke on his journey to Inverness, who then absented themselves, would immediately be under suspicion.

The Duke summoned his butler, a man by the name of Neacal O'Keefe, to make arrangements for the trip to Inverness. The butler had been the Duke's best friend in their former navy days and they had served together on several ships. This, Janine noted, made for an unusual working relationship. Janine had lost count of the number of times she had seen O'Keefe, one moment, behaving formally and touching his brow in deference to the Duke and then, the next, slapping him on the back and falling about laughing with him.

"I will be taking the big red coach that requires a team of six," the Duke announced, "I will forego the use of the smaller, faster coach. I would have preferred to favour speed over luxury, but making an impressive appearance on our arrival seems appropriate for this trip."

"As you wish, Your Grace," replied O'Keefe.

"Besides," the Duke noted, "The roads are bad at the best of times, so the extra pulling force of six weighty horses won't go amiss if the roads turn out to be particularly wretched."

"Exactly so, Your Grace," O'Keefe acknowledged, "I will make the necessary arrangements."

The Duke paused and rubbed his chin, looking deep in thought, and then slowly raised his hand and, absentmindedly, wagged his finger in the air to countermand his order.

"No, wait," he said, "I want you to make pretence of me travelling in the smaller, faster coach and make it known that the servants who accompany me will follow behind in one of the regular, slower coaches."

"Very well, Your Grace," replied O'Keefe, with slight puzzlement on his face.

"I do not want you to tell the stable master that I will be just taking the big red coach, and nothing else, until tomorrow morning. Let him think that it will be two coaches, until then. That is important."

"I understand, Your Grace."

"I want you to draw up your list of staff as if it were for two coaches, O'Keefe, and I want you to advise all of the people on that list that they are going," the Duke instructed, "This is irrespective of whether or not they will actually be making the journey."

"Very well, Your Grace," O'Keefe replied, looking even more puzzled.

"I have a very particular reason for this deception and I rely upon your discretion."

"You have it, absolutely, in all matters, Your Grace," O'Keefe assured him.

"In the morning, I want you to assemble all of the staff on your full, two coach list, and give them the normal kind of briefing that you would give them for such an event. I then want you to take to one side the staff who won't be going and tell them that there has been a change of plan and that they will be staying. I want you to have Missus Keltie with you when you do that."

"Yes, Your Grace," O'Keefe replied, now – despite his best efforts – appearing both baffled and intrigued.

"I want the two of you to watch them closely as you make the announcement. I want you to make a note of anybody who looks to be particularly relieved or particularly disappointed at the news."

"It will be done, Your Grace.", O'Keefe confirmed.

"I also want to know of anybody who, overnight or in the morning, suddenly claims to have fallen ill or becomes otherwise unavailable to make the journey with us, whatever the reason they give."

"Most certainly, Your Grace.", O'Keefe enthused, now looking pleased to be involved in a matter of some secrecy.

"I want you to tick off on your list, the staff who will actually be travelling with us in the heavier coach. When it is complete, I want you to bring it to me, in person."

"You can be assured, Your Grace, of my complete discretion."

"You are the very backbone of Brech Woorlach, Mister O'Keefe."

O'Keefe, already stood straight, miraculously managed to straighten still further.

"I am most grateful, indeed, for you to say so, Your Grace."

O'Keefe, after assuring the Duke, again, of his best endeavours, made to leave the room to go about his allotted tasks. As he reached the door, the Duke called him back.

"Mister O'Keefe, I want you to arrange for the portrait of Angus Percival to be moved from the Under Gallery to the Entrance Hall. I want you to ensure that you make room, next to it, for another picture of the same large size."

"Yes, Your Grace."

"I will let you know, on our return from Inverness, when I will require you to sit for it."

His butler, Neacal O'Keefe, gaped in surprise and his face displayed genuine astonishment.

"Your Grace," he replied, "That is such an honour!"

"It is, indeed," agreed the Duke, "But one that you have most definitely earned by your long, loyal and exemplary service."

O'Keefe expressed his profuse gratitude and, upon being excused, departed glowing with pride and looking at least two inches taller. When he was gone, the Duke returned to the fire and stood beside it with a worried look on his face.

CHAPTER 18

"I have either played an ace or I have played a dud," the Duke announced, "For instead of a full staff of six accompanying us to Inverness – four maids and two footmen – we will now have only half as many."

His wife, The Duchess, gave him a questioning look, which prompted him to explain.

"There are two possible outcomes: If my action has just excluded the two culprits from making the journey to Inverness with us, then I have given them what they want and they now won't need to make excuses not to accompany us."

Janine and the Duchess both nodded.

"If, on the other hand," the Duke continued, "The culprits are on O'Keefe's list to travel with us, they may now feel unable to avoid going, for fear of compromising themselves. As a result, we will have our enemies with us on the road, which might give them new options to observe us and act against us."

"It is very likely," Janine asserted, "That they have no idea that we have learned of their treachery. This, if we watch them carefully, may lead them to give themselves away."

"Either way," the Duchess declared, standing in front of the Duke and taking hold of both his hands, "Your wonderful idea to flatter and show our esteem for O'Keefe is a stroke of genius!"

The Duke broke into a huge grin, happy to be congratulated. The Duchess kissed him on the cheek.

"I know, full well," she proclaimed, "That you regard O'Keefe as utterly beyond corruption, and I agree, but commissioning a portrait of him is such grand gesture that any possible bribes from other parties are rendered piffling and inconsequential to him!"

The Duke beamed at her.

"Yes, indeed, my love," he replied, "While O'Keefe is anything but vain or conceited, this portrait is something that cannot be matched by any kind of material wealth."

Janine applauded and the Duchess promptly joined in. The Duke glowed with pride and basked in their adulation.

The Duchess fixed the Duke with a long, measured look and his face promptly dropped and his shoulders slumped.

"You feel disgusted with yourself," she told him.

"Yes, I do."

"Because O'Keefe is so beyond reproach that even one drop of doubt in a whole vat of certainty is painful to you."

The Duke nodded, miserably.

"Then let his portrait be in recognition of your total and absolute trust in him, Dear Husband."

The Duke's glow instantly returned.

"It may surprise you, Your Ladyship," the Duke suddenly declared, turning to the Queen, "To know that when O'Keefe left the navy, he had achieved the rank of Captain."

"That's interesting," Janine replied, "I am sure that a man of that kind of character must prove a great asset to Brech Woorlach."

"He is, indeed, an asset," the Duke enthused, "Frankly, he is irreplaceable."

The Duke smiled to himself, appearing to mull over some pleasant recollection.

"Despite his age," the Duke added, "He can handle himself in a fight with astonishing ease!"

The Duke rubbed his hands, savouring the tale he was about to tell.

"I sometimes dress anonymously," he confided, "And go into one of the villages in these parts for a mug of ale in the local inns. I am not averse to such a thing. When I go, I take O'Keefe with me. While I can defend myself with no real problem, O'Keefe is an accomplished fighter! There was once a brawl at one of these establishments and he launched himself into the troublemakers like a raging bull. His arms and fists were flailing like a windmill. The louts who had caused the trouble were taken unawares by his fighting ability and he soundly trounced all three of them."

Janine and the Duchess smiled and nodded appreciatively.

Presently, they all sat back down around the fire and the Duke put another couple of logs onto it. Janine was pleased that he had not rung for a servant to do this for him. In her opinion, it showed good character.

They watched the new logs crackling and spitting and enjoyed the wonderful aroma of the sap from the wood drifting from the fire. They all gazed into the flames, totally absorbed by their hypnotic dance, each lost in their own thoughts.

After several minutes, the Duke sighed a momentous sigh, shook his head wearily, then groaned.

"Your Ladyship," he said, looking apologetic, "There is a matter that I have not mentioned, but which it is important to discuss. I wanted to think it over, before bringing it to your attention."

The Duchess looked at her husband with dismay.

"You are the Queen of the West," the Duke affirmed, "It is your birth right. You were born to this role. You are the heir to your mother's title. However, Your Ladyship, when I spoke with him, the king's courier who delivered the warrants from King James, made reference to another person....."

The Duke hesitated and the Duchess slumped her head forward and looked down into her lap. It was easy to see that she was displeased. She exhaled a hiss of exasperation through her teeth and then clenched her jaw.

Janine glanced from the Duchess to the Duke and he gave her a little, apologetic smile.

"I regret to tell you, Your Ladyship, that matters in Inverness would appear to involve another party. A party who is a pretender to your throne."

Janine was both confused and astonished.

"A pretender!" she exclaimed in horror, "How can that be? Who is it? Who is this person?"

"While you have been unavailable, Your Ladyship, due to being safely hidden under another identity, there is a claimant who has been flaunting themselves as if they were the rightful queen."

Janine was dumbfounded.

"If I am Queen," she said, "Then I am Queen!"

The Duke opened his mouth to speak, but Janine cut him off.

"How can this be any other way?" she demanded.

"In your absence, Your Ladyship...."

"My absence?", Janine snapped, "I haven't been living in Africa or on the sea bed beneath the Atlantic Ocean!"

The Duke scowled. It was clear that, lately, Janine had become far more comfortable with her status as Queen of the West. It was also clear that her former reluctance to assert her authority was waning rapidly.

"Your Ladyship," the Duchess interjected, "We thought it safer to allow the pretender their 'day in the sun' and let them draw away from you any potential threat to your life."

Janine paused and it was apparent, from her face, that she was processing this information.

"I see," she said and made no further protest.

"Your Ladyship," the Duke implored, "These days, there are politics in every aspect of our lives and in everything we do. This matter is no exception."

Janine had turned to the fire and was watching the flames dancing and cavorting as the new logs began to blaze in earnest, but – at this remark – she immediately looked back to the Duke and eyed him with undisguised suspicion.

"Go on," she said.

The Duke looked unsettled and took a deep breath before replying.

"The Duke of Cumberland has left no stone unturned to cultivate a positive relationship with King James. I have reports, from my people, that his behaviour is almost too obsequious and fawning for words."

The Duke pressed a hand to his forehead as though his explanation were hard work.

"This, in itself, would normally be just something irksome and tiring, nothing more than that, but the Duke of Cumberland has also recently become a little too friendly with Clan Campbell."

Janine wrinkled her brow questioningly.

"Clan Campbell," the Duke continued, "Are far from well disposed towards the Queen of the West and have, historically, begrudged her the right to rule the Highlands."

Janine nodded, slowly, and made a gesture for the Duke to proceed.

"I have information, Your Ladyship, advising me that Clan Campbell marched a large number of troops towards the North East in the direction of Aviemore a few days ago. On nearing that town, they turned to head North. Their trail appears to be taking them towards the bank of the Spey, where the false Queen of the West is camped."

"They believe themselves to be marching on me?" Janine asked in alarm.

"Yes, they do. They will, of course, find only the pretender."

"But if they are friendly with the Duke of Cumberland and if the Duke of Cumberland is friendly with King James and if he is the very same King James who sent a warrant to me, here, at Brech Woorlach...."

Janine left the sentence incomplete, allowing its inference to echo in the minds of her listeners.

"Then," said the Duchess, insisting on declaring the conclusion aloud, "It is inevitable that The Duke of Cumberland will eventually learn that you are here."

Janine put a finger to her lips in a thoughtful pose.

"Unless," she said, "They do not know that she is merely a pretender to my throne."

Her expression wavered for a moment, before she suddenly grimaced, "Unless, on the other hand," she cried, "They think that it is me who is the pretender!"

The Duke and Duchess stood by, helplessly, looking vexed and concerned. They shared the benefit of having already worked through those very possibilities, themselves.

"Or," Janine cursed, "Neither Cumberland, nor The King, nor the Campbells know which of us is the real Queen of the West!"

"In which case," the Duke interrupted, "You may well both be in danger!"

"There is, beyond that," the Duchess offered, "The chance that King James and the Duke of Cumberland know of you being here, but that the Campbells do not."

"I am the Queen!" Janine proclaimed.

Janine looked troubled and closed her eyes for a moment, struggling to bring back a memory.

"I know I am the Queen!" she exclaimed, proudly holding up the middle finger on her left hand, "For I have the mark of the Queen!"

The Duke and Duchess both drew close and examined the scar she showed them, above the first joint of the middle finger, was a white line in the shape of a double arch, like a Cupid's Bow.

"How did you know that?", the Duchess asked in amazement.

"I have always known," Janine replied, sounding distinctly dubious about the statement, and then added: "Apparently."

"If you are at risk, we need to take measures to protect you," the Duke announced, "I will summon the Torch Men from the neighbouring lairdships to ride with us as escort."

The Torch Men – Janine had learned – were the equivalent of the Rangers in the Highlands and the Lantern Men in Glasgow and Edinburgh and were tasked with the keeping of order in the countryside. Their methods could be violent, their punishments could be harsh and their application of justice did not always encompass the finer points of the law. Despite all this, their activities allowed the average citizen to sleep easier in their beds.

The Duchess reached for the bell rope, hanging next to the fire, and pulled it. Around twenty seconds later, a page boy knocked and entered the room. He was promptly sent to alert Mister O'Keefe to the Duke's request. Five minutes later, the page boy returned with a note from Mister O'Keefe. The Duke scanned the note and announced its contents:

'Riders have been dispatched and are on their way to summon Torch Men from each of the five nearest lairds. They have been requested to attend at first light tomorrow. That should be around ten or fifteen of them, by my best guesswork. I will feel safer to have them with us!'

The Duchess reached and rested her hand against the Duke's cheek, demonstrating her concern. She then rested a hand on Janine's arm.

"I must confess that this whole business fills me with dread, Your Ladyship," the Duchess declared, "And the thought that we have traitors in our midst is most disturbing."

"You are right," the Duke agreed, "It makes me extremely uncomfortable. We have operated our college to the highest possible standards, studiously infiltrating others, but we are now the victims of the same kind of thing, ourselves. We will have to take steps to get to the bottom of this matter and root out anybody involved."

"Shall I send for Lachlan Balloch?" asked the Duchess.

"Yes, please, if you would," replied the Duke, "As my Head of Security, I do not think he will mind having his holiday interrupted for this."

"Will he know about me being Queen?" asked Janine, a little hesitantly.

"Yes, he will indeed," smirked the Duke, "For, in a house built around spying and espionage, the Chief Architect of it all will doubtless have his own private channels of communication!"

The Duchess nodded her agreement and Janine, after a pause, did likewise.

"Tomorrow," the Duke told them, "We set off for Inverness. There, I feel sure, we will be stepping into the lion's den."

CHAPTER 19

Constable Ewan Burberry winced as he relived the moment he had been hurriedly dragged from the relative comfort of his wagon and unceremoniously bundled into the undergrowth at the side of the muddy track that led up a steep hill to the village of Killiecrankie. Though it was deeply rutted, slippery and rock strewn, this thoroughfare was the main route leading from Perth to Inverness.

Burberry sat and grumbled to himself, resigned to enduring whatever wait might ensue. As he awkwardly tried to adjust his position to relieve the hurt of his scrapes and bruises, he winced and groaned in pain. Despite his struggling, he was unable to accomplish the move. Caitlan Pottle looked concerned and gestured to offer help, but he shook his head to decline.

Burberry counted to ten. Taking a deep breath, he tried again, his efforts punctuated with another bout of groans. After much exertion, he managed to push his elbow into the ground and raise himself far enough to slump against a tree stump. Caitlan mimed applause.

Caitlan Pottle was happy to sit quietly while her fellow passenger punctuated his gloomy silence with groans, moans and the hissing of air through his teeth.

Abruptly, they both jolted, from the shock of the sound that assailed their ears.

A screeching whistle was piercing the air as the second pair of scouts issued a further, urgent warning.

Moments later came the unmistakable sound of many horses galloping from beyond the summit. As they approached, their pace slowed from gallop to trot, and finally to a deliberate walk.

Destination: Inverness

Two anonymous riders appeared at the brow of the hill and halted in the middle of the road. They both held a long pole aloft with pennants fluttering from them in the breeze. They were mounted soldiers, but the bright morning sun behind them rendered them little more than dark shapes, their details completely indistinct and their allegiances impossible to discern.

An eerie quiet fell over the scene. Burberry could hear only his own pulse in his ears as he tried to control his breathing.

To his surprise, McCleary's original scouts casually rode out from the tree line and positioned themselves on either side of the mysterious strangers. Rather than showing hostility or alarm, they simply sat and watched the opposing soldiers.

Soon after, the second pair of scouts emerged from the trees, appearing equally untroubled as they stood observing the scene.

The confusion among Captain McCleary's troops was palpable. Nothing about this encounter made sense to them.

The two unknown riders drew their swords and raised them vertically above their heads, clearly aware that they were silhouettes against the sky. Still, McCleary's scouts showed no distress.

With deliberate slowness, the two horsemen began descending the hill. As they moved away from the skyline, the morning light gradually revealed their features.

A moment later, more mounted troops appeared on the horizon to their rear, stark outlines against the blue sky.

When the lead riders were about fifteen paces away, they sheathed their swords and returned their arms to the air, signalling peaceful intentions. Their elongated shadows now stretched to the feet of the men standing before them.

Suddenly, as their comrades behind them blocked the glare of the sun, their appearances transformed from hazy silhouettes to full colour.

Instantly, their identities became unmistakable.

Captain McCleary and his Second-in-Command grunted in recognition and disbelief. Rather than remaining in cover, they stepped out onto the road, deliberately placing themselves in the path of the riders.

Burberry watched, puzzled by this seemingly dangerous move. Was it foolishness? Was it fearlessness?

Understanding dawned on him: McCleary and his lieutenant knew these men. From their dour expressions, there was some unpleasant history between them.

Crossing his arms, McCleary let loose a distinctly irate oath in broad Gaelic before switching to English.

"What in Holy Hell are you doing here?"

The two MacDonald horsemen sat tall in their saddles, clearly enjoying the reaction their theatrical arrival had provoked. Captain McCleary pressed his palm to his forehead as though nursing a headache. Then, he raised his arm in a signal. His troops emerged from cover and moved onto the road, relief evident in their postures and expressions.

The men who had bundled Constable Burberry into the foliage, despite Caitlan's protests, now returned him – with many times more care – to the back of his wagon and drew it up the road a distance.

The newcomer, Allan MacDonald, spurred his horse with a delicate lightness of touch and it walked forward a couple of paces. The rider, now within an arm's length of McCleary, smiled down at him. The smile was disarmingly genuine and completely devoid of guile or cunning.

Hamish and Alex flicked a glance at each other. Their eyes met for a mere second, but eloquently conveyed a mixture of caution, worry and suspicion.

The Captain reached out to the new arrival's horse and stroked its muzzle. The horse immediately whinnied its delight and snuffled at the man's hand and arm, before gently tugging his cuff.

Hamish and Alex flashed eye contact, again, this time sharing mutual surprise. The horse and McCleary appeared to be acquainted! They watched as McCleary stroked the animal fondly and reached up to tussle its ear. This was evidently to the creature's utter bliss.

Captain McCleary spun his head and looked directly at Hamish. It was as though he knew, for certain, that he had been watched. It was also as if he could read their thoughts. The Captain's eyes now moved to Alex and then to Constable Burberry. No words were exchanged, but it could not have been clearer that he was telling them that he needed them to trust him.

Allan MacDonald coughed, loudly, to draw their attention.

"The MacDonald," he said, looking to McCleary with a wicked grin, "Has charged me with your safe arrival in Inverness."

Despite Allan MacDonald's mocking tone being edged with amiable good humour, McCleary gave him a sour smile. The bitter irony of the other's remark was most certainly not lost on him. The rest of his audience, however, unaware of the two men's unfortunate history, had no clue as to the darkness of his caustic wit.

"I am charged by the king," McCleary replied, jauntily, "With a similar mission to yours. Except that it is in respect of a certain Constable."

McCleary motioned to Burberry, who shuffled more upright in the back of the wagon and nodded his acknowledgement. The lead rider, Allan, clapped himself on the side of his head, as if delivering a reprimand, and contorted his face to mimic embarrassment.

"Forgive me for my feeble memory!", he said, smiling broadly, "I am also here for that very purpose, too!"

The Captain and the two MacDonald riders all laughed and took turns shaking hands with each other. Burberry was puzzled that, despite their original animosity, the three men seemed remarkably relaxed and at ease with each other. They were nothing at all like strangers.

"We have our own force to keep watch over us on our journey," McCleary assured Allan MacDonald, waving an arm towards his soldiers, who had now lined up in ranks on the road.

"If I were to return to the MacDonald," the horseman protested, "Without discharging my mission to his complete satisfaction, he would cut off the tips of my fingers and feed them to his hounds!"

"I am sure that King James will be heartily grateful for his concern!" the Captain said, with a heavy dose of sarcasm, "Especially considering that both Clan Mac Donald and Clan Campbell are his loyal allies. A curious situation, then, that he regards *me* as needing *your* protection against *them*."

"Three months ago the Campbells were the king's sworn enemies," Allan MacDonald replied, twirling his hands in the air to indicate confusion, "Six weeks ago they became his loyal allies. Perhaps he fears they might forget which week it is and be thrown into confusion as to whether you are their friend or their foe?"

McCleary pursed his lips. Allan, the lead MacDonald let slip the merest hint of a smile. No words passed between the two men and neither of them moved.

Eventually, McCleary sighed a profound sigh and shook his head, as if gripped by sudden melancholy. He addressed the other man with the inflection that a long suffering parent might use to reason with a misbehaving child.

"Your Laird MacDonald has recently put a lot of Campbells into the ground at Boat of Garten. Three hundred at least, I am told, but very likely two or three times that number."

Allan MacDonald stuck out his bottom lip in the fashion of a temperamental child on the brink of tears.

"King James," Captain McCleary persisted, "Will very likely, before too long, be hearing from the Campbells on the subject, begging for some form of vengeance."

Allan MacDonald looked reproachfully at the Captain, rubbing his chin as he spoke.

"If the king were to send forces against the MacDonald and his clans, the nearest armed body of men at his disposal would be...." he looked around pretending to be seeking inspiration, then snapped his fingers to indicate he'd found it, "Of course! It would be *yours*, right here!"

The other rider, Allaster MacDonald, put a long thin tube to his mouth. As he blew it, everybody visibly winced at the ear-splitting note. The two horses in front of them twitched and trembled, seemingly on the verge of panic. After a slight pause, a rumbling sound could be heard in the distance, just over the brow of the hill ahead of them. It was the sound of a cavalry in full charge.

CHAPTER 20

"Desist!", McCleary shouted furiously at the top of his voice, knowing that the MacDonald cavalry had been summoned to '*attack*'.

Allan raised a thumb. At the sight of it, Allaster promptly blew hard on a smaller whistle, this one made of brass, and a slightly lower – but no less penetrating – note reverberated through the air. The ominous noise of hooves slowed and stopped. The two distressed horses instantly calmed and the closest one stepped nearer to McCleary and pressed its face against his shoulder for comfort. McCleary reached up and stroked it. The beast gave a snort of gratitude and relief.

Constable Burberry, Caitlan, Hamish and Alex all looked at each other with a wary concern. Allan MacDonald addressed them apologetically.

"I am here to escort you to your destination," he assured them, "And not with any intention of doing you harm if it can be avoided. I give you my word on that. I have, all the same, brought with me a force equal to any eventuality."

Folding his arms, defiantly, at Allan MacDonald's threat, McCleary looked up at him, atop his horse, with a stern and sombre look. It was like cold iron on a frosty morning. The speaker's face faltered and slowly turned into a look of genuine remorse.

"Sir," the rider said, holding out his hands, palms down, "In truth, I would rather drive a spike through the backs of both my hands and nail them to yonder tree than do you harm."

The rider's horse snuffled McCleary's ear, playfully.

"And, of course," Allan MacDonald jested, "For the additional reason that my horse is plainly besotted with you!"

The tension broken, everyone laughed heartily, with several of the soldiers closest behind them joining in.

It was evident that the words of their leaders had been whispered back through their ranks, as the laughter that erupted from the troops moved progressively rearwards in a ripple. The infectious amusement rebounded like an echo as the two MacDonalds and Captain McCleary now laughed at the reaction of the soldiers to their humour. Very soon, nobody was quite sure if they were laughing at the original remarks or at the enjoyment of the reaction to them!

"The Captain," Allaster MacDonald announced, "Has, in the not too distant past, had the privilege of being an honoured guest of the Laird MacDonald."

McCleary groaned.

"The arrangement," Allan MacDonald, rejoined, "Was not one that he greeted with any particular enthusiasm, despite our boundless hospitality. His detention was a circumstance that endured for some nine months before being resolved."

McCleary was silent. Allan MacDonald saluted him.

"I would die for this man," Alan proclaimed.

Allaster, sensing the gloom his brother was provoking, decided upon levity.

"One day, when we were camping out in the mountains, it was Allan's turn to cook and, after tasting his porridge, the Captain must have written to complain about it to King James!"

Allan looked theatrically offended and hung his head.

"Because," his brother continued, "Within no time at all, our dispute was settled and the Captain was galloping back to London at full speed!"

"With a poorly belly!" Allan added.

They all laughed and Burberry winced at the resulting pain in his ribs. Again, the retelling of their words, back through the ranks, inspired still new peals of laughter and some bawdy shouts.

"I apologise for the circumstances of our meeting," Allaster assured, "But it is forced upon us by events. Your men are, indeed, probably sufficient to get you through to your destination and, while the risk of failure is small, the price of it would be catastrophic. I would ask you to accept our MacDonald troops to go ahead and behind your own."

Captain McCleary threw both hands up to shoulder height and let them flop back down in dejection.

"So, am I to be a hostage, again?" he asked, making no attempt to disguise his ire.

"A *'guest'*, again, you mean? Surely!"

"Hostage sounds a lot closer to the truth of it."

"As far as I recall it, *'guest'* sounds even closer, still," the horseman asserted, "For the MacDonald has a great fondness and respect for you."

McCleary, mockingly, approximated a ceremonious bow, as though he were being introduced at court. The action seemed to amuse the two MacDonald riders, who replied with a little chuckle and both made a flamboyant salute.

"This," Allan MacDonald announced, "Is nothing when set beside the fact that my sister is head-over-heels in love with you and shuns any other man!"

"She does?"

"Yes, she does."

"You say this truly?"

"I say it truly."

Allan MacDonald lowered his head, seemingly in order to speak to McCleary in confidence, but promptly smirked like a rascal and raised his voice to the crowd.

"My sister's love for you, Sir, is of such intensity as to almost rival the affections of my horse!"

Much to Allan MacDonald's amusement, McCleary leaned forward and planted a noisy kiss on the muzzle of his horse.

"The blatant truth," Allan confided, wringing his hands and scowling, "Is that while I am most definitely here for the safety of the Constable, I cannot avoid bloodshed if your orders are to resist us."

Captain McCleary said nothing.

CHAPTER 21

The two corpses lay crumpled and contorted on the ground. Their sightless eyes staring vacantly up at the overlapping panels of sailcloth suspended from criss-crossing lines over the forest clearing. Their finely tailored clothes were soaked in blood. A steady stream of blood continued to well from their wounds. Their faces were contorted with the shock and disbelief that had filled their final moments.

Until a minute ago, Robert Taylor and Victor Haviland had been, without question, the finest exponents of sword craft in the whole of England. In over ten years, nobody had come close to equalling their ability to fight with a blade. That was until just now.

A nineteen year old girl had just slain the two distinguished swordsmen and, to add insult to mortal injury, she had taken on both at the same time.

When compared to the girl's astonishing ability, the two men had seemed like bumbling amateurs. The two were victorious, both individually and as a pair, in a hundred and fifty tournaments across Europe. They had relished the prospect of hacking this impudent young upstart of a girl into pieces.

When these fine noblemen had taunted her with their scathing words: *'You're only a woman!'*, she had warned them of their mistake. They had taken no heed.

"I am not just a woman!" she had retorted, angrily.

Then, shouting each word as if it were an entire sentence she had berated them:

"I..."

"Am..."

"A..."

"Woman!"

The nineteen year old Queen Annis of the West of Scotland, had given them no time to process her rebuke. She had not bragged at them nor showered them with insults and denigrated them, as she had seen men do to rile themselves up in readiness for bloodshed. She had simply executed them. She had not done this for herself. She had done it for all women.

Annis looked around her at the assembled audience.

She looked at Gavin Crombie, her First Officer. He was wide eyed with astonishment.

She looked at her maid, Morag. She looked completely stunned.

She looked at her maid's two young assistants, Jet and Jade. They were staring, open mouthed, in wonder.

She looked at Bobbins, the young boy who tended her horse as her groom. He was utterly spellbound.

She looked at the royal courier, William Cox, who had carried a message to her from King James. He was gaping in awe.

She looked at her soldiers and her followers, who travelled with her camp to attend to her. They appeared dazed by what they had just seen.

She looked at the McRory soldiers whom the Laird MacDonald had sent to bolster her own troops. They gazed in open amazement.

She looked at her Honour Guard, the seven McRory soldiers, amongst the best of the Laird MacDonald's army, dressed in shining bronzed armour, helmets and plumes. As they met her eye, they stepped forward, each raising an arm in the air, and began to shout her name, over and over.

"Annis! Annis! Annis! Annis!"

The other McRory warriors immediately took up the chant. Moments later, her own fighters and followers were chanting, too. Then, after a few seconds more, absolutely everyone was shouting her name. Leading their raucous calls was the tall, handsome, muscular figure of Balgair McRory, the Captain of the McRory force and of her Honour Guard. As their eyes met, Annis felt her heart perform a double backflip in her chest and she had to catch her breath. He beamed at her with an almost impossibly wide grin. She smiled back, unrestrained in her glee, her heart pounding at the sight of him.

Queen Annis, the Queen of the West, felt hugely proud of herself for not having let her people down, for not having let herself down, and – far more importantly – for not having let her mother down. She also felt a desperate wave of relief that she, as a descendant of Kiffan the Defiant, had been good enough for the moment.

The cheering and shouting and laughing and singing seemed to go on forever. Her Honour Guard raised her aloft on their gleaming shields and carried her around the edge of the wide clearing where she had set up her court. After what seemed like an age, they set her down and reluctantly allowed her to retire to her huge round tent. Several of her closest people, still giddy from her victory, imposed on her to seat themselves in a semi-circle around her.

"I have something important to do," said Annis.

"After what you have just done," Captain Balgair McRory replied, "I should think that nothing else is important in comparison."

"You were wonderful!" Gavin enthused, beaming at her.

"The thing I need to do is personal," Annis protested.

"You're saying that what you just did to those men wasn't personal?" Balgair exclaimed, getting up from his seat and bumping his head on the roof of the queen's tent, "You just killed two of England's greatest swordsmen who ever lived and you made it look easy!"

Annis crumpled her lips in a bashful smile and pretended to wriggle with embarrassment.

"Those two animals, aside," she said, dismissively, "I need to fulfil my promise to the warriors who died during the battle at Boat of Garten. Only days ago, they gave their lives for me when the Campbell's and their allies attacked us as we made our peace with the Clan Grant, ending an eight hundred year feud. I need to place flowers on the graves of the fallen."

"We need to go to Inverness, without delay," Gavin replied, "For you have many friends and close supporters there, especially among the Frasers and the Munros, and they will prove most valuable allies whatever King James wishes of you."

"I made a promise to those who fell."

"You did, Your Majesty, and you will keep your promise," a little girl argued from the doorway, "You will do as you have said you would do."

Everybody turned to look at the new arrival.

The tiny figure of Wild Flower, the mysterious potion maker, soothsayer and fate-seer, was dwarfed by the towering stature of Balgair. Turning to her, Balgair smiled, tolerantly. Gavin also turned to look at her and he, too, smiled. It was impossible not to like Wild Flower.

Wild Flower had been a cause of fascination for Annis and her close companions ever since she had abandoned the Clan Grant to join Annis and her supporters. Wild Flower was an oddity that nobody could quite fully fathom.

"Your Majesty," Wild Flower insisted, "Other matters are urgent, right now. Any man who is slain leaves only

161

his bones and his decaying flesh behind. Their spirits will live on and will be with you wherever you go."

Balgair and Gavin were delighted at Wild Flower's words and looked to the queen, nodding their heads in agreement, hoping that she would be persuaded.

Wild Flower continued.

"If the dead feel that you are still in peril, they would rather continue to walk with you than be set to rest," Wild Flower told her, "Do not condemn them to depart from this world when their watch is not yet complete."

Annis looked at the little girl disapprovingly.

"You, my little one, could convince me to hack off my fingers and replace them with my toes!" Annis scoffed in exasperation.

Wild Flower stood still and looked virtuous. Annis toyed with her argument in her brain, then smiled and gave a weary sigh.

"It would appear that I can defeat the best of swords but not the best of tongues!" Annis complained.

"I am your humble servant," said Wild Flower, bowing.

"As am I," said Gavin.

"And I," said Balgair.

Annis shrugged and ran her fingers through her hair, frowning at what she encountered.

"I hate to set out on a journey when my hair is such a mess," Annis grumbled, "Since I am surrounded by so many *humble servants*, where is my humble servant Morag?"

"I am here, My Lady," Morag replied from just outside the tent doors.

"And Jade and Jet, your assistants?" Annis asked.

"I have one either side of me, My Lady."

Annis turned to Wild Flower and gave her a churlish smile, "Who else do you have assembled beyond my doors in readiness for a decision that you seem to have already predicted?"

Wild Flower dropped to her knees and lowered her head.

"If I have offended you, Your Highness, have my head taken from my shoulders and hung from a tree!" she cried.

Annis reached and drew her sword and then gestured for everyone to leave her alone with Wild Flower. Gavin and Balgair both gave her a slightly anxious look as they departed. Annis held her sword and flicked her fingernail on its cutting edge, causing it to ring. She then gently laid it onto a sheepskin-covered bench and moved to stand in front of Wild Flower, whose head was still meekly bowed.

Annis waited for a moment, but did not have sufficient cruelty in her heart to delay any longer. She quickly knelt and drew Wild Flower into an embrace.

Annis reached and took hold of her sword. Lifting it up, she embedded its blade into the wooden tree stump that served as a stool.

"Gavin!" Annis shouted, "Pick up her head from the floor and take it away!"

The flaps of the tent rapidly parted and an ashen faced and horrified Gavin looked in. Seeing Wild Flower still alive and well, he guffawed. Balgair's head suddenly popped through the entrance, beside him, and he began to laugh, too.

"I will forego my hair being attended," Annis declared, "And require that we make ready to leave as soon as possible. We will move on and make camp at nightfall."

"Your Highness," said Gavin, reproachfully, "You are queen and you have privileges. There is not one of us who would not willingly wait for you and your…"

Gavin hesitated, juggling in his mind the words he might use. Balgair, however, waited for only a single heartbeat before finishing the sentence for him.

"We will wait for your beautiful hair!" he declared.

"I and my *beautiful hair* thank you," said Annis, fighting to overcome a blush and smirking at Balgair's sudden awkwardness.

Gavin bowed and, taking Balgair's elbow, dragged him along behind him as he left the tent. Wild Flower caught the queen's eye and gave her a knowing smile. Morag entered, with her helpers, and exchanged a broad grin with their queen.

"Come," said Morag, mischievously, "Let the three of us get to grips with your beautiful hair!"

CHAPTER 22

The camp of the Queen of the West bustled with furious activity as everything was packed up and stowed away into wagons, carts and donkey panniers. Well-practiced in their roles, each person went about their allotted work with speed and diligence. Within half an hour, nothing remained unready except for the round tent, belonging to Queen Annis, with its iron stove pipe thrusting skyward through its roof.

Annis vacated her tent – her hair now impressively brushed, combed and set – and was ushered into her personal transport, which looked as much like a wagon as it did a coach. Morag boarded the vehicle with the queen, while her two assistants went to sit under the nearby trees with her groom, to await the word to set off.

Annis looked at Morag and nodded to the doorway of her wagon.

"Tell everyone I am not to be disturbed."

Morag went to the door of the vehicle and issued instructions for the guards to stand several paces off and to allow no-one to disturb the queen. Annis extended an arm, her hand indicating to Morag the padded bench opposite her own.

"Sit," she instructed.

Morag sat.

"What is it that disturbs Jet's sleep?" Annis asked, gently.

Morag frowned.

"That need not concern you, My Lady."

"It does concern me. I have heard her whimpering, these past few nights."

Morag shrugged her shoulders and let out her breath in a desolate sigh.

"Her parents, as you know, My Lady, both starved to death. They forced their daughters to eat while they went without. You took them in, as orphans, and gave them shelter. They love you and love to be with you, but Jet is tormented by thoughts of death."

"Does she not know that the Messiah banished death?"

"They were brought up with a more basic form of faith, My Lady, and taught notions that were fashioned from superstition and folk lore."

"Her sadness crushes my heart and her distress, at night, is like a knife thrust through it."

"I have cried over it many times, myself, My Lady, but she feels she must be brave and puts up a wall against my attempts to talk with her or console her."

"If she had our faith, she would know that she has nothing to fear."

"I have taught her of God and of the Messiah, My Lady, but after she first accepted the faith, she allowed it to wither to nothing. She finds herself unable to believe in anything."

Annis looked sad and forlorn.

"She adores you, My Lady, and there is nothing she would not do for you. If you told her she should believe, then..."

"No!" Annis snapped, "If she does not believe, I will not have our faith foisted upon her. If she cannot feel God's presence, I will not have her pretend."

"Yes, My Lady," said Morag, lowering her head.

"I will not give up on her and I will not let her suffering go unrelieved," Annis insisted.

Morag nodded, dully. Annis sighed and regretted the harshness of her words. She moved closer to her maid and rested her head on her shoulder. Morag immediately reached and stroked the queen's hair. Morag, Annis reflected, had been the closest thing she had known to a mother for the last seven years. Her real mother, Queen Cydara – the previous Queen of the West – had been betrayed and murdered. Morag's husband had lost his life defending Annis and yet Morag had never blamed her for it and had never allowed it to come between them. In fact, Annis realised, she had never even mentioned it once, since that fateful day.

"Jet and Jade have no mother," said Annis, tenderly, "Except the same mother that I have, who is a fine and wonderful mother."

Morag looked up, startled. She regarded Annis with eyes that were wide and bewildered. She lifted a hand to her mouth to restrain a sob that still managed to escape. The tears, brimming in her eyes, suddenly overflowed. Annis pulled her close and hugged her and said the words she had wanted to say for so very, very long.

"I am so very sorry about your husband."

Morag made a gargled sob and cried still harder.

"No! No!" she replied, "He would have been a broken man, a mere scratch in the dirt, a shadow of himself, if he had lived and you had died. He would never have forgiven himself. He would never have wanted to be alive if you had perished."

"He was so brave!" Annis wept, "I remember!"

Morag hugged her close and, gently guiding her head, returned it to rest on her shoulder.

"The Campbells were astonished!" Annis declared, "He made them doubt themselves. He fought like two men, Morag, I swear he did!"

Morag made another choking sob.

"Thank you, My Lady. Thank you for telling me so."

They both cried some more and Annis began to reminisce, recounting things that Leslie – Morag's husband – had said or done when she was just a little girl and the things she remembered as she was growing up. Then abruptly, she stopped and looked aghast.

"My Lady?" said Morag, tentatively.

"He told me something, once, Morag," said Annis, in something approaching wonder, "He said that the deadliest blow comes from where you least expect it."

Morag looked at her queen blankly.

"I'm going to do something to honour your husband," Annis announced.

Morag arched her eyebrows and look expectant, inviting Annis to continue.

"The deadliest blow comes from where you least expect it," Annis repeated, triumphantly.

Morag's face was a picture of confusion.

"Come," Annis demanded, taking Morag by the elbow and leading her to the door of her wagon, "Let us find Jet and Jade."

As Annis strode across the grass to the trees, where Morag said she would find them, she beckoned Bobbins who came running to her at full speed.

"Go and find my armourer and have him send me two light swords," she instructed.

"Yes, Your Majesty," replied Bobbins, saluting and rushing away to do her will.

Annis spied Jet and Jade a little way off and came to a stop. Jet and Jade, noticing their queen's approach, jumped to their feet and stood anxiously wringing their hands.

A young boy, sprinting ahead of her groom – who adopted an uncharacteristically solemn pace to emphasise his seniority – brought her the two swords she had wanted. The boy bowed furiously, several times, before throwing himself to his knees and dropping his gaze to the grass.

Annis stopped and gazed at the boy for a moment.

"Look at me," said Annis, softly.

The boy looked up, timidly.

"Who am I?" asked Annis.

The boy looked astonished by the question.

"You are the queen!" he said, looking at her with adoration, "You are the Queen of the West."

"Am I *your* queen?"

"Yes! Truly! With all my heart!" the boy declared.

"It makes me happy to hear so."

To demonstrate his loyalty, the boy placed his hand on his chest, over the top of the organ in question, which was beating at four times its normal speed. Annis smiled at him, swept his hair from his eyes with her fingers, and dismissed him with a wave. The boy marched off, looking immensely pleased. Bobbins clapped him on the shoulder in congratulations and sped away to tend to Annis' horse.

"That boy will be telling everybody that he spoke to the queen, today," said Morag, clearly amused.

"And, from that small tale, spread far and wide," Annis responded, "Everyone will know that I am not conceited, arrogant or aloof."

Morag nodded and bowed.

With her maid at her elbow, Annis walked across to the two young girls, beneath the trees. Jet and Jade both appeared over awed at being sought out by the queen, rather than being summoned. They had not been sent for, they marvelled. The queen had come to them.

Annis lifted up one of the swords and, throwing it like a dagger, landed it a hand span away from Jet's right foot. The girl took a step backwards in shock and gawked at the weapon as if it might spring to life and bite her.

"Pick it up," Annis commanded, pointing to it with a fierce stab of her finger.

Jet's eyes widened and she took another half step backwards.

"Pick it up," said Annis, in a voice that invited no quarrel.

Jet's eyes were as large as a pair of full moons.

"I can't," murmured Jet, apologetically.

Annis repeated her throw, landing the partner to the first sword at Jade's feet.

"Pick it up!" shouted Annis, sternly.

Jade gave a little moan of panic and stared at the sword as if beholding a wildcat. Annis knew that neither of the girls would have ever touched a sword, never mind having got to hold one in their hand. Swords were something that men used. Swords were not a thing that any female might have cause to encounter. Swords were something from another world.

Annis glared at the two girls and then, suddenly, realised that they were both close to tears.

"I dare not!" sobbed Jade.

"Why?", asked Annis, adopting a soothing tone.

"I'm….. I'm…..," hesitated Jade, "I'm just a girl."

"That's right!" cried Annis, jubilantly, "That's what men will think!"

Morag's little assistants looked at Annis with total bafflement. Annis knew what they were thinking. They presumed that a queen could hold a sword because she was a queen. They presumed that men could hold a sword because they were men. Being a queen bestowed rights and a permission from men to be something like, but never quite the same, as a man.

"My fine girls," said Annis, softly and soothingly, "Pick up your swords."

The girls' mouths sprang open and their eyes shot to the size of duck ponds as they goggled at each other. They were utterly dazed by swords being described as *theirs*.

"Please, pick up your swords," repeated Annis, solicitously.

Jet looked at Jade. Jade looked at Jet.

"**Our** swords?" asked Jet, timorously.

The two girls eyed the weapons longingly, as a pair of starving dogs might eye a tray of sausages.

"Jet! Jade!", called Morag, intervening, "Your queen commands you!"

Jet and Jade both sprang to the swords and obediently pulled them from the ground. Then, regarding them like live cobras, held them away from themselves. They were paralysed with fear. Annis hurried to the girls, for reassurance, and pulled them together, an arm around each. Jet and Jade held the swords out, their tips now drooping to the ground, so as not to endanger their queen.

"I will, one day, give you warrior names," Annis declared.

Morag smiled and gave a little chuckle. She could see that Annis was working on a plan in her head.

"When you have trained to handle these blades," announced Annis, "You will not be Jet and Jade. You will be the unexpected versions of yourselves. The ones that no man would think to predict."

Morag's grin was from ear to ear.

CHAPTER 23

Janine squinted at Lachlan Balloch through narrowed eyes, fighting the glare of the sun that was streaming through the curtains of the morning room. Seeing her predicament, Balloch obligingly stepped into the shade.

The man was nothing like Janine had imagined. She had, for no particular reason, visualised him as tall and slim. In reality, he was small and a little overweight. He had a head of strangely reddish-blonde hair that was rapidly turning to grey. The thin band of distinctly fiery red hair that stretched from ear to ear, along the length of his jawline and up the edge of his cheeks, was a mere finger width. It appeared so narrow that it was almost as if he'd wiped strawberry syrup from his fingers onto his chin and it had turned into a beard. His eyes were kind and humorous and not at all like the cunning and devious ones she had imagined.

"I am honoured to meet you, Your Ladyship, as a grown up," Lachlan Balloch said, bowing deeply, "For I have not seen you since you were this high."

He gestured with a hand to indicate a point a little above his knee.

"A lot has happened, Sir, since then," Janine replied, "A lot more than I could have ever imagined or foreseen."

The irony was not wasted on Balloch and he gave a thin lipped smile that was tinged with regret.

"Alas, Your Ladyship, while fate has been less than kind to you, I assure you of my best possible efforts to change these current times for the better."

Janine nodded, graciously, to acknowledge his concern.

"Your Ladyship," the Duke declared, "I have fully informed Mister Balloch of recent events and I have appraised him, this morning, of our journey to Inverness."

Again, Janine nodded.

"Mister Balloch is of the opinion that the sooner we depart, the better," the Duke concluded.

"Everything is ready and prepared, Your Ladyship," confirmed the Duchess.

"And our unexpected situation with staff?" Janine asked.

The Duke looked to Lachlan Balloch for him to reply.

"Nobody has attempted to excuse themselves from this journey and the reduced number of staff have been selected and they stand ready. I will, as instructed, be keeping a sharp eye open for anything of interest."

"You are accompanying us, Mister Balloch?" queried Janine.

"Yes, Your Ladyship," replied Balloch, bowing to her, "The Duke and Duchess thought it a wise precaution for Mister O'Keefe and I to travel with you."

"When you said we would take the big coach," Janine asked the Duke, "You meant something of greater size than the one in which I arrived here?"

"Very much so, Your Ladyship," responded the Duke, "For the coach in question has a less open driving position at its front, compared to most, allowing two people to ride with its driver, while nine ride within its body."

"Yes, very well, I see," replied Janine, framing the words so that it was obvious she didn't see at all.

"The three crew will ride atop," the Duke explained, "And you and I, along with Francesca, Balloch,

O'Keefe and Chang will ride in the front of the coach. A footman and two maids will ride in the rear. That will be twelve people aboard in all."

"Very good," said Janine, still looking a little puzzled.

"The main part of the coach has a front and rear compartment, Your Ladyship," the Duchess obligingly pointed out, "So it is like two cabins, one behind the other, with a separating wall between them."

"I understand," Janine replied and, this time, she actually meant it.

"The journey will likely take four or five days," Balloch advised, "Depending on the condition of the roads. I am certain that they won't expect you in Inverness any earlier."

Balloch went to the windows and looked out, surveying the final loading of the coach. After a few moments, the Duke went across and stood beside him.

"There will be no kind of preparation for the second coach until a quarter hour after we have departed," Balloch announced, turning to Janine, "So that nobody has any inkling about it, beforehand."

"A second coach?", Janine asked.

"Yes, Your Ladyship," Balloch explained, "Mister Chang and I will not be accompanying you straight away. I have arranged for a second coach to set off, purporting to take us, on separate business, to Edinburgh. Anybody giving away information on us will not know that we are actually only going as far as the ferry crossing. We will meet you, there, and join you on your journey to Inverness."

Janine nodded.

"In order to enhance the deception and ensure that our '*secret*' becomes common knowledge, Your Ladyship,"

Balloch continued, "Our false destination of Edinburgh will be '*accidentally*' disclosed to a servant known to have a loose tongue."

Janine smiled at his plan.

The Duke and Lachlan Balloch remained observing the progress of the coach through the window for a little longer, before announcing that everything was in place for departure.

CHAPTER 24

Outside, their group assembled on the sweeping, tiled causeway in front of Brech Woorlach. Bruce and Brian came to bid them farewell. After Janine had exchanged hugs with them, and the Duke handshakes, they quickly boarded the coach. The Duke, O'Keefe, Francesca and Janine climbed into the front compartment and the chosen footman and two maids took up position in the rear. The two armed guards clambered up the steps to flank the driver. Once harnesses and wheels were given a final check, they set off.

The coach clattered away down the drive. It soon passed under an imposing archway with stone gargoyles, and out through the gates. Here, on the broad, sweeping apron that bordered the highway, they were joined by a dozen Torch Men. These armed riders, brandishing clubs, swords and pistols, assembled themselves into two groups, six forward of the coach and six to its rear.

With a thunder of hooves, the coach and its escort turned onto the highway, heading along the bank of the River Forth towards Queensferry. The vehicle, pulled by no less than six horses, made an unusual and prestigious sight on the road. A decision had been taken to fly the flags of the Duke of Bo'Ness for the first part of their expedition. In the lowlands, there were fewer bandits who might be brave enough or stupid enough to seek to interfere with them. For extra safety, the guards atop the coach prominently displayed muskets and spears as an extra line of defence.

No sooner had they crested the first rise than the Duke held his finger to his lips to implore silence. Turning, theatrically, to the left and right to make his gesture plain, he produced a small knife. It was the kind used to sharpen writing quills. He used it to gently remove a slat of wood fitted into the wooden barrier separating the front of the coach from the rear. Beyond it, where the footman and maids were sat, was a metal grill that disguised the other side of the aperture from prying eyes. Urging silence, again, they all sat and listened to the now clearly audible conversation of the three servants.

They all listened, diligently, for over fifteen minutes, but heard nothing more than gossip, small talk and occasional bickering. These were not, they decided, the conversations of people involved in a secret mission. The Duke replaced the panel and they all looked glum. Clearly, they had nobody of interest accompanying them. Nobody confessed to their disappointment, but they all felt it.

CHAPTER 25

The second coach departed from Brech Woorlach in the midst of mock secrecy. As planned, their supposed destination of Edinburgh was carefully leaked to their chosen gossipmonger. This, for certain, would ensure that news of it would promptly begin to circulate.

The coach emerged onto the road and turned right in pursuit of the first coach. The driver kept up a modest pace, ensuring that they did not follow too closely in the wake of the larger coach.

Lachlan Balloch and Mister Chang were installed inside the carriage and both stretched themselves out between the front and rear seats, certain that the luxury of such space would not be available to them for much longer. In what seemed far too short a time, the coach slowed and came to a halt. Balloch leaned out of the window to check on their whereabouts and found they had already reached the water crossing over the River Forth at Queensferry.

"We have made it to the ferry," he announced.

Waiting down by the pier was the Duke's imposing big red coach. With the assistance of the coach driver and his guards, Balloch and Chang unloaded their baggage and stowed it in the back of the larger transport.

The passengers travelled over the river first, along with the guards and six of the Torch Men for possible protection. Using his skill and the judgement of several decades, the ferryman then divided up the remaining Torch Men, horses and the coach into three more trips across the water. Once everybody and everything had reached the far bank, the Torch Men got back into their saddles and the team of six were hitched up, again.

Eventually, they were able to set off north.

The coach had, so far, flown the flags of the Duke of Bo'Ness, but – once the ferry crossing was thirty minutes behind them – they stopped to replace them with the flags of King James. They would have to encounter exceptionally bold or reckless robbers for them to dare to waylay a coach associated with the king. Especially one that had a dozen outriders protecting it. On this particular section of road, running between Edinburgh and Perth, such a conveyance and impressive accompaniment were not entirely unusual.

Nine hours after having set off from Brech Woorlach, having stopped twice for fresh coach horses, they were very glad to see the staging inn at Bridge of Earn come into sight. Everyone was looking forward to a meal and the comfort of warm beds. Janine, the Duke, Francesca, Balloch, O'Keefe and Mister Chang were assigned chambers at the front of the inn on the first floor, which they found to be surprisingly well furnished. The servants were allocated cabin rooms at the rear of the premises and the guards and the coachmen were given bunks in the adjoining the stables.

The Torch Men, who had brought three huge tents with them, sternly declined the frivolous luxury of sleeping indoors. They opted, instead, to camp out behind and to either side of the inn. Having lit fires in buckets, they attached lengths of interconnected metal drums – looking very much like a stack of gentleman's top hats – to form a chimney, which they poked out through a hole in the canvas roof.

The Duke's immediate party opted to dine in their own rooms and were served chicken cooked in wine and white barley bread. Once they had eaten they climbed, gratefully, beneath cosy quilts atop feather beds and were asleep within minutes.

The general staff and the Torch Men hurried to the mess room and stacked their plates with thick slabs of beef, chunks of turnips and potatoes and wedges of dark bread. They all ate hungrily and then staggered, exhausted, to their respective quarters, inside and out.

True to their name, the Torch Men lit torches to declare their presence. These were sited at strategic points that allowed them to be visible from far away in all directions. The torches were left to eventually burn out and another form of illumination, to last through the night, was provided by a set of huge lanterns that were suspended atop lofty poles.

Before long, the inn keeper searched out O'Keefe and protested, in grumpy tones, that the light from the Torch Men's lanterns was causing a nuisance to some of his other guests. From the warmth of their quilt, Janine and Francesca elbowed each other in their ribs, trying to provoke laughter, as they listened to the gruff exchange in the hallway.

The confrontation ended, abruptly, with a few stern words from O'Keefe. Janine was fairly sure that, as their exchange concluded, she had heard the distinctive clink of silver. Following that noise, the inn keeper's concern for the welfare of the other guests appeared to be suddenly forgotten.

CHAPTER 26

The following morning, the coach and its escort made an early start. During the morning portion of their journey there were only a couple of minor incidents, where the coach wheels got trapped in ruts. The coach crew and the Torch Men managed to free it up and got it moving again without too much trouble. Everyone was feeling grateful for the ability of six horses to haul them with such formidable force.

"These are not your dandy horses from Edinburgh," the driver had boasted to all who would listen, "These are half carriage horse and half labouring horse. If they were tasked with it, they could pull a plough as easily as any beast bred for the furrow."

As their expedition progressed, however, the advantage of six horses proved, on one point, to be a profound disadvantage. At the point where the previous staging inn was an hour and a half behind them and the next one two hours ahead, they had a major incident. Their six magnificent steeds, who were so capable of pulling the carriage at speed uphill, managed to pull it against, rather than over, a large stone in the road. They did so with such force that two spokes in the front wheel broke under the strain.

The driver and guards unhitched two of the horses and, saddling one of them to ride it, they strapped the damaged wheel to the other. One of the guards then rode off to engage the wheelwright at the previous staging inn. It was almost three hours later that he returned.

After re-attaching the wheel, now repaired, they were able to set off again. Their final stop of the day was at Pitlochry. Their delay caused them to arrive in the late evening, rather than late afternoon.

The servants, guards, coachmen and Torch Men gathered in the large dining room with a weariness that was almost palpable. The day had felt like a very long one and they all ate ravenously from the buffet that was provided. The Duke and his senior party ate in a room just off the kitchen, served by waiting staff, and were no less weary than the rest.

An hour after their arrival, their bellies full, everybody trudged off to their assigned sleeping quarters and, under the watchful protection of the Torch Men, they fell asleep promptly and slept soundly until the morning.

CHAPTER 27

The next day, the Duke's party made it to Kingussie by nightfall. The Duke had agreed with the driver to push the horses a little less and travel at a slower pace.

The roads proved to be somewhat more challenging than they had anticipated. Parts of their route had suffered some heavy rain and sections of the road had become so muddy that they were almost impassable for a heavy vehicle.

At one point, a foraging party had to be assembled to gather heather and bracken from the surrounding hillsides. These were then bundled up and deposited onto the track to quench the mud. This, the driver assured them, was the only way they could get the coach up some of the hills. Even this proved to be a struggle!

In the end, they had to employ the assistance of several of the Torch Men's mounts, roped up to the coach, to provide still more pulling power. Much to everyone's relief, they eventually got to the top of the long incline without any kind of accident.

CHAPTER 28

It was with some trepidation that the Duke set out, the following day, from Kingussie. The sun was shining and there was a thin haze of steam rising off a lot of the fields. The roads a few miles ahead of them had received less rainfall and were relatively easy going.

They got stuck on only two occasions, which was quite a good achievement considering the conditions. They changed horses twice, along the route, as a precaution. The horses, being less strained and better rested, were of benefit but proved not to have been essential. If there were such things as Weather Gods, the Duke decided, then they were definitely smiling on them.

The driver continued to boast the virtues of his beloved 'Tramping Horses' and the Staging Inns who were able to provide them were delighted to oblige. These elite animals were an expense that most travellers could not afford and were usually only hitched to royal vehicles or the weekly mail coach.

At one of the inns, to the absolute delight of the driver, the stable master had to recall two of this kind of horse from a nearby farm, where they had been lent to pull a pair of ploughs.

The coach made it to Carrbridge by dusk, as they had hoped, but – once there – the Duke made the decision to stop only to change horses and opted, instead, to press on to Findhorn Bridge, a half hour or so distant.

When they pulled off the road onto the apron of the staging inn at Findhorn Bridge, the feeling of relief, felt by everyone, was plain and clear. This was their last stop of their expedition and only a single rise remained between them and the blessing of a long, gradual descent down to Inverness.

As everyone assembled to eat, there was a celebratory atmosphere in the air. As was the Duke's tradition, he insisted that everybody ate together at the last stop. This met with no objection from anyone, for they all knew that it would mean that the fare laid before them would be the best of the journey. They were not disappointed, as the Duke's fabled generosity was more than evident.

There were around a dozen other people at the inn, sat at various tables, and the Duke made sure that each of them was furnished with a drink, at his expense, to raise a toast to a safe conclusion to their respective journeys.

At one side of the room, four tables had been pulled together into one long line, to seat the twenty-five diners of the Duke's party as a single throng. The Duke and his close troupe sat together, in the centre, but – in blatant disdain for the fanatical snobbery of most aristocrats – the layout was arranged so that there was no break, either side, between them and everyone else.

To their left, a footman sat next to Lachlan Balloch and the coach driver was sat next to O'Keefe. To the right, a Torch Man sat next to Mister Chang and Francesca sat alongside a maid.

The whole party laughed and joked and exchanged stories. This was refreshing, Janine thought, because each group of people – on top of the coach, in the front of the coach and at the rear of the coach – had, long ago, talked themselves to a standstill with each other. The interaction with new people seemed to have reignited everybody's conversational abilities! There seemed to be at least a dozen things that each person simply had to say and a dozen stories that they simply must tell.

After eating, the lower status staff were permitted to move into a corner to drink beer, while the higher status members of their party retired to one of their bedrooms to drink wine and spirits. The Duke, in his wisdom, had thought it best not to interfere with this particular arrangement, but had taken definite steps to ensure that nobody was short of liquid refreshments.

No sooner had Lachlan Balloch's room door been closed than he motioned to his five guests to be silent and sat them in a circle on the carpet in front of his bed. Sitting in a space between them, he reached into a sack and took out a bundle of six tubes. The looks of puzzlement that greeted this action seemed to amuse him. The tubes appeared to be lengths of pig intestine with metal hoops sewn around them at intervals. The hoops, it was clear, were designed to keep the channel running through the pipes open and prevent them from collapsing when they were extended.

Gathering the ends of the tubes in a bunch in his cupped hands, he held them to his mouth. This done, he gestured for the others to hold the opposite ends of the tubes to their ears. Once in position, their purpose became plain. Lachlan Balloch's quiet whisper, at one end of the tubes, was heard loud and clear in his listeners' ears at the other.

"I need to tell you something disturbing," he told them, "My blood chilled and my heart fell still for a moment when my gaze fell upon one of the other diners, this evening."

The faces of his audience lit with a look of enthralled expectation.

"I quickly averted my eyes, so as not to draw his attention," Balloch explained, "But – with the utmost care – I observed him twice more to make sure that my eyes had not deceived me."

The Duke and O'Keefe exchanged expressions of foreboding, as did Janine and Francesca.

"I know him only as 'Dallington'. Surely not his true name. Tonight, his presence on the road to Inverness fills me with dread. He is a most skilled assassin."

Destination: Inverness

Balloch's audience exchanged looks of horror.

"The thing that concerned me most was that he was trying not to look at *you*, Your Ladyship," he divulged, addressing Janine, "He gave the rest of us several brief glances, casually casting his eye on us from time to time, but he seemed dead set against looking at you for a second time."

The Duke and Janine traded puzzled expressions and raised their eyebrows at each other. Mister Chang signalled that he wished to speak and the tubes were quickly rearranged, between mouths and ears, to allow him to do so.

"How is it possible that you can recognise him? Would he not be in disguise? Why would he not conceal his identity so as to render himself anonymous?"

Again, the tubes were swapped around to accommodate the reply.

"I fear," said Balloch, ominously, "That he has no care to remain hidden, for he holds his skills of camouflage, concealment and disguise to be so perfect that he can disappear at will."

The Duke motioned to speak and tubes were, once more, shuffled in their positions.

"It seems to me," said the Duke, "That this man's behaviour is either a bluff or a double bluff. He may wish to be seen because he doesn't intend to turn up, next, where we would expect him to be. On the other hand, he may wish to be seen in order to trick us into thinking he has nothing to do with us or our plans."

They all sat pondering this proposition for a few moments, before Mister Chang indicated that he would like to speak, again.

"Should we send word, with one of the Torch Men, to warn our hosts in Inverness?"

"No," replied Balloch, "After the horses have been switched about in the morning, we should let the Torch men set off south and return home. I have a strange feeling that the fewer people who know about this new development, the better."

Lachlan Balloch's listeners lowered their pipes from their ears and looked at each other, dubiously, then back across to him. In response, Balloch lowered the pipes he had cupped to his mouth and gazed reproachfully at each of them. When he returned the pipes to his mouth, they returned theirs to their ears.

"This man is almost certainly on his way to Inverness," Balloch assured them, "And, knowing his trade, we can be sure that he is going there to kill someone."

The looks that flitted around the room made it evident that everyone was thinking the same thing. Balloch decided to voice their thoughts for them.

"The question is," Balloch declared, "Who is he going to kill?"

They all brooded over the question, Janine looking uncomfortable, while everybody else awkwardly avoided eye contact with her. Balloch observed their dilemma for a few moments and then raised the pipes to his mouth. The others obediently put theirs to their ears.

"I confess that you, Your Ladyship, may be the target," he said, looking directly at Janine.

The group looked back and forth between each other, expectantly, waiting for any further offers of wisdom, but nobody moved to speak. Lachlan Balloch raised his eyebrows first to Mister Chang, then to Francesca, then to the Duke, then to Janine and – when they all shook their heads – he took their pipes from them and stashed them back in his sack, along with his own.

Francesca opened her mouth to speak, then thought better of it. Balloch held up the bag containing the pipes and tilted his head in question. Francesca shook her head and went to the little desk in the corner of the room. There, she picked up a quill and, removing the lid from the ink pot, dipped it in. Picking up a fragment of parchment, she wrote the words: *'He is still very dangerous'* and held it up, briefly, to her compatriots. They all nodded in agreement. Janine went to the fire and, holding a corner of the parchment into the flames, she set it well and truly alight before dropping it into the fire.

Suddenly Francesca laughed, gleefully, and tapped a little jig with her feet on the wooden floor. Everybody looked puzzled.

"Thank you, Mister Balloch!", she cried, "You are, indeed, a master at the art of playing cards but I think we will all end up poor and broke if we play another hand!"

Everybody picked up on her cue and made appropriate comments of their own, laughing cheerfully, their earlier silence in the room needing an explanation if anybody were to have been listening.

"Your money feels more at home in my pocket than in any of yours!" Balloch told them all.

"I apologise that I am not such an accomplished player as either you or Mister Lee," Francesca said, pointing meaningfully at Mister Chang to confirm his new identity.

"I have been a valet for many years," Mister Chang lied, "And I have learned to play cards with at least a little skill, in order to boost my income, but I was outclassed, tonight."

Everybody laughed.

"Perhaps so, Mister Lee," the Duke exclaimed, "But I have never seen anybody play their hand so swiftly!"

"My nickname was *'Lightning Lee'* when I was with my last employer!" Mister Chang improvised.

"Well," Balloch retorted, "If you would make like lightning, now, Mister Lee, and scorch your way to your bedroom, along with the rest of our party, I will sit and gleefully count my winnings!"

Mister Chang bowed.

"At once, Sir!" he replied.

"And you, my sweet niece," Balloch said to Francesca, "I bid you, too, a good night."

"Good night, Uncle."

"And get some good sleep, Marie. It will be a long day, tomorrow."

"I will, Uncle Laurence," Janine replied.

Celebrating and mocking their own performances, in equal measure, the six impromptu players made ridiculously formal and elaborate bows to each other. This caused further mirth and huge grins.

"If it pleases you, Sir," Mister Chang declared, addressing Lachlan Balloch, "I will see your guests to their rooms."

"I am obliged, Mister Lee. I will retire, myself, this instant."

Further grins were furnished at his mockery of aristocratic speech, and their company duly dispersed. True to his word, 'Mister Lee' took each of them to their door.

"I will wake you good and early in the morning, Ma'am, just as you have instructed," said Mister Chang, delivering Francesca to her room, last.

"Thank you, Mister Lee," said Francesca, first waving her fist at him for overplaying his role, then kissing her finger and pressing it playfully to his nose before she closed the door.

Mister Chang turned and began walking up the corridor to his own room.

"Mister Lee!" shouted a voice behind him.

Mister Chang turned round and, continuing his performance as her servant, caught the lady's blouse that was sailing through the air towards him.

"You would oblige me by having this ironed for the morning,", Francesca commanded, putting out her tongue, "There's a good man."

"Anything, Madam. Anything you wish is my pleasure," replied Mister Chang, playfully baring his teeth at her while clawing the air as if to scratch her.

CHAPTER 29

Allan MacDonald regretted the harshness of his words. He was under no illusion that he was in a precarious position, but was having second thoughts about the wisdom of making it worse.

Allan's father had tasked him, and his brother Allaster, with getting Constable Ewan Burberry to Inverness safe and alive. He had sent with them a large number of troops to achieve that objective. Unfortunately, the Constable already had a reasonably sized armed escort, provided by King James and led by Captain Iain McCleary and his Blue and Greys. The Clan Campbell were the MacDonald's sworn enemy. King James, however, was currently flirting with an alliance with the Clan Campbell.

Allan MacDonald sighed, heavily and, taking a deep breath, decided to address his problem head on.

"If the Campbells should decide to spring an ambush on us, I need to know your orders, Captain McCleary," he demanded, "Would your loyalties to the king oblige you to fight against us or your loyalties to Scotland oblige you to fight with us?"

An acrid murmur of distaste ran through the Blue and Greys.

"I think you have your answer!" Captain McCleary replied.

There was a rumble of agreement from his troops.

"These men are Scottish and they are Lowlanders," McCleary declared, "But they know what counts as right and what counts as wrong. They can tell good from evil. We are under orders, and we will obey our orders, to a man…"

McCleary paused and glanced at his soldiers before continuing.

"But I can assure you that we would join you against the Campbells, if they attack, be they allies of King James or not."

There was a roar of agreement from his men.

"That almost sounds like treason!" Allan MacDonald replied with a wink.

"My orders are specific," McCleary replied, "So if the Campbells get in the way of my orders, then the more of their corpses strewn along this road, the better."

This statement was met with enthusiastic applause and cheers of approval from his troops. Allan and Allaster MacDonald looked pleased and sat a little more at ease atop their mounts.

"Your mission, Constable," Allan proclaimed, looking at Burberry and addressing him directly, "Has the potential to displease the MacDonald, but the unease it seems to provoke among the Campbells gives him comfort."

There was a stark silence that hung heavily in the air.

"I am the King's Man," said Constable Burberry.

"You are," conceded Allan MacDonald, "But let us hope, for the sake of Scotland, that you are God's Man first."

"As a Constable, empowered under royal warrant, I know my duty."

"One man's duty is another man's betrayal."

"I am to convene a special Court of Justice at The Fortress of Inverness. King James wants his justice to be both done and to be seen to be done."

"Now that *is* an onerous duty."

"I will do the right thing."

"Will the court do the same? Will it do God's will? If it does, the MacDonald won't find it wanting," Allan MacDonald replied.

His brother, Allaster could not resist making an observation.

"The more likely it is that the right thing is done," said Allaster, "The less likely the Campbells are to approve of it."

Hamish Pottle noisily cleared his throat.

"I have no idea what either of you are talking about," Hamish complained, "And it leads me to realise that I can only *presume* both of you are talking of the same thing."

"For my part," McCleary declared, cutting off the MacDonald brothers from answering, "I only know what I *need* to know."

Allan MacDonald folded his arms and grimaced at McCleary, as if resigning himself to receiving a lecture.

"The one thing that I *always* know is all I ever *need* to know," McCleary affirmed, "It is that I am required to carry out my duty as a soldier. I leave politics and plotting to those who have command of me."

"A noble idea," Allan MacDonald assured him, "But I, for my part, do not have a dozen ranks of officers stacked above me, like a tower of brass and bronze. Nor do I have a formal process of discipline enshrined in law. If I should fail in my duty, a hand over my mouth and a blade drawn across my throat, from one side to the other, serves as my reprimand."

"I go about the king's business," Burberry reiterated, "Sometimes, my knowing only enough can be dangerous in itself, but knowing too much can be fatal."

Everyone nodded.

"Our father, The MacDonald, has a loyalty to God, to his family, to his clan, to Scotland and to King James," Allan MacDonald told them, "It makes life a little more complicated that, in the opinion of his people, God's work and God's purpose happen to be served so very well indeed by *another* sovereign."

Constable Burberry laughed a hollow laugh, with no trace of humour. He fully understood the reference to the Queen of the West. Allan MacDonald sighed a longer and even more dramatic sigh before replying to the Constable's scorn.

"King James is King of England. King James is King of Scotland. That is the *whole* of Scotland. There is a monarch, who is the Queen of the West, who is queen of *part* of Scotland. She believes that James is king by the Holy Will of God. She recognises that his right to rule is divine."

"She is a fine example to her people," Burberry declared, unable to suppress a smile.

"The king would say she does God's will," McCleary added.

"She does, indeed, do God's will,", Allan MacDonald responded, "She cares for the sick, for the poor, for the hungry, for the elderly and for all those who suffer. She fights for what is right. She stands beside her soldiers in the mud and filth, her sword drawn, and her life at risk just like their own."

Allan MacDonald and Iain McCleary stood looking at each other for a full minute without saying a word. Eventually, McCleary broke the ominous silence.

"Many years ago," the Captain began, "My father was found at the side of the road, just north of Aviemore, by a previous holder of the title 'Queen of the West'. He was badly wounded and bleeding to death."

It was as if everyone in his audience had stopped breathing at once. The silence was so absolute, they could all have been stood beneath a glass dome.

"My father had been heading south from Inverness, with his two lieutenants, when they were robbed by Eastlanders who had come raiding across the Spey. She commanded her Healer to tend to their wounds. She then took them to a local stronghouse and beat on the door, demanding entry. The Laird was not best pleased that she should impose upon him to host officers of the Blue and Greys under his roof."

The tension amongst his listeners was so thick in the air, that it could have been dragged down with two hands and knotted like a rope.

"She told him that none of the King of Scotland's armies had lifted a weapon against her or her people in over fifteen years. She told him that there had been talk amongst her small folk that, on his way north, at Kingussie, my father had given a silver coin to an inn keeper to pay for the lodging of an elderly couple. He had found them on the road, poorly clothed and freezing to death. They had fallen on hard times and had no money."

There was a ripple of approval through the Blue and Greys.

"She said that my father had shown charity and been a Good Samaritan, just like in the bible. She said that a kindness done to even the lowliest of her people was as good as a kindness done directly to her. The Laird relented and obeyed her. He agreed to take in my father and his companions and to tend, further, to their injuries. All three eventually mended and recovered. They were given horses to continue their journey to their barracks at Perth. Two years later, my father married. Two years more and my twin brother and I were born."

Captain McCleary stood tall.

"I must serve King James. It is my duty. It is my obligation. It is my privilege. I have taken an oath upon my honour, but do not think that it binds me to think badly or with disrespect of the great woman of whom you speak."

Allan MacDonald looked at McCleary for a long moment, his gaze steady and thoughtful, then his face broke into a smile.

"If you had told me that tale about your father, back when we first made our acquaintance, you might have got double rations of porridge the following morning!"

The resulting laughter was infectious and spread like wildfire throughout the whole throng of onlookers, the soldiers being the most enthusiastic.

Caitlan Pottle, who had rejoined Burberry in his wagon, leaned and whispered into his ear, "If this is a potentially deadly confrontation, then it is an absurdly jovial and good natured one!"

Constable Burberry smiled and nodded as he whispered back, "It's just two little boys, who have crossed paths in the forest, seeing who can piss highest up a tree."

Caitlan gave a little giggle.

"My men," McCleary announced, "Have acquitted themselves admirably in combat, as recently as just the other day. They were, and they are, as fierce and fearless a group of men as I could ever wish to command."

The Captain paused to acknowledge the mutters of goodwill that passed through the assembled group.

"They will get us all to Inverness, without a doubt, but if you are offering your own men to *accompany* us, we would have no cause to gripe or grumble."

Allan MacDonald got down from his horse and bowed ceremoniously. He even added a twirl of his fingers in the air as a final flourish. McCleary applauded him, with his hands lifted to head height, in acknowledgement of being imitated so ludicrously well.

"That," McCleary confessed, "Was, for all the world, like looking in a mirror!"

Everybody around them laughed heartily. Allan MacDonald climbed back up into his saddle and turned his horse to face uphill, in readiness to be off. Captain McCleary waved to his troops. In response, they began to clamber up into their wagons and onto their horses.

Hamish raised an arm while making a loud and ostentatious affair of clearing his throat. Allan, the lead MacDonald, turned his steed around, again, and looked puzzled. McCleary, who was stood poised to swing up into his saddle, with one foot in his stirrup, returned his foot to the ground.

"Sorry to be the cause of delay," Hamish apologised, "But, I am still a little puzzled about something."

With this, he looked toward Burberry with an eyebrow raised. Burberry cocked his head, as an invitation to speak.

"I hope that I am not a complete dimwit and that I haven't simply lost track of the conversation," he said, looking to Alex for support, "but I am worried that I still don't know the precise reason why we would need such a large force to go to Schnecky."

Everyone smiled at Hamish's use of the slang name for Inverness: '*Schnecky*'.

Allan and Allaster MacDonald looked at each other and Burberry looked at Captain McCleary. Seeing these silent consultations, Hamish and Alex were unable to resist the urge to look at each other, too. Caitlan watched, completely baffled.

Without the need for words, Hamish and Alex conversed. It was odd, they felt, that everybody should feel such an irresistible compulsion to check with one another, on this particular topic. They both began to wonder, exactly who amongst them, knew what.

"I am, as I said before," Constable Burberry explained, "Commanded to convene a special Court of Justice in The Fortress of Inverness and, in addition to my own warrant of office, I have an additional warrant for that specific purpose."

Noticing that Hamish's expression had remained unchanged, he decided to expand further.

"That warrant urges and obliges all those who might encounter me to give me their full and unlimited assistance in performing the work of the king."

Seeing Hamish's expression still not relent, he gave a hearty sigh. Looking around at the assembled people, he shook his head, gravely.

"I'll not be speaking more on the subject without a little privacy," he cautioned.

McCleary obligingly ordered his troops to finish the ascent of the hill and to then wait for them at the other side. The MacDonald brothers did the same. The wagons and riders began to move off. They all processed away into the distance and gradually disappeared over the rise.

CHAPTER 30

Once they were quite alone, Burberry reluctantly addressed them.

"The king recently lost a courier in these parts, between Perth and Pitlochry," Burberry began, addressing himself initially to Captain McCleary, then to the two MacDonalds, "The courier was carrying documents relating to the matters that I will be investigating."

"The king lost a courier?", McCleary asked, unhappy to accept such a gross liberty without confirmation.

"Aye," Burberry replied, "That's the truth, I'm sorry to say."

McCleary looked pained and shocked.

"They are either fools too foolish to appreciate the true scale of their own stupidity," the Captain snarled, "Or they are knaves and scoundrels with no concept of honour."

"I suspect that it is both of those things, together!" said Burberry, with a face like thunder.

McCleary turned to Hamish and opened his mouth to speak, but Hamish replied in advance of his question.

"No," Hamish said, "The courier never arrived at my inn and it is certain that he would have been heading there."

"There's nowhere else he could have stopped?"

"It's too far to go, beyond Pitlochry, to reach another stopping place in any kind of reasonable time."

"He'd not camp in the forest?"

Hamish laughed, causing McCleary to scowl.

"A rider bearing a royal warrant," Hamish advised, "Would shun everything but the very best accommodation. Since, on a king's errand he is permitted to spoil himself, he would most certainly take advantage. He would come to me for the best food on my menu and insist on one of our feather beds."

"Did they find the courier's body?" McCleary persisted.

Burberry cringed, as if the recollection disturbed him.

"They found **parts** of the body," he said.

McCleary nodded, obviously still appalled by the matter.

"These documents," the Captain enquired, "Having fallen into somebody else's hands, how much would they know of your mission?"

Constable Burberry shrugged.

"They would know less than me," he complained, "For, as a precaution, they had sent two despatches. The second and most important despatch being used to make sense of the first. When the first didn't arrive, the second made very little sense. Furthermore, my knowledge about this whole matter is extremely limited. The king was keen that I should know only what I needed to know. My instructions were only enough to explain my going."

"So," Hamish asked, cautiously, "The question has to be: *How much of what you know are you at liberty to tell us?*"

Burberry flinched and it was hard to tell if this were from the pain and discomfort of his injuries or from the prospect of imparting his secrets. Caitlan helped him into a more comfortable position and, taking a blanket, she folded it and placed it behind his head as a cushion against the boards.

"The sharing of information," Constable Burberry cautioned them, "Was strictly forbidden, but I feel certain that nobody could have foreseen *these* particular circumstances. Nor could they have accounted for their impact. More to the point, nobody could have predicted the involvement of each of you."

Nobody spoke.

"The most important thing to know," Burberry insisted, "Is that I do not know, and have never known, who is to be tried in the special session of court, and I give you my word of honour on that."

He paused, to allow for any protests, and, when there were none, he continued.

"The offence that concerns the court *has* been disclosed to me. It is the most grave and serious offence of all."

Burberry paused to look at each of them in turn. His face was stern and earnest and his eyes grim.

"The offence is that of Treason."

The Constable's audience looked at each other in stunned silence. Even the two MacDonalds appeared to have been taken completely by surprise. Alex and Hamish were unsure if they had misheard what had been said and they both spoke at once, asking the same question.

"Treason?"

"That's right, treason," confirmed Constable Burberry.

"Who?" asked Hamish.

Constable Burberry shrugged his shoulders, for he didn't actually know who King James proposed to try for the offence.

"That is something the king has, so far, omitted to communicate," Burberry responded, sarcastically, "I'm sure he will let me know in his own good time."

Alex and Hamish locked eyes but didn't speak. Allan and Allaster MacDonald looked at each other but they, too, had no words. Captain Iain McCleary looked from each of their faces, one to the next, but could think of no comment to make.

"Don't all cry out at once!" Burberry shouted, in mock annoyance, "You will deafen me trying to talk over each other like that!"

They all returned him glum expressions. Treason was a serious accusation and nobody appeared to appreciate his attempt at humour.

"Shall I ask the question that everybody has already asked themselves?" Allan MacDonald offered.

"What might that be?", the Constable asked.

"If nobody knows who is to be put on trial, how does the MacDonald know that it is in his interest to ensure that you, Constable Burberry, arrive in one piece and unmolested?"

"And the answer?"

"The king knows that you, Constable, will do your job properly and well," Allan replied, "The MacDonald, too, knows that you will do your job properly and well. In fact, as well as he could ever hope it to be done."

Constable Burberry gave him a long, steady look that stopped just short of reproach, before responding.

"The MacDonald feels that he knows me well, then?"

"He feels that he knows you very well, indeed."

"How so? Has he been consulting rabbit bones?"

Allan MacDonald looked at the Constable icily.

"I think, good Constable, that you know I did not mean that."

Burberry raised his eyebrows in query.

"The MacDonald....", said Allan, pausing to calculate his next words and, perhaps, regretting them *before* saying them, "The MacDonald has seen it in the flames."

"It sounds as if The MacDonald enjoys staring into the campfire every bit as much as me!" Burberry replied, in a dead flat tone.

"I think, good Constable, that you know I did not mean that."

Burberry gave a slow and considered nod in appreciation of the other's use of dramatic repetition.

There was a long silence.

"I have seen the fire," said Hamish Pottle, at last.

"I have seen the fire, too," Alex Brennan admitted.

"I have also seen it," said Caitlan Pottle, from her perch behind the Constable.

"I, too," added Burberry, "Without a doubt I have seen it."

McCleary looked at each of them in turn, his brows furrowed dubiously. His reaction could scarcely have been any different, Constable Burberry mused, if they had all just claimed that tapping their noses could make it rain.

Captain McCleary prided himself on being a man of logic and common sense. He shunned superstition and had no time for fanciful ideas. Yet, he had just witnessed a group of perfectly rational men talk about seeing things in a fire. He briefly contemplated the idea that he might be asleep and dreaming, but this didn't have anything like the feel of a dream. He wondered, then, if this were a cleverly contrived joke, but felt quite certain that he would have had at least a vague inkling of it.

McCleary screwed up his eyes and grimaced. He then shook his head, vigorously, as if it were a keg and the mention of *fire* were a bean that could be ejected with the right amount of effort.

They all watched McCleary's consternation with cruel amusement. Here was a Lowlander, floundering like a fish out of water, in the company of a bunch of superstitious Highlanders. In these parts of Scotland, so the folk of Edinburgh and Glasgow would have it, belief in witch craft, magic and hocus pocus was rife and untamed. Here, it was said, otherwise sane and reasonable men placed great trust in such farcical things as ghostly horses without heads, forest imps and other such childish nonsense. They held steadfastly to these notions as if they were utterly real.

"Just like you," McCleary told the two MacDonald brothers, "My job is to get the Constable to Inverness. I do so in order that he can perform whatever business he has there, in the service of King James."

The MacDonald brothers nodded their acceptance of his statement and made no protest.

"To do my job," McCleary continued, "I don't need a belief in anything that is not of this Earth. I just need to do my duty as a soldier."

"Well," Allaster grinned, "Let's hope that we have no encounters with either the ghostly horse they call '*Headless Neddy*' or the pixie they call '*Will of the Woods!*', on our way to Inverness!"

Unlike the MacDonalds, the Captain found nothing amusing about this proposition.

"Whatever his reasons might be," Allan maintained, "The MacDonald is sure of his faith in you, his faith in the Constable and his faith in the mission you share."

Constable Burberry kept his tongue still, deciding to portray himself as a 'safe pair of hands' and left any discussion unrelated to the law to the others. For their part, the MacDonald brothers were happy to leave Burberry worried and uncertain about exactly how much they and their laird knew about him, about his loyalties and about his past.

Hamish Pottle and his wife had no doubts and were fully committed to this venture. They felt that there was something important to be done. To them, this was an opportunity to make their lives count for something, at last, and it was one not to be missed.

"It is the Quickening," said Hamish, firmly.

There was an awkward silence, as people considered what might constitute a suitable reply.

"I agree," Alex announced, after a little reluctance, "I can't explain it any other way. It has to be the Quickening."

The MacDonald brothers stole a conspiratory glance at one another before committing themselves.

"The MacDonald believes that the flames he has seen are, indeed, a sign of the Quickening," Allan affirmed, relieved to have finally said it.

"The Hebrews saw a burning bush when God communicated with them," his brother agreed, "This strange thing – the inexplicable curling tongues of fire – is a sign, too. A sign appropriate to our own time."

McCleary didn't need to shout: *'Hocus pocus!'*. His expression said it for him.

"If any of you truly do believe in magic or in miracles," the Constable requested wearily, "I wonder if you could have this cart lifted up and transported on a bank of clouds to Inverness, so that I don't have to be thrown around like a rag doll in the back of it."

"You do not believe?" Allan asked him, fixing him with a solemn look.

Ewan Burberry returned a vacant gaze that gave no clue as to his feelings and left a long moment before replying with absolute conviction.

"I truly believe," he confirmed.

Allan appeared to cogitate over his answer before seeking reassurance.

"You believe that this is the Quickening?"

"The Quickening? Well….. I wasn't alone when I was a prisoner in the McArthy stronghouse. I believe that there was a force there with me. A powerful force that was not of any Earthly kind."

The Constable's audience listened intently, as if transfixed.

"I have seen the fire – the form it uses when it wishes to appear to us – and there is nothing about it that is evil. Its presence is good. Its aura is completely benign. There is a feeling of calm and of holiness about it. I don't know what force it might be, but it didn't just happen to be there, it didn't just appear on a whim….. it was made to happen. It was sent."

Apart from the noise of the horses' breathing, there was only reverent silence.

"I don't know if this is the Quickening," Burberry went on, "What I do know is that the flames are a manifestation of goodness and that….", he paused, searching for the right words, "And that they seem to be crossing a barrier. It is as if they are leaking from another world."

There was a long pause before anybody spoke and when, at last, the silence was broken it was by Captain Iain McCleary.

"Well, let's not mention this to any holders of high office we may encounter in Inverness. Please keep it to yourselves, if you will. The last thing we need is for any of you to be condemned to an insane asylum!"

There were some subdued snorts, a murmur or two of begrudging laughter and a couple of polite grunts of acknowledgement at McCleary's words, but no expressions of support for his disbelief.

"It's a strange thing!" Burberry chortled, shaking his head in amusement.

"What is a strange thing?" asked Allan MacDonald.

"It's a strange thing that I am blessed with the trust of both the Laird of the MacDonalds and of King James! Surely, by all the power of logic, this cannot end well for me!"

There was spontaneous laughter at this remark, for the irony of it was not lost on any of them. When the laughter had died away, Allan MacDonald slapped his thigh and shouted for them to come to order.

"We must gather ourselves and be away," he cried, "Or my men, up on yonder rise, will think that my brother and I have deserted them and run off to join the Blue and Greys!"

CHAPTER 31

Unsure of the faith of the two men that Annis had slain, logs and branches were stacked up and capped with brushwood. The two bodies were then placed on top. Much to everyone's annoyance, a party of seven traditional mourners was assembled. None of those chosen showed the least bit of enthusiasm to be participating.

The mourners begrudgingly assembled and the pyre was lit. It did not take a great deal of guessing to know that, if the queen had not commanded this, it would not have taken place.

The soldier who was selected to say the traditional prayer for departed souls, on being bestowed this 'honour', looked as if he had been invited, instead, to be shaved and whipped.

"Dear Lord," said the unlucky soldier, "Take into your care these souls, newly departed, and show mercy to them in your judgement as, one day, we beseech you to show mercy to all of us. Let them account for what they have done and for what they have not done. Let us all be wary of that day of judgement and mend our ways. Fill our souls with devotion to Your service and strengthen us from temptations. Let us act bravely and well. In Your name, we shall feed the hungry, clothe the naked, befriend the friendless and give support to those who suffer. At the end of days, when this world has ceased and all human matters are done, permit us to dwell with You in Paradise."

There was a sullen and half-hearted murmur of 'Amen' and everybody turned around and headed off, leaving the fire to burn unattended. Whatever destination was awaiting the souls of these foul and wicked sword fighters, nobody seemed to care.

The birds quickly stopped singing and the skies above the spot began to darken. At tree top height, a murky, gloomy vapour started to gather and, from it, a billowing bank of mist descended to surround the fire. The ground instantly became hard and a white frost formed, in all directions, for a distance of five paces.

A minute later, a dark shadow rose from out of the soil. The flames burned a ghostly blue as tendrils of black smoke wrapped themselves around the two charred corpses. With a dull, rumbling like a waterfall, the two men's souls were dragged, kicking and screaming, to Hell. The potential clemency of awaiting Judgement Day – that had been prayed for and beseeched on their behalf – had not, as it turned out, been granted.

CHAPTER 32

An hour later, Annis called for her caravan to stop. When Jade and Jet leapt from their cart and came to see of what service they could be, Annis sent them to fetch the king's courier. The man, no longer blighted by the presence of his 'escorts', appeared to be in much better spirits.

Annis recalled her mother's advice to her about talking to people in such circumstances as this.

'Pretend that it is not you, but another person who is speaking. Pretend that you have to translate everything they say because they speak a different language. Now, make believe that the person to whom you are speaking has a knife to your throat and that any timidity or weakness in the words you convey to them is likely to get you killed.'

The man, one William Cox, sat down and Annis looked at him levelly. Morag turned away and busied herself with some non-existent task.

"Tell me," enquired Annis, dispensing with formalities, "Where did you learn to speak French?"

William's cheery disposition was dispelled in an instant. He sat and reflected on the question.

"I have served my country in different ways," he offered, eventually, "One of them required me to speak French."

"List the ways," demanded Annis.

William looked desolated and swallowed several times before he could speak.

"Stop!" Annis commanded as he finally began to answer, "Just tell me about the thing you know I want to know."

William appeared to deflate in front of her.

"It was when the French were plotting against the English. This is a regular thing, for them, of course," the courier explained, not enjoying his own humour in the least, "The French had recruited some ill-treated and disillusioned English soldiers to supply them with information in exchange for rewards. I was sent, in my role as a military courier, to pose as one of them. This was because I had mastered some basic French. They thought I would be more convincing than somebody who was fluent."

Annis nodded, "Go on."

"I was stripped and flogged for some invented charge and this punishment was delivered deliberately within sight of where we knew the French to have one of their observation hideouts, forward of their lines. I was left in a wooden hut overnight and, in the early hours, my escape was faked. I ran parallel to the French lines and was captured by one of the French scouts."

At this point, William winced at the memory and bit his lip.

"I had been promised that the man wielding the whip would be advised of my innocence. Instead, he was never told, and the flogging I received was real. Whatever the invented charge, the punishment for it was severe. My back was a wretched, bloody mess, just as my superiors had intended to be."

"Go on," said Annis, a little more gently.

"I was beaten and tortured by the French and it was, in fact, with very little pretence that I eventually gave in to their interrogation. I supplied them with information that had been agreed. Some of it was real. Some of it was a hoax. In any event, it was no more accurate or detailed than could be expected, coming from an infantry man of humble rank. I am happy to believe that no English lives were lost on my account."

"Let us hope so!" said Annis, sternly, "Carry on with your story."

William looked a little shame-faced, but continued.

"It was agreed with the French that, for the second time, my escape should be faked. I made my way back to my own lines and rejoined my unit. As the French had instructed, I went back to my job but took routes that would allow me to show them sight of some of the documents I carried. These were carefully chosen, by my English officers, and never contained anything of momentous importance."

Annis nodded, solemnly, and – after having Morag ply him with some wine for his throat – she had him resume his tale.

"It wasn't long before we had to feign my being caught by English scouts. My officers had decided that we needed somebody to spy for them within the enemy's ranks. Additionally, constantly finding low level information to leak to the French had become a chore. I told the French that I had become aware of being watched by my own side and overheard a conversation between my officers that alerted me to having been discovered. As I fled, it was arranged that I would be shot at, to make it seem more genuine."

William shook his head and sighed.

"However….", he began, dismally, but Annis interrupted him, clapping her hands with glee and laughing out loud. William joined in her laughter.

"As you have already guessed," he said, grinning, "I fared no better in terms of my health with the second 'escape' than I did the first, and one of my comrades managed to hit me with a musket round in the leg!"

This time, Morag laughed, too, and took quite a while to recover her self-control. Before long, Annis and the courier were laughing more at Morag trying to control herself than they were at the original story.

"I was imprisoned by the French, far from the front lines of the war. There, I met another English courier. I despised him for betraying England and allowed him to think that I was a fellow traitor. Under his tuition, my grasp of the French language hugely improved. The French officers spoke excellent English, but they decided that a better command of their language would allow me to report to them in French, once I was sent back to England to spy. Because I was a courier, I knew all sorts of important locations and the names of important people."

Annis nodded and spun her finger in the air to indicate that he should continue.

"I made my mind up to remain a double agent, working for King James, and decided that, once they sent me back to England, I would report myself to the English Army and resume sending the French false information. I would also advise them about the English traitor I had met. The war lasted longer than anybody had expected and I became such a natural French speaker that my English accent virtually disappeared."

The courier shrugged, indicating another twist to his tale.

"My run of bad luck continued! I was seriously injured, one day, when some nearby French troops were being trained in the laying of explosives. They set off a charge by accident and brought down a wall and part of the roof of the hostel where we were staying. I was moved to a hospital to be treated and to recuperate."

Annis lifted her hands from her lap, palms upward, to request if there were more to tell.

"I became friendly, in the French hospital, with some other wounded soldiers and got to know some men who, it turned out, were members of "L'épée de la Nuit *(The Sword of the Night)*". By a twist of fate, they included the English traitor I had met earlier."

The courier shook his head in disbelief at the bizarre path of his own life.

"These men were a secret society. They were a force who regarded themselves as being more knights than simple soldiers. These men decided that a pair of English traitors would be fine people to teach them about England and English life. Then we learned of their intentions. Their Grand Order – and that is how they referred to themselves – had the objective of assassinating the King of England and his highest ministers of office."

The courier took a deep breath.

"As it turned out, the other Englishman was no more a traitor than I. Although we carefully never discussed this point, for fear that we would be discovered, it gradually became obvious to both of us. We worked together to train their spies exceptionally well, but we built in some ingenious verbal flaws that we hoped would give them away and lead to them being discovered."

Annis held up her hand for him to stop.

"In the finest schools of England and Scotland, and – of course – in France, children are taught about the Sword of the Night and their bold adventures. They are known. How did you manage to escape?"

The courier shrugged and looked apologetic.

"It appeared to be fate, Your Highness. L'épée de la Nuit were fond of infiltrating the French Army, whom they regarded as soft, stupid and undisciplined. One day, the other Englishman and I were on such a mission. We were in a coastal town on the English Channel, spying on the French army while disguised as a pair of their senior officers. We were having tea, sat around a table in a café, when a group of English

Commandos swooped on us, taking us by surprise. Believing us to be actual French officers, they drugged us both, put us in sacks, kidnapped us and sailed us back to England."

Annis clapped her hands.

"A free ticket home!" she declared.

"Yes, Your Highness, though the fishing boat they used stank of rotten fish and we were treated violently by the commandos who disliked the French military vehemently."

"Not your first time being assaulted by your own side!"

"No, Your Majesty."

"To be frank," Annis confessed, "I believe that a lot of the English gentry dislike Scottish Highlanders as much as they do the French."

"Their dislike stems from ignorance, Your Highness."

"Ignorance of the Highlanders or of the French?"

"Both, Your Highness, but most regrettably so in the case of the Highlanders."

"I fear that many regard my people as being nothing more than primitive savages."

"The more educated some people become, Your Highness, the more loathsomely stupid they become. It would not surprise me if some of them thought that those north of the rivers Forth and Clyde were cannibals!"

"Ignorance is bliss, where to know is folly," she quipped.

They both laughed.

"The English taste delicious, by the way!" she quipped.

They laughed a whole lot more.

"Tell me," Annis asked, "The two men who travelled up from London with you – your '*escorts*' – did they know you had been a member of a fanatical French secret society?"

"No, Your Majesty, but they did suspect that there was *something* amiss."

"Perhaps it was you having manners, not being unbearably arrogant and not treating women like filth that put them on their guard?"

William smiled but ventured no reply. Annis motioned to Morag to serve them more wine and their cups were filled.

"I do not know what acrobatics and fiendish contortions you learned as a Secret French Knight," Annis teased, "But the art required here, in this vehicle, is to drink your wine without it ending up either down your front or in your lap!"

Everybody laughed and, at that moment, the wagon obligingly descended into a deep rut, causing further amusement. Annis caught the courier's momentary questioning glance at Morag as she, as a mere servant, poured a cup of wine for herself.

"In my service," the queen told him, "Nobody is a worthless inferior."

William appeared a little embarrassed at having been observed.

"The Messiah washed the feet of his disciples," he replied.

Annis raised her eyebrows and inclined her head to show her approval of his words and nodded thoughtfully at them. They all rocked, bounced and swayed, holding their glasses away from themselves at each rut or pothole, and the courier quickly honed the skill of staying dry.

CHAPTER 33

The journey continued for almost an hour in amiable, companionable silence. It was the kind of silence that was not strained and where nobody felt obliged to say anything just for the sake of saying something. Nobody spoke because neither Annis, nor Morag, nor the courier, had anything to say that was of any greater value than silence.

Annis had not worn anything of any particular elegance or finery. She had persuaded Morag to let her don a loose blouse and a little tunic with a laced belt and a pair of roman sandals. Whilst her attire made no attempt to offer anything up to the eye of the beholder, it didn't particularly seek to hide her physique, either.

As their journey progressed she had been unable to ignore that the courier had looked her up and down several times and that his eyes had lingered, here and there, with evident pleasure. To her surprise, she found that this didn't make her feel at all uncomfortable, as it normally would in a man's company. Oddly, she had found herself, now and again, adopting some poses that would emphasise her body and was pleased to note that the courier found it necessary to swallow more frequently and breathe faster when she did so. At one point, stretching herself and stifling a yawn, she caught Morag raising her eyebrows at her and realised that the amount of bare thigh that was on display was, perhaps, a little immodest.

Annis smoothed down and rearranged all of her clothing, then shuffled to the front of her bench, opposite the young man.

"Tell me," she asked, looking the courier directly in the eye and completely masking her mischievous humour, "Would you like to witness me completely naked?"

The courier shuddered as if she had just physically slapped him and looked around in panic. Morag raised her eyebrows at Annis, again. William had swallowed most of a cup of wine in his panic and was now spluttering and gasping for breath.

"It is okay," Annis urged him, "There is no need to speak. Please, just shake your head or nod it to give me your answer."

While studiously not looking at Morag, William suppressed his coughing long enough to manage a nod of his head, though with some evident trepidation.

"Very well," said Annis, sitting tall, placing her hands on her knees and leaning forward slightly, "I fear that I will never be anywhere near as good as my mother and that, because of this, I am letting everybody down. I fear that I cannot compare, in any respect, to the glory of my ancestors and this regularly makes me feel wretched."

William looked at her, blankly. Then his eyes became gentle and amused. The soft, kindly hint of a smile on his lips became more distinct.

"If Your Majesty would allow me to say…."

He paused for permission and Annis nodded.

"You are a beautiful woman, My Queen, and the more naked your heart the more beautiful you become."

Annis looked deep into his eyes and she felt she could see his soul. This man was, without doubt, a good man. He was a very good man, indeed.

"You said '*My Queen*'," Annis told him.

"Yes, I did," he replied.

Annis was relieved that her heart did not beat, when she looked into his amazing eyes, the way it did when she looked into those of Balgair.

"I have good news for you," Annis told him.

William inclined his head to the side in question.

"I am sending word to my cook that you will not be appearing on the menu for supper, tonight."

All three of them rocked with laughter and, after a minute, they all began to hold their sides for the ache it caused them, there.

The driver of the queen's wagon turned and looked down at its roof, as if he might hope to see through it, and shook his head in puzzlement.

CHAPTER 34

The closer they got to the village of Moy, the lighter Annis grew in her mood, the easier she laughed and the more often she smiled.

When her wagon finally pulled off the track and down to 'Caisteal nan Cnocan Iarainn' (Castle of the Iron Hills), it was obvious to all that she was very happy to arrive. The Duke of Moy, otherwise known as The Laird MacKintosh or, more personally, 'Gregor' to his close friends, was waiting for her.

The Duke of Moy had assembled his entire staff outside the entrance to the castle and had lined up his men at arms either side of the cobbled approach road. Judging by the volume of armed warriors, Gavin guessed that he had called on a number of his bondsmen to supply extra foot soldiers.

There were flags hung along ropes and pennants flying from poles. There were flowers in baskets and maids with wicker troughs of bread, meat and fruit. There were dancers in fine costumes and players with their instruments.

Annis stepped down out of her wagon and Morag watched, with dismay, as her expression slowly changed to a more serious one. This change did not escape the notice of the Duke and, with a worried look on his face, he quickly hurried to her to make his greetings.

"Your Highness," he said, bowing deeply, "I am most proud and honoured to receive you."

Annis looked pensive and then pursed her lips before speaking.

"I am most grateful for your kind reception, Duke, but…."

The worried look on Gregor MacKintosh's face turned to one of concern, "Your Highness?", he asked.

"I regret that we have buried many of our fallen, this past week, and I have not yet had time to show them my full respects. There are widows, orphans and other kin who will have only just learned of this dreadful news. My heart is heavy with the grief of it and the shock is too recent to be contemplating dancing, music or any kind of banquet."

"I apologise for my folly, Your Highness. I will disband the entertainers immediately. I will have the tables prepared with a more humble fayre."

"It is *I* who must apologise," Annis said, provoking a stunned look from the Duke, "For I should have thought to send word ahead."

The Duke looked embarrassed at the kindness of her words and pained at her wish to take onus for the situation.

"Nay! Nay! Nay!" he exclaimed, "I will not hear of it!"

The queen waved a hand to dismiss his objection, but he was determined to declare her blameless.

"Your Majesty, I have not taken into proper consideration the things that have happened and my wish to supply merriment is a woeful error of judgement."

"Gregor, no,", Annis insisted, placing her hand on his arm for reassurance, "There is no finer, more loyal, or more good hearted man than you from Berwick-on-Tweed to Orkney."

Gregor MacKintosh swelled with pride at this praise. Gavin, Balgair and their Seconds-in-Command all saluted the Duke to add their own esteem. The mind of William Cox, however, was elsewhere. He had been caught in a state of distraction. He was looking up at the tower of 'Caisteal nan Cnocan Iarainn' with a gaze so intent that there could almost have been a dragon perched at the top of it. Coming back to his senses, he hurriedly bowed, appearing slightly flustered.

"Your Grace," said William, bowing to the Duke, again, "I am to give you my sword."

"What?", asked the Duke, looking intrigued.

"The king, Your Grace," said William, apologetically, "He commanded that I should give you my sword."

"Did he now?" mused the Duke, holding out his hand.

William surrendered the sword and the Duke hefted it in his hand and made a couple of practice sweeps with it.

"It is a fine sword," said the Duke, slashing with it back and forth.

"Yes, Your Grace. It is magnificent. It is the best I have ever held."

"The king must trust you," the Duke confided, "He must trust you very much indeed."

William looked puzzled.

"It is only a sword, Your Grace," he replied.

"Yes. Just so."

"I believe it must be intended for you as a gift, Your Grace."

"Yes, it is. It is, indeed, a gift. I realise that, now," the Duke agreed, "But I am certain that the gift is meant for *you*."

William looked thoroughly confused at this.

"Good Sir," said the Duke, "The king, I think, only intends that I should borrow it. I would not deprive you of it longer than overnight."

"I am unworthy of such a sword!" William protested.

The Duke looked serious and put a hand on the courier's shoulder.

"No. You are wrong.", the Duke insisted, "You are every bit worthy of this wonderful blade. There is no doubt."

The Duke looked at the sword and stroked its beautifully carved wooden handle, bound with the finest deer skin threads, and capped, at its end, with a dragon's head.

"What is your name?" the Duke asked.

"William Cox, Your Grace."

"William, I will use this sword, later, in my regular sparring practice with my Man-at-Arms and then return it to you in the morning."

"Yes. Yes, of course, Your Grace. Whatever you wish."

William looked back at the tower. The structure was just as King James had described. There was no doubt about it. He had given the sword to its intended recipient, exactly as the king had instructed and, just as he had said would happen, they had declined to accept ownership.

As a thin rain began to fall, Jet and Jade appeared and lifted a waxed, canvas canopy over the queen's head, holding it taut at each end by a pair of poles, which they carried aloft.

"The sky cries for my dead," Annis told her entourage.

Annis was escorted into the 'Castle of the Iron Hills' and up to her chambers where Jet and Jade made rapid work of getting her changed into a gown. Annis descended the steps to the banqueting hall wearily. More out of courtesy and good manners than any wish or desire to do so, she had agreed to eat a formal meal with her hosts, the Duke and Duchess of Moy, her officers and her close staff.

After they had all eaten and drunk their fill, the Duke and Duchess, invited Annis to withdraw with them to their lounge. Annis accepted their invitation and was pleased to relax into an easy chair before a roaring log fire.

The Duchess served them whiskey from a finely carved decanter, which Annis duly admired, and they all reclined with their feet raised on little buffets, warming their toes in the heat from the fire.

"Gregor," said Annis, dispensing with any preamble, "I respect your opinion as highly as any man alive."

"I am humbled by your kind words, Your Majesty," the Laird MacKintosh of Moy replied.

"Tell me, if you would, Gregor, why – in your opinion – would King James wish me to attend a trial at The Fortress of Inverness?"

"Your Highness," he replied, "I cannot think that King James has any reason to wish you harm. The Highlands are unsettled and troublesome enough for him, with all the disputes and quarrels that already exist."

"So they are!" the Duchess agreed with a smile.

"If it were not for you, as Queen of the West,", the Duke declared, "The Highlands might already have descended into open revolt!"

Annis nodded, thoughtfully.

"Strangely enough, Your Majesty," the Laird exclaimed, "That could actually be the reason! For King James is known to have a habit of spending far more money than he gathers in taxes. I have heard it said that many a Duke, Earl and Baron has been appointed to their position directly after making a substantial contribution to the royal coffers."

"I have heard so, too," Annis agreed.

"I think that, perhaps, King James' shortage of money might have driven him to listen to greedy fools who would have him dispense with the Queen of the West."

"A folly if it were to ever happen!" his wife declared.

"A folly, indeed," the Duke concurred, "But he might do this in order to cause a conflict in the Highlands. He could then resolve it by appointing English Dukes, Earls and Barons to put down the ensuing clashes. Such people, having received their titles and accompanying Scottish lands – seized for them to own – would, of course, be expected to donate generous volumes of gold to the king's treasury as a token of their gratitude."

"Why would he not simply appoint them, anyway, and have done with it?"

"Because," the Laird MacIntosh explained, "As queen, you are a focus of loyalty in the Highlands. Without you, the clans would be too divided to rise up, to any real effect, against rich Englishmen grabbing swathes of Scottish land."

"This is not the work of the king," the Duchess declared, "His mother was a strong woman. She was unafraid of asserting herself. She was toppled by men who hated the idea of a woman having authority over them. I do not think he would do this."

"If not the king," the Laird responded, "Then it must be somebody in very high office. They would have to wield huge influence within his court."

"I regard that as a more likely explanation," Annis conceded.

"A king's love for gold," the Duchess observed, "Has often led them turning a blind eye to things done in their name."

"I still think that, for all King James is said to have become more English than Scottish," Annis defended, "He still has heather and thistles in his blood."

"His mother, Your Majesty, was a cunning, clever and resourceful woman," said the Duke.

"She had to be in order to survive," Annis replied, "I would think that with her blood still flowing in his veins, the king might be similarly able to outsmart those who are dangerous to him."

"Yes," the Duke agreed, "He may well be a man it is difficult to outwit."

"He is, more importantly, a Scot first and a king second," Annis enthused, "In fact, he is his mother's son before anything else."

Gregor looked troubled and Annis got the distinct feeling that he knew something that he wasn't telling her.

"Your Majesty," he said, after a long silence, "Perhaps the king fears for your safety, if you were to know too much."

"You say this truly?"

"I do. I cannot think he would willingly keep you in the dark."

Annis looked at the Duke. He had been a good and dear friend to her mother, she recalled, and to her mother's mother before her. His family, for centuries, had been resolute in their loyalty to the Queens of the West and unswerving in their support during times of crisis.

His eyes held a steadiness that suggested conviction, yet something in his manner – perhaps the way his fingers tightened slightly around his whiskey glass – made her wonder if he was hoping rather than believing his own words.

Annis turned, deliberately, to the Duchess, "How do you feel about this, Your Grace?" she asked, using the formal address with pointed significance.

The Duchess met her gaze evenly. Not a muscle betrayed her thoughts, yet in the slight pause before she spoke, volumes were communicated. "Your Highness," said the Duchess, her voice calm and measured, "I believe that my husband speaks the truth as he knows it."

The careful choice of her words was subtle but unmistakable. For Annis, it rang like an alarm bell. The Duchess had avoided vouching for the King's intentions, but only for her husband's honest belief in them.

"I am certain that you are right," Annis responded with the faintest hint of a smile.

A look passed between the two women that was brief but laden with understanding. As women, the ability to talk over the head of a man was something they absorbed with their mother's milk.

As soon as she could, delaying only long enough to cause no offence, Annis excused herself and retired. When Morag attempted to follow her to her chambers, Annis dismissed her and sent her back to sit down, eat and socialise with the other staff.

If Morag were allowed, she reflected, she would tend to her queen's wants and needs from morning till night without a moment's hesitation. Annis felt weary and exhausted. She could only imagine how tired Morag must feel after the day's labours.

"Go and enjoy yourself," Annis commanded.

CHAPTER 35

Neacal O'Keefe had seemed preoccupied since they set off from the last staging inn, that morning, at Findhorn Bridge. He had stared out of the window in silence for most of the last half hour and, eventually, his travelling companions had begun to find this a little annoying. Even their driver's argument with a drover, at the bridge over the river, hadn't stirred O'Keefe from his inward thoughts. Any attempt to engage him in conversation had borne little fruit, despite repeated efforts by both Janine and the Duke.

In the end, unable to restrain himself, the Duke decided to challenge him directly on the subject.

"What is it that troubles and distracts you?" he asked.

"The man," O'Keefe replied, at length, "The one who raised Lachlan's suspicions. I have a feeling, gnawing away at me, that tells me I should know him, but I simply cannot place where I might have seen him."

"Should I have noticed this man at the inn?" enquired the Duke.

"There was no reason you should have taken note of him," O'Keefe assured him, "He was dressed in drab clothing and was sat, for most of the time, in the shadows."

"He was, indeed," Lachlan Balloch confirmed.

"At the inn, I dismissed the idea that I'd seen him before," replied O'Keefe, still somewhat distracted, "But, having slept on it, my mind has been half recalling some things that deeply puzzle me."

Janine and the Duke looked at each other, plainly mystified.

"It was just that...." O'Keefe said, absentmindedly, "Now, a good while afterwards, I feel that I might, indeed, know him."

The Duke and Janine traded puzzled expressions and raised their eyebrows at each other.

O'Keefe resumed his silent brooding and contemplation but, try as he might, no matter how he strained his memory, he simply could not bring to mind the name he sought. The name of Derek Ramsbrook.

The Duke of Bo'Ness raised his cane and tapped it on a sliding panel in the roof of the coach. He then placed the end of his cane in a hole in the panel and slid it to the side. The driver lifted the outside of the hatch and doffed his cap as he peered into the body of the coach.

"How long to Inverness?" asked the Duke.

"Two hours and a quarter, I believe," replied the driver.

"When we come to the top of the last hill, pull over. We'd like to stretch our legs and take a look at the view over Inverness."

"Yes, certainly, Your Grace."

The Duke moved the panel shut and the driver dropped the door back down on his side of it.

"I will be glad when this whole sorry business is behind us," complained the Duke.

"Yes, so will I," Janine replied, "These are strange circumstances that I will be happy to be over."

Shaking her head in amusement, Janine gave a little laugh as a thought struck her.

"The irony, of course, is that I – as Queen of the West – am being summoned as holder of a title I had no idea was mine, not even in my wildest dreams, until less than two weeks ago!"

"We are all but pieces on a gaming board, if I may say, Your Ladyship," O'Keefe bemoaned.

Janine laughed again, this time without a shred of mirth.

"Yes," she agreed, "A boardgame where a pawn becomes a queen."

CHAPTER 36

Half an hour later, Lachlan Balloch, in response to a gentle tapping, slid the window of the coach open a little way. A guard put his head through. The man had climbed down from his seat by the driver and, despite the pitching and swaying as the coach rumbled along the track, had skilfully made his way along the running boards.

The guard conversed with the Duke's Head of Security in hushed tones. Mister Chang and Francesca sat quietly, waiting for the conversation to conclude. Eventually, Balloch turned to them to deliver the news.

"Is there something wrong?" asked Mister Chang.

"It is something and nothing," explained Lachlan.

"Go on," Mister Chang urged, clearly intrigued.

"Once or twice, when we have been approaching the brow of a hill, our guards have seen, just cresting a previous hill a mile or two behind us, a large group of soldiers, both in wagons and on horseback."

Francesca knitted her brows and Balloch hurriedly interrupted to reassure her.

"There is no cause for alarm, Your Ladyship," he advised, "For it would have taken little effort, on their part, to have remained hidden. It is because of their lack of caution that there is no cause to think of them as a threat."

"If I may say, My Lady?" offered the guard through the window.

"You may."

"The distance is too great to study anything in detail. As they fall behind us, little by little, making anything out clearly becomes more of a challenge, but…."

The man hesitated.

"I see, and…..?", replied Francesca, gesturing for him to carry on.

"The soldiers behind us seem to be of two kinds, My Lady. Some are mounted troops, in uniform, carrying what looks to be the flag of King James. There are others, also on horseback, but without uniforms. They are displaying flags, too, but we can't identify them for certain."

"I see," said Francesca, motioning to hear more.

"The troops without uniforms are wearing armour. That's not all. It looks a lot like the armour from the time of the Romans."

"*Roman* armour?" asked Janine.

"Of that general style. I've seen it in drawings in the blacksmith's forge. Our blacksmith studies the history of armour. He is not just a man of huge muscles, My Lady, he is a man of huge books, too."

Janine nodded seriously, realising that the man had a great respect for the reading of books.

"The armour these men are wearing, My Lady, is a style favoured, in days of old, by the MacDonalds. That isn't to say that they *are* MacDonalds, mind you, but it seems most likely."

The guard thought for a moment and then added a final observation.

"We know they have at least two wagons, My Lady. They are visible from time to time, but they probably have a greater number further behind them."

The Duke, O'Keefe and Lachlan Balloch all nodded and exchanged looks, each studying the other to gauge their reaction. They all appeared content and none gave any indication of being unduly worried.

"Thank you for letting us know," Balloch told the guard.

Daringly, the guard took one hand off the pair of handles he was gripping and gave a quick salute, before clambering back along the side of the coach to return to the front.

"We could stop our coach," Mister Chang declared, "And pretend to be having a problem with one of the wheels and see how these troops react?"

"No," replied Balloch, "We are making good time and we don't want to delay. More importantly, we don't want to draw their attention any more than we may have done, already. Six horses is an uncommon sight anywhere, but especially so far north of Glasgow and Edinburgh."

"I'm sure you're right," the Duke interjected, seeking to reassure everyone, "Let's try to make it to Inverness without being waylaid or accosted."

"And when we get there," Janine added, impishly, "We need to avoid being waylaid or accosted, for the duration of our stay."

Her travelling companions gave her a doleful look.

"If we can deduce who it is that is working against us, we can take steps," Francesca told them, earnestly.

"I haven't been much help in that, have I?" Janine apologised.

"While we cannot be sure who you overheard in the passageway at Brech Woorlach, Your Ladyship, we can presume that if they are not in the rear of this coach, then they are on their way to Inverness or have already arrived."

"Through your endeavours and good offices, Lachlan," remarked the Duke, "We have, until now, always had the luxury of being able to spy on others without being spied on, ourselves."

"Having traitors in our midst is infuriating!" Balloch agreed, "So much so that it *almost* makes me feel sympathy for the victims of our own spying."

"We have successfully helped others deal with infiltrators, in the past," Mister Chang observed.

"It's a case of *'Physician! Heal thyself!'*, I'm afraid!", Balloch quipped.

"We are family," Francesca reminded them, "It is the strict and unvarying tradition, handed down from generation to generation at Brech Woorlach, that from the mightiest to the meekest, we are all one family."

CHAPTER 37

At the summit of their gradual climb, the Duke's coach pulled off the road onto a well-worn area of flat land. The ground had been churned up by the wheels of countless vehicles. The coach drew to a halt and the occupants all climbed out, glad for the opportunity to walk around and exercise their legs.

"The view across to Inverness is impressive!" Janine gasped.

"It is, indeed, Your Ladyship," the Duke agreed, "This is a wonderful vantage point and a well frequented location along the highway."

Their party spent several minutes gazing down across the land below them, the woods and meadows stretching on and on, the varying shades of green random and haphazard, like hundreds of scattered tiles.

The Duke held Janine's arm as she climbed back up the steps into the coach, then he ascended, too. His butler, Neacal O'Keefe, performed one last reach for the sky, accompanied by a yawn, before boarding. The rest of the senior party clambered into the front of the carriage and the footman and two maids got into the rear. The driver raised his voice to speak to the horses and they obligingly set off.

"I know that I have said it before," Janine began, "But while the prospect of these matters in Inverness does not fill me with joy, I will endure them and I will come through them stronger."

"I am certain that you will," the Duke agreed, "Whilst I feel no great foreboding, about this, I don't feel the least bit of enthusiasm for it, either!"

"Let us hope that our host, for our stay in Inverness, has no sense of foreboding," O'Keefe suggested, with a grin.

"Thank you for your words of encouragement," replied the Duke, sarcastically.

Janine looked at the Duke quizzically and he grimaced before speaking.

"Our host in Inverness is the Laird of Raigmore.", he said, "He is a very good and loyal friend of mine."

Janine nodded, appearing to be reassured.

"While he knows that I am asking him to put up a guest of considerable importance, he does not know your identity and, from the way I have worded my correspondence, he will presume that we are travelling ahead of you rather than accompanying you."

CHAPTER 38

The coach made good time to Inverness and, when it slowed to a walking pace on the last length of road, the occupants were surprised to find that they had arrived. Almost stopping to make the final turn, their coach then swung across a short stone bridge built over a steeply sided ditch. The ditch was one of two dug around the imposing Raigmore Castle. The first ditch ran the length of the road and, whilst it was dry, it had hundreds of wooden posts driven into its bed, each sharpened to a vicious point.

"They don't like unwelcome guests!" O'Keefe chortled, gesturing to the ominous ditch.

A second, deeper ditch – constructed in parallel – was filled with water and circled the entire perimeter of the building. Spanning it was a longer wooden bridge that could be raised or lowered by a set of sturdy winches and chains.

The moment the wheels of the Duke's coach rumbled onto the drawbridge, they were greeted by a pair of pipers who played them through the majestic gates of Raigmore Castle. Their coach passed under a second stone archway and, as it came to a halt, a fanfare rang out from musicians stationed on a balcony above it.

Janine could see at least fifteen, possibly as many as twenty, servants gathered in the courtyard. They were all standing tall with their chins in and their chests out. A little way ahead of them stood a man and a woman, their arms linked. As the Duke and Janine disembarked, the couple – the Laird and Lady Raigmore – came forward.

"Welcome to Raigmore Castle," said the man.

"We are honoured to receive you," said the woman.

"Thank you," replied the Duke, "I am most grateful for your hospitality."

Their hosts assured them that they were very welcome, indeed.

"This place looks finer every time I visit!" exclaimed the Duke.

"It is a labour of love!" the Laird replied.

"Raigmore Castle extends to Your Grace and his companions every possible service and indulgence," beamed Lady Raigmore, dropping into an elegant curtsey.

"I am overwhelmed by your kindness," replied Francesca, curtseying.

Janine said nothing, realising that neither the Laird nor Lady Raigmore had any idea who she might be.

"If there is anything whatsoever that you might wish, please do not hesitate to ask," the Laird assured.

"We would be honoured," said Lady Raigmore, "If you would allow us to escort you inside to view your chambers and recover a little after your journey."

The Duke of Bo'Ness and his party walked towards the fortified entrance of the castle, stepping onto a red carpet that had been laid for them. Beyond the entrance was a short passage that traversed three different types of stone, one after the other.

"The roof to the entrance tunnel has been carved out slightly higher," Laird Raigmore explained to the Duke, "And, also, the floor beneath our feet has been dug down deeper. Before that work was done, it was necessary to walk with heads bowed."

"I take it that the different bands of stone are the work of different generations?" asked the Duke, pointing to the innermost layer of stone, which was darker and rougher than the two outer layers that came before it.

"Yes, this is Raigmore as it was first built," Laird Raigmore declared, pointing to the stone in question, "And the other two layers of wall were fortifications added in later ages."

Having passed through both an outer and an inner set of iron gates, the light – which had grown progressively dimmer – was now relieved by oil lamps set into the walls. The passage widened out into a round room with a domed ceiling and, to Janine's great surprise, it was flooded with daylight.

"A little miracle!" the Laird announced, raising his hands to indicate the ceiling above them.

Arranged around its domed structure were windows from which bright sunlight flooded into the chamber below.

"On the roof of the castle, there are a dozen arches, arranged in a circle to face in every direction," the Laird explained, "The light they capture travels down the shaft, above us, by means of a series of reflecting mirrors. These mirrors bring the light into this 'illumitorium'."

"The effect is utterly amazing!" the Duke declared.

The Laird Raigmore beamed with evident delight at his praise and, leaning towards his wife, kissed her on the cheek and squeezed her shoulder.

Turning back to the rest of his party of guests, Laird Raigmore shrugged off all formality and allowed his face to break into a huge grin. It was apparent that, once they had duly admired the illumitorium, they were elevated to a higher level of friendship.

"Lachlan!" he cried, "It's good to see you again!" and promptly gripped Balloch in an enthusiastic bear hug.

"You, too, Mister Chang!" he called, grabbing his other guest and drawing him into a similar embrace, "It feels like only yesterday that you and I were aboard a ship together, tying up in Glasgow Harbour!"

"It will be fifteen years ago in just a few weeks," Mister Chang laughed, patting his old friend on the back.

"Malcom!", the Laird shouted, grabbing the hand of the Duke and shaking it furiously, before pulling him into a hug.

"And you!" he laughed, hugging O'Keefe with the same enthusiasm, "You old sea dog!"

"Welcome, again, to Raigmore Castle.", he told Janine, kissing her hand twice.

The Laird then turned to Francesca and stared at her for several moments, uncertain of himself, before clapping a hand to his mouth in astonishment.

"Francesca!" he exclaimed, "Is that you?"

"It is!"

"You've grown! You're so tall! I can hardly believe it!"

"I only came up to your elbow the last time you saw me."

"Yes! That's right! You're still as pretty as ever, though!"

Francesca raised her hands and covered her face, pretending to be embarrassed and there was much genial laughter at her comic expression.

Janine remained in the background, with her eyes cast down, leaving the Laird and Lady Raigmore to presume her to be merely a personal maid.

Once all pleasantries had been exhausted and reminiscences exchanged, the Laird and Lady Raigmore led them to the far end of the room and to a huge wooden door that swung open as they approached it. Beyond the door was a grandly decorated reception room. At the far end of the room was another pair of double doors, both pinned open. These gave a view into a very sizeable dining hall.

"It would be our great pleasure," Laird Raigmore announced, waving a hand towards the dining hall, "If you would be our guests of honour at a banquet to celebrate your stay."

"We would be delighted," the Duke replied.

"But first," the Laird Raigmore announced, "As promised, we will conduct you to see your accommodation. Our servants, as we speak, are assisting your own to unload the trunks and bags from your carriage and transport them to your chambers."

"I feel certain," Lady Raigmore confided, "That you may all wish to retire, temporarily, and take the opportunity to change out of your travelling clothes before we dine?"

All their party confirmed their agreement.

"If I may escort you?" Lady Raigmore asked Francesca, extending her arm in the direction of a nearby door.

Francesca accepted the invitation and Janine tagged along behind.

"And if I, gentlemen and your Grace, may likewise escort you?" Laird Raigmore entreated, with a similar gesture.

The Laird Raigmore led the way up two flights of twisting stone steps to the second floor of the castle and into a tastefully furnished room. The walls were hung with tapestries and regimental flags and a sumptuous carpet covered the floor. The Duke, O'Keefe, Balloch and Mister Chang followed him in.

"Your daughter will, no doubt, take considerably more time to ready herself than us," the Laird told the Duke, "So let me show you all into the morning room, here, where we can relax for a few minutes."

They all sat down, politely. None of them had any doubt that the Laird's purpose of assembling them, there, was so that he could speak to them in private. They looked at each other, questioningly, each undecided how they might introduce the subject of exactly why they had come to Inverness. The Laird did not miss their wordless consultation and spoke to assure them.

"Please feel free to speak plainly and openly," he urged, "The message you sent me said that you were arranging the travel of somebody of note to Inverness."

"Yes, we are," the Duke confirmed, looking earnestly around his companions, "And we find ourselves facing a difficult situation. One that will, by its nature, prove extremely challenging to resolve."

"Tell me more."

The Duke looked to Balloch and tilted his head, questioningly.

"Laird Raigmore," Balloch said, guardedly, "You are friends with the Duke of Cumberland..."

"Friends?" scoffed Laird Raigmore, with a contemptuous laugh, "Well, I have his acquaintance and he has mine, if that is what you mean. I don't think that our relationship has ever extended as far as friendship. In truth, when we cross each other's path, our meetings tend to be more than a little strained. All too often, we find ourselves on the opposite sides of important issues."

"I thought as much, but I was reluctant to presume," Balloch admitted.

"I must protest!" mocked the Laird, "You can presume that I am not friends with the Duke of Cumberland as often and as brazenly as you wish!"

Balloch grinned and gave a little snigger. The Duke reached out and rested a hand on Laird Raigmore's arm, for a moment, to emphasise their common situation.

"I am relieved to hear it," the Duke proclaimed, "For I have endured the exact same predicament for many a year. I have found my acquaintance with the Duke of Cumberland extremely awkward and vexing on numerous occasions."

"I wager that even that assessment is painting a rosy picture!" the Laird mused.

The Duke guffawed, "Yes! To be sure! If he were on fire, I don't think I would rush to put him out, even if it meant me emptying my bladder on him!"

The Laird Raigmore exaggerated a look of indecision.

"I must confess that I would find the opportunity to piss on the Duke of Cumberland a hard one to resist!"

At this, everyone in the room hooted with laughter. When they were settled, Balloch's demeanour took on a grimness that seemed to draw light and warmth from the room.

"The Duke of Bo'Ness has always been a staunch patriot," Balloch told Laird Raigmore, using an upturned palm to indicate his employer.

The Duke bowed his head to acknowledge the accolade.

"The Duke," Balloch continued, "Once took on the role of guardian for a child that was brought to him, in distressing circumstances, a number of years ago."

"He has a good heart," the Laird declared, nodding approvingly at the Duke.

"The Duke of Cumberland," Balloch disclosed in a deliberately hesitant manner, "Had given the impression that he was also a supporter of her cause."

"Cause?" the Laird queried, evidently uneasy at the choice of words.

"The girl was of a very particular importance to certain people."

The Laird Raigmore's expression became darker and his brows creased.

"The girl had been kept hidden for her own safety," Balloch continued, "The Duke of Cumberland became aware of her location and we believe he tried to have her killed."

The Duke held up a finger to indicate that he would take up the story, himself.

"The child arrived at Brech Woorlach in the dead of night," the Duke disclosed, "Snatched from the jaws of death."

"Why am I getting the idea," the Laird Raigmore asked, warily, "That this story is not just going to be just something and nothing?"

The Duke frowned and gave a thin lipped smile before resuming the tale.

"The girl arrived at Brech Woorlach at the tender age of one year old. She stayed with us for two years, growing up as a sister to my own daughter, Francesca."

The Laird Raigmore nodded, slightly puzzled, and raised his eyebrows, bidding the other to tell more.

"When the child was three years old, she returned to her mother, the situation being judged, by then, to be relatively safe, but....."

The Laird held up his hands to indicate his resignation to bad news being imminent.

"But," Balloch cautioned, picking up the tale, "She had only reached the age of seven when another attack was launched on her. While she very narrowly escaped, they managed to kill her father as she was being bundled away."

"The work of the Duke of Cumberland, again?", asked the Laird, one eyebrow arched.

"The Duke of Cumberland could only be linked to the first assassination attempt by circumstance and strong suspicion, but – as far as the second attack was concerned – those who know about such things are absolutely certain it was him."

"Am I right in assuming," the Laird enquired, "That this girl – this child – must have been somebody of grave significance?"

"Yes, indeed," Balloch confirmed, "She was, and is, of momentous importance for Scotland."

"And it is she who is coming here?"

"It is she, Laird Raigmore, who will be your guest," Balloch replied, choosing his words carefully.

The Laird's face flooded with a look of consternation and he lifted a palm to Balloch, imploring him to urgently complete the tale.

"The girl's mother went to great lengths to remain anonymous. Her efforts to keep her identity hidden, while cunning and resourceful, were – in the end – to no avail."

The Laird fumed with impatience as he waited for the conclusion of the story and, after sighing loudly, he made a rumbling sound in his throat.

"The Duke of Cumberland," Balloch quickly resumed, "Managed to learn the identity of the woman and, thus, the significance of the previously anonymous child."

"Which," the Duke revealed, "Was why he attempted to assassinate her."

"Assassinate her? That's a weighty word.", the Laird exclaimed, "You talk of her as if she were royalty!"

The Laird Raigmore took one look at the expressions on the faces of the four men before him and froze.

"Her mother," the Duke declared, "Was Queen Cydara, the Queen of the West."

The Laird's mouth fell open in shock and his eyes stared in undisguised amazement. After a few moments, he managed to find his voice.

"It is Queen Annis who is coming here?" the Laird gasped, clearly shocked.

"No," advised Balloch, "The girl was Janine."

Laird Raigmore looked completely mystified and clapped his hands to his head in consternation.

"Janine," Balloch proclaimed, "Is the real and genuine heir to the title 'Queen of the West' and Annis, it turns out, is nothing but a usurper."

CHAPTER 39

Everybody not yet on their horse began to mount up. Slowly, they all moved off. The two MacDonald brothers moved to take up the lead with McCleary and a half dozen of his men in their general quarter.

The convoy slogged up hill and downhill for the next hour and a half. They halted, from time to time, to dig one or other wagon out of a pothole or rut and then clattered away again, bouncing and sliding, until the next mishap.

Periodically, Captain McCleary would bring everyone to a halt and send a dozen of his Blue and Greys into the trees, either side of the road, to hide in wait to ambush anybody who might be following them. Before too long, these men would catch up with the main group, only for McCleary to repeat the process a little further up the road.

Soon after midday, their column dispersed – left and right – into the fields either side of the road for everyone to eat and rest.

Alex and Hamish helped Caitlan to get Constable Burberry down from the back of his wagon. The three of them managed to move him with the minimum impact on his injuries. The Constable gave a joyful sigh as he made contact with the soft, cool grass.

Before long, the army cooks came round with huge cauldrons of stew, which they ladled out into stout metal pots. With each pot of steaming stew came an enormous chunk of dark bread and a spoon of bright yellow butter. Most of the troops, they noticed, put the butter into the stew rather than onto the bread. Deferring to their wisdom, the Constable's own little group did likewise.

An hour passed as if it were fifteen minutes and everybody clambered back into their vehicles or onto their horses in preparation for the word to set out. They didn't have long to wait. A few sharp notes on the pipes rang out and they all reassembled on the road, riders to the front and rear and wagons in the middle.

It took only a half hour before the first of the wagons yielded to the grip of a deep rut. A rescue party was rapidly assembled. Riders roped their horses to the front, soldiers deployed poles and spades beneath the wheels and half a dozen of the strongest men pushed from behind. After some initial difficulty, the pulling and shoving was successful and the road reluctantly relinquished its prey.

No sooner had they crested the next rise, than a second wagon succumbed to the fearsome grip of a gulley in the highway. This time, it took considerably longer to get it moving again, but – having practised the routine around twenty times already – they managed to get the better of the situation in the end. As the wheels started turning, once more, the sun came out from behind the clouds and everybody's spirits lifted.

A little while later, Allaster MacDonald surrendered the lead to Captain McCleary, and fell back to walk his horse alongside the Constable's wagon.

"My brother is of a like opinion to me," Allaster told Burberry, "In respect of you having the trust of both the MacDonald and of the king."

"And what is that?" Burberry asked.

"He agrees that you are in an unenviable position and that….."

"Thank him for being so frank!" Burberry interjected.

Allaster laughed and continued his explanation.

"And that, at the end of the day, irrespective of who is *meant* to be put on trial, it will end up with an additional defendant. *They* will be on trial for their supposed *'crimes'* and *you* for what they will claim are your divided loyalties!"

Burberry laughed, but it was a dark, gruesome laugh with not one jot of actual humour in it. It was more like the rattling of a condemned man's shackles.

They continued, in silence, to the top of the next hill, where their convoy halted to fill in a treacherous rut in the road with pebbles and stones. Allaster slapped Burberry's shoulder and bade him farewell as he headed back to the head of the column.

It wasn't long before Burberry had another visitor. Allan MacDonald, the older of the MacDonald brothers, had been slowly progressing forward from the rear of the convoy, performing an inspection as he went. Allan now spurred his horse to trot up to the Constable's wagon and greeted its occupant cordially. The Constable replied in kind. It appeared that the two men had decided to like each other.

"I hope that you didn't think I was mocking you, earlier, Constable Burberry," Allan enquired.

"You spoke your mind," Burberry assured him, "And said nothing that I hadn't thought, myself, already."

Alex, Hamish and Caitlan – at the front of his wagon – kept themselves discretely out of the conversation, not wishing to intrude on this tactful bridge building. This, they all knew, might turn out to be a very important friendship for all their futures.

"It says in the Bible," Allan ventured, "That 'no man can serve two masters, for either he will hate the one and love the other, or else he will hold to the one and despise the other' and that sounds like a cruelly accurate description of your dilemma."

It was clear to everyone, from his tone, that he was being genuinely sympathetic and that he did not intend his words as a taunt or jibe.

Caitlan cleared her throat. Having attracted Alex and Hamish's attention, she asked if they might escort her and stand guard while she answered the call of nature in the undergrowth by the road. The relevant parties dismounted from the wagon and made off into the greenery, leaving Burberry and Allan MacDonald alone.

"Your companions are good people, Constable," Allan told him, "And are hugely well mannered to allow us to talk in private."

The wagon driver gave Allan a sideways glance and then excused himself to go and make water, too.

"You need to start calling me 'Ewan', if you will, MacDonald."

Allan MacDonald laughed at the formality of the one name stacked atop the informality of the other.

"I would be honoured to do so," he replied, giving the Constable a salute, "And you must call me 'Allan'," he said, before hurriedly adding, "And call my brother 'Allaster'."

"I, too, am honoured," Burberry advised, bowing his head and touching his forelock.

Allan MacDonald adopted a confiding tone as he leaned closer to Burberry.

"I hope – and I mean this sincerely – that this doesn't turn out to be a poisoned cup that your king is giving you to drink from."

Constable Burberry made a dull rumble in his chest and nodded gravely before sighing heavily and uttering a curse in bawdy French.

"Pisse sur mon âme! *(Piss on my soul)*!", he said.

Allan, who had been looking up the road at that moment, whirled his head around in a sudden snap and stared at Burberry in disbelief. His eyes were wide with alarm and his mouth gaped open in abject astonishment.

"Are you insane?" he asked, incredulously, "This cannot be!"

Burberry froze, realising that he had just made a grave error.

"I am no fool!" Allan MacDonald brayed in cold fury, "I am no untravelled buffoon, some country dimwit, a brainless dolt who would fail to understand! I was schooled in Dublin, in Paris and in Winchester."

Burberry hardly dared to breathe.

"I *know* who swears like *that*!" he snarled, his face contorted with fury.

Burberry looked up and met the other's gaze. Immediately he wished that he hadn't. Allan MacDonald's eyes were glittering with something close to madness. All the blood drained from Burberry's face. His guts clenched as if they were in a vice. He had just committed an unforgiveable blunder! His casual slip of the tongue could be potentially catastrophic to his whole mission.

Allan MacDonald sat astride his horse, breathing deeply, almost panting, as if he had just run up a hill.

"Do *they* know your secret?" he demanded, stabbing a finger, venomously, in the direction of Alex, Hamish and Caitlan who were just emerging from the undergrowth.

"No," Burberry replied, feeling like a small schoolchild in front of a headmaster.

"Have they any reason to suspect?"

"No."

"Are you absolutely certain?"

"I am."

"I am here to protect you. I am here to extend to you the protection of the MacDonald Clan. I have brought soldiers who would lay down their lives to safeguard you! Now, I discover *this* about you! This *abomination!*"

The Constable looked down at his gun, its muzzle peeking from under a fold of canvas. He wondered if he could reach it. He wondered if he could attain the dreamy slowness of ancient combat and move at blistering speed. His heart spasmed and he felt pain. It was a pang of despair. It was a jolt of shame. He could not kill this man. He could not kill the man who pledged, on oath, to protect him.

Burberry looked back to Allan MacDonald and it was as if his mind had just been read.

"It would be best if we were *both* dead if this is true!" said Allan, mournfully, "Best that neither of us were even born if it is, in fact, *you* who is guilty of treason."

Burberry looked sullen and dejected and made no attempt to defend his reputation or his honour from what appeared to be a shocking revelation. Allan's face crumpled into half a dozen expressions as he tussled with the magnitude of his discovery. Then, he appeared to come to a sudden resolve.

"You're *not* with the French!" Allan growled, "I cannot believe it to be true! Tell me, now, to my face, that you are not a traitor to both your king and my queen!"

"I am not a traitor. I cannot be one if I am a betrayer of traitors. I betray whom I must, but I do not betray her."

"Words!" scoffed Allaster, haughtily.

Burberry watched as Allan appraised his situation. He was watching the approach of Alex, Hamish and Caitlan. All three carried pistols in holsters. He was performing a calculation. He was working out, at this distance, how many of them he could kill before he were slain himself.

"Words," repeated Allan, flatly, as if toying with the sound.

Burberry looked back, blankly, and waited to die. Abruptly, Allan straightened, as if taken by an idea and cupped his chin in his hand. He mulled over, in his head, what Burberry had said: *'I betray whom I must, but I do not betray her'*.

"Tell me, Constable," he asked Burberry, "What would you wish to be buried with? What possession do you prize most highly?"

The MacDonald horseman looked at the Constable, imploringly.

Burberry thought. His mind staggered and rocked in his head. What was he being asked? Was the question *no more* than what it sounded to be? Was he, perhaps, being offered a concession that might allow for a fitting burial? Or did he dare to believe that he was being asked something else completely?

Alex, Hamish and Caitlan came to a halt, sensing the danger of the moment.

The MacDonald horseman looked at the Constable with desperation and slowly laid his hand upon the butt of his pistol with a reluctance that almost made the air itself cry out in pain. Burberry looked back and felt the sands of time running out in the hourglass of his life.

CHAPTER 40

Burberry sighed and, like a card player staking everything in the world on the turn of a single card, made his play.

"I have the petal of a violet," Burberry declared, quietly.

The MacDonald horseman drew in a shuddering breath.

"I keep it in a glass thimble," Burberry explained.

The MacDonald horseman swallowed, with difficulty, blatantly battling with his emotions.

"I keep the thimble in a pouch,", Burberry said, "I keep the pouch in a box."

The MacDonald horseman put his head back and closed his eyes, the palpable surge of relief sweeping through him like a tidal wave.

"It is my most precious thing because it is the symbol of my one true love," Burberry finished.

Allan MacDonald reached across to the Constable's wagon and gripped the side of it firmly. He then pulled himself towards it, causing his mount to stagger sideways. The beast snorted and, despite objecting, shuffled up so its flanks were against the wagon. Allan MacDonald reached out and put his arms around the Constable. The Constable, staggering painfully up onto his knees, put his own arms around the rider.

"I would have had to kill you," Allan said, dismally.

"I would have expected nothing less," Burberry replied.

At that precise moment there was a fluttering and a blur of tiny wings as a butterfly flew between them and hovered in the air. The tiny form hung there, its wings throwing off the most beautiful sparkling colours as the rays of the weak Autumn sun struck them.

"It is far too late in the year and far too cold for butterflies!" Allan remarked in astonishment.

Suddenly, as if it had heard his remark, the butterfly seemed to fade and flicker. The place it had occupied suddenly sparkled, again, but this time with a dozen tiny tongues of flame that danced and shimmered as if alive. The swirling fronds of yellow, red and orange fire coiled and twisted, holding the same position, pulsing with a magical aura.

"If you were not true," said Allan, with absolute certainty, "This spectacle could not occur."

"I feel its power," replied Burberry.

Alex, Hamish and Caitlan appeared beside them, the noise of the feet as they advanced having been inexplicably muffled and rendered almost silent.

The flames floated across to position themselves midway between the old and new members of their little group and flared up to become brighter and more vivid.

"It is stronger when we are together," Caitlan said.

Hamish turned and looked up and down the road, to where soldiers on foot and on horseback were sat, idly gazing around.

"Do *they* see it?" Hamish pondered aloud.

"No. Only us," Alex said, unable to describe why he knew it to be so.

"It is the Quickening!" exclaimed Allan.

"Yes. It *is* the Quickening.", Wild Flower confirmed, her voice taking them by surprise from the bushes behind them.

They all turned to see her stood at the edge of the forest. Her slender form somehow fixed by a misty aura that slowly whirled and eddied around her.

"It's an angel!" said Alex, not realising that he was speaking aloud.

"No," said Wild Flower, smiling, "Not quite an angel."

They all looked at her blankly.

"You have been called," Wild Flower told them, "Be strong and believe."

The group looked at each other, checking that they were all seeing the same thing. When they looked back, Wild Flower was gone, a tiny spark hovering, for a brief second, where she had stood.

The flames in the air, tumbled and spiralled for a few more moments, brighter still. Then they, too, were gone.

They all gaped at the spot where the apparition of the girl had appeared and looked at each other for reassurance that it had not just been a product of their imaginations.

"Who was that?" asked Hamish, still partly mesmerised.

"How could she just appear like that?" asked Alex, equally dumbfounded.

"How could she *disappear* like that?" asked Caitlan.

"Please!" Allan MacDonald pleaded, "Don't let me hear the breakfast gong and find out that this has all been just a dream!"

"If I, too, am asleep," quipped Constable Burberry, jovially, "Let me wake up in a cosy bed in a nice, warm inn!"

"We have slept in tents in the fields, these past three nights," moaned Alex, "On bedding that prods and pokes me every time I move and in fear of having our throats slit during the night by marauding Campbells. Hearing the army breakfast gong in a morning is a refreshing reminder that I have survived another night!"

"Do they have breakfast gongs in Heaven?" asked Burberry, with a grin.

"No!", responded Allaster, "That's Hell you're thinking about! It's a huge, huge gong where each blow echoes for a full minute!"

They all laughed and the wagon driver, now returned to his post, joined in the laughter, amused simply by their amusement.

"I saw the little girl with my own eyes," Burberry announced, abruptly, "And I know, for certain, that she was there."

"She was there," Hamish confirmed, "And then she was gone."

Hamish made a gesture in the air that approximate a spark flashing.

"We have been called. This is the Quickening. She said so," Alex declared, looking stern and serious.

Allan, a few paces ahead of them, held up a finger to draw their attention and then pressed it to his lips for them to be quiet. He then leaned his head to the side, quizzically, and put his finger behind his ear, pushing it forward to capture any sound.

Suddenly, everybody heard the birds in the trees singing gloriously loudly. It was like the Dawn Chorus. It was far too late for that! Yet the birds were gripped by an overwhelming urge to chirp, trill and call at the top of their voices in one huge, feathered choir.

"Don't tell me that *that* isn't strange!" Allaster demanded.

Everybody nodded their agreement. At that moment, Allaster, at the front of the convoy, called for them to move off and the ordinary world took over, again, as they resumed their journey.

They hadn't gone far when they encountered a small scale farmer with four bags of turnips strapped to his horse. He was heading south.

"Hello!", Burberry called out, "How far to Inverness?"

"I don't rightly know," the man replied, shrugging his shoulders, "But I reckon that you'll make it there by this time tomorrow, Sir."

"Heaven save me!" Alex moaned, "Another night of beef so tough it makes my teeth ache to chew it."

"Another morning," Hamish grumbled, "Of porridge so thick you can set stones in a wall with it."

Alex laughed, Hamish laughed, Burberry laughed and Caitlan laughed, too.

Behind them, one of the senior soldiers stopped the man with the turnips, purchased them all, and sent him back the way he had come.